A QUEST OF FIVE PRINCES

Paresh P. Rana

HOLISTIC Publishing

Published by "The Great Indian Book Tour"
Imprint : Holistic Publishing
www.tgibt.com
106/91, Ashok marg, Vijay path
Mansarover, Jaipur, Rajasthan-302020
Phone : +91-72400-68114
email : prashant@tgibt.com

Title : A Quest of Five Princes

Author : Paresh Priyadarshan Rana

First published in 2025
First Edition 2025
Printed in India
Printer : Manipal Technologies Limited, Manipal
ISBN : 978-93-49571-30-3
Price : INR 360
Cover design by Kubra Pandit

"The self is the friend of the self, and the self is the enemy of the self."

— *Bhagavad Gita, Chapter 6, Verse 5*

The Summon

IN the olden days, Pandhar was a mighty and wealthy kingdom, lying in the north of the land. It maintained peaceful alliances through commerce with kingdoms lying to its south and east, even with lands beyond the western sea. Lush forests and lakes lay to its east, rich in wildlife and evergreen trees. Though they harboured threats such as beasts or creatures of ancient times, a vast part of the kingdom was kept safe, the border villages being protected by the army. Bandits were not unheard of, but their influence was minimal, or so was the news in the kingdom. Besides, it helped keep neighbouring kingdoms from interfering with their lands, a buffer zone that acted like no man's land. To the west was the Great Sea, a means of trade with distant kingdoms and harvesting pearls. Pearls were the biggest trade for Pandhar, along with marble for palaces or temples, snail colours as dyes for royal banners and attires, and mustard oil for its sacred value.

When one moved beyond the northern border of Pandhar, dark and deep forests began after a little barren land. Many stories were born from these parts, legends known all over the continent. Some spoke of spirits running foul, while other stories were of more tangible creatures, monsters nonetheless. Folks who lived near borders still burned incense and herbs outside their houses to keep evil spirits from entering. Heroic stories of monster slayers were quite popular in Pandhar, thanks to the eerie lands beyond its northern borders. Whether in plays performed by theatres and travelling troupes or stories told by old wives around a fire, the monsters were brought to life many times in the kingdom.

Beyond these forests rose the gigantic, snow-capped Dharataj mountain range (Crown of Earth, *Dhara*: Earth, *Taj*: Crown). Its snowy and rocky slopes were filled with creatures, plants of many kinds, and tales or mysteries of old. It stretched from the western sea to far in the east. Even with all this, many people visited it for pilgrimage, traversing the dangerous forests or seeking paths around them, such a holy site it was considered. It was a long hike to reach the top, braving snow and stone, with barely any air to breathe at its peaks. There were tales of gods who, in eras bygone, would descend from heaven to speak with mortals, granting them wisdom or great boons. A few heroes were believed to have prayed to gods at the peaks of Dharataj to gain favour and enchanted weapons capable of slaying demons. However, no one knew where these weapons were now, perhaps lost to stories and songs only. Whatever the stories might be, the faithful ones still made their trek up the mountain now and then, merely as a pilgrimage from which they might not return. Some visited for long meditation with the hope of *nirvana*, the freedom from the cycle of death and rebirth.

Many others would go there seeking the medicinal herbs that could cure many diseases. So potent was the medicinal strength of those herbs that rivers coming from Dharataj could heal body and soul. The greatest of these rivers was Neri, named after a divine lady from years of yore. River Neri flowed southwards from Dharataj, splitting into two at the centre of Pandhar. One kept moving south, passing among the tall hills and flowing beyond the borders. The other branch moved almost orthogonally, escaping the kingdom from its eastern border. People flocked to take a dip in the river, and even citizens from other kingdoms were allowed to visit this holy river. Some years, when the stars aligned, a great festival, a procession one might call, happened at the river Neri that brought pilgrims from all over the land. Many festivals were celebrated throughout the year, all across the land.

It was quite a week every year at the beginning of summer when a play was organised in every city to village throughout the kingdom. Actors dressed as warriors and demons danced around, as priests – or *pandits* as folks called them – would sing the songs of forgotten days. It was a week to celebrate the victory of light over darkness, of good over evil, as through these songs, the *pandits* recounted the victory of a warrior prince over a demon king as he rescued his beloved princess. No theatre was needed for this, as people would gather in the streets and roads to watch a play under the open sky if needed. As much fear as those northern forests might instil, they were still part of everyone's memories. The kingdom had a few poets popular worldwide, their plays and poetry reaching far from the east to the lands beyond the sea in the west. Some were even claimed to have been blessed by the Goddess of Knowledge after they spent years meditating.

Such pilgrimage through its land, along with big festivals, helped boost the economy and geopolitical position of Pandhar. Its abundance of natural resources, added with access to the sea, had made Pandhar prosper and stand tall as an influential kingdom, at least until now.

*

King Dharmendra ruled Pandhar with justice and fairness. The cities maintained good wealth from trade with other kingdoms. The might of his kingdom on the battlefield had kept more aggressive kingdoms at bay. There hadn't been a war in a long time across the entire land, but it would be a lie to say that every kingdom had taken the peace for granted. Yet, it wasn't bad enough yet for rising border tensions. He hoped that it would remain so for a long time. Dharmendra preferred peace over warfare, though he understood the necessity of strength to maintain balance. His major philosophy was doing his duty with justice, as his name translates to Lord of

Duty (*Dharma*- Duty, *Indra*- Lord of heaven and sky). In truth, light cannot exist without shadow. Even with all his efforts, conflicts were happening now and then in the kingdom. Wealth disparities still existed, too. He made his best efforts to counter these social evils, yet he was only a mortal king.

Many other kings showed him respect, even scholars and philosophers visited his halls on their pilgrimage to Dharataj. It was one such scholar, *Pandit* Bhimsen, who sat by the King's bed that day. The scholar was filled with life and wisdom, his eyes shining with a light of knowledge. His head was shaved, except for the tuft of hair at the back of his head. He was dressed in bare minimum clothing to travel the lands along with a jute bag. He had a saffron *dhoti* and another cloth draped over his shoulder. It was such a contrast to the King lying on the bed. A scholar with no possessions, yet rich in life, on the other hand was a king, ruler of an entire kingdom, yet struggling to breathe or speak as sickness consumed him.

Dharmendra had fallen sick, getting weaker every passing day. He was still in regal clothes, though his old body was marked by many wounds from battles of his youth. His beard and hair were getting grey, marking his time to retire from the throne. All his life, he had worked to lift his kingdom to its glory days. While his wife lived, she often claimed he should spend more time with his children, but he usually remarked that the citizens were his children too – he couldn't be partial just to his blood. Now, lying alone without the love of his life on his side, nor his sons in the palace, he wondered if he was wrong all those years ago. It didn't matter, his time would come sooner or later to join his love again. For now, he needed to ensure that the kingdom didn't fall into chaos. He didn't have much strength to rule from the throne, illness or not, age would soon catch up to him, nonetheless.

There were still flames in his eyes, as he had his five able sons after all. Yet, it troubled him that the kingdom he had worked so hard for would fall into despair and chaos if a successor were not there to guard its stability. A successor, a Crown Prince, was considered the second most important person in the kingdom. If a kingdom lacked a suitable Crown Prince, people believed that *Devas*, the Lords of heaven and elements, would stop blessing that kingdom. Even though Dharmendra did not believe in such tales, he was wise enough to know that without a true successor, the kingdom would become unstable and insecure, as forces from inside and outside would try to tear it apart. When Dharmendra came to know that Bhimsen was passing by the kingdom, he requested the *pandit* to come and discuss that matter with him.

Pandit was not a mere title for priests or scholars – often, they were advisors in royal courts and teachers to princes and princesses. It was their primary act to offer prayers in temples or shrines and carry out holy rituals, but they also had a myriad of skills. They were experts in philosophy, medicine, astrology and the arts. While the princes were away from the palace, Dharmendra kept wondering about the best way to select a successor. The coming of a *pandit* to his kingdom was like the first breeze of spring. He summoned him to ask for advice on suitable ways to select a Crown Prince. First, he needed an objective to drive the princes, given how some of them could be so laid back. He had heard tales and accounts of the achievements his sons had achieved, and also their spoils. He then needed a way to challenge them, bring out the best and worst from them, like the strongest of steel tested with the hottest of fires.

*

It was a night with a half-moon – the clear sky was decorated with stars and constellations. The chamber was dimly lit with earthen and brass lamps, casting long shadows. The King's bed was soft and wide, the sheets and covers pristine and luxurious. On the walls were paintings from great artists, some depicting scenery from worldwide, while others were about tales and myths. Rarely were *Pandits* invited to such a luxurious chamber, yet Bhimsen sat there with the king to plan the future of the kingdom. He looked at the stars, not doing any astrological counting, just staring at their beauty as he contemplated the suggestions from Dharmendra.

'Is this not too harsh a test, my king?' Bhimsen questioned as he looked at the ailing king. *A quest like that has not been tried in centuries*, he thought to himself. He continued, 'We want to test their skills, yes, but no need to make it this brutal. Besides, it will be better if they work together to achieve this goal, a test can be done separately if you wish.' King Dharmendra tried to speak, but his cough interrupted him. He gestured towards a grail filled with warm water, honey, ginger and medicinal herbs. The grail was decorated with ruby and opal – it would have been worth more than Bhimsen's entire possession. Yet, the most precious thing about it was the simple liquid in it.

Bhimsen brought the grail from the nearby table and helped Dharmendra take a few sips. The flames danced in their lamps while a soothing breeze filled the chamber, bringing respite on that warm evening. The chamber had a big window, perhaps to look at the capital city or to gaze at the infinite sky. The ceiling was decorated with many designs, fractals and patterns. None of it mattered to them at that moment. Even with all the glorious display of the chamber, the king's condition made him look like a broken man waiting for his final hours.

There were flowers on the table, flowers carefully picked by his daughter, Geetika. She believed flowers represented health and growth. They lay there to give her father the mental strength to live on. There were many summer flowers there, the most common being *Champa*, a symbol of immortality and long life. But those flowers were not the ones that could heal Dharmendra – he needed something more potent. Flowers whose kind had passed into stories, the ones which could do miracles of bringing back people from the doorway of death, could cure all wounds and illnesses.

As the scholar helped the king to sit up, Dharmendra answered, 'It is a test to test the competency to rule an entire kingdom. It can't be done on playgrounds and theatres, O' Wise One. Thousands of lives will depend on the hand of a Crown Prince, the future king. Thus, he must be tested through the harshest of challenges, like the best gold or steel.' The king was silent as he recalled his five sons. He looked at the portrait of his sons hanging on the wall. First from the right was his firstborn, with his rough hair and subtle beard, holding his bow as he stood on his chariot. The king remembered his first son, *the many battles he had fought for the kingdom, and so many victories he had brought. Yet, as headstrong as he might be, he needs to find kindness in his heart. He worried for his firstborn, as ruthless and mighty a warrior as he might be, he would lead the kingdom to doom with his iron fists. A protector, a defender, a true warrior was what the kingdom needed, not a conqueror.* His thought wandered off to the second prince. A sharp mind who was quite observant, always thinking ahead of others. Yet, the king felt that his heart was not bold enough, hoping he would find courage in that quest.

A smile tugged at his lips as he thought of his third son. Bhimsen looked at him as if asking him to speak what he wanted. The king sighed and said, 'My third son, the heavens must have been happy with me when they blessed me with him. A ruler in making, I must admit, even if that makes me sound partial. I must say that I won't recall all the laws and rules he has managed to remember and follow to the letter. I worry sometimes that he might put himself in danger to live up to the honourable heroes he idolises. He would not even take drinks, given how he considers those vices as sins. I would have been concerned if he were all talk and no skills, but I have not seen or heard of an archer better than him in these lands. Even with a blindfold, he can shoot at birds flying above, though he would refuse to take a life unless necessary and only through a fair challenge, such are his honours. So honourable and wise, yet honour is not all that is needed to rule a kingdom. He needs to find his true strength, then perhaps I will happily give my crown to him and lie in peace, knowing that the kingdom is in safe hands.'

Bhimsen looked out of the window, to the star-filled sky and houses with faint lamplights outside their doors. 'Yes, Your Majesty, indeed your sons were taught and brought up well. Each one is unique with the skills they have honed. Every one of them is equal to each other in one way or another.'

'I doubt that O' Wise one,' Dharmendra said, 'My fourth child, as dear as he might be, I barely see him in the capital, forget the palace. Always wandering off to indulge in distractions, avoiding court and royal affairs like the plague. My last son, my second youngest child, is skilled and a beloved one, but he has much to learn, most importantly to stand up for himself. Even though I speak such, I hope the test will bring forth their best skills. I must ask thus, to help me test them with fire and ice, so not only do I find the best suitor for my throne, I hone all my sons so they can aid their brother in ruling the kingdom fairly.'

Bhimsen took his time to think, then said, 'I will do my best to help you, O' King, but in the end, I pray that your judgement is right. Young souls are like an open canvas, easy to paint in many colours. I pray to heaven that the colours which painted and will paint them are vivid, colours of warmth and strength.'

'Yes, for now, we can only wait for my sons to arrive,' the king said, 'And I hope that they arrive before I pass away, I need to see all of them and ensure they are happy with this selection method, to avoid any conflict later. I know my last son will be one of the first to arrive, sometimes it gets hard to send him away from the palace itself.'

The *pandit* said, 'My lord, if you wish, we can declare the quest to whoever makes it first, that will be a test in itself, as time is of the essence now and will be for any ruler.'

'No, no, that will be unfair and unjust. They are all my sons, no matter what. They all have the right to the throne, so they must get a fair chance. Thus, I have made it clear that none may even enter my chamber, till all five have gathered.'

Bhimsen took his leave, giving a generous bow, 'Send for me if you need anything, Your Majesty. I will retire for the night now.'

'I will, and thank you very much for your kind support, dear friend. Here begins the long wait, till my five stars illuminate my halls again.'

The *pandit* walked through the throne room on his way out. Maps were decorating the wall. He looked at the kingdom's map, river Neri splitting almost at its centre. South-east of that part lay the capital, a few leagues from the split point. The map on its side showed a detailed view of the capital. Three concentric circles, the centre being the royal palace and home of noble lords and the warrior class. The next ring was where most of the merchants lived. Lesser-born farmers lived in the outermost circle, so they could have easy access to agricultural fields, or so was the narrative. Bhimsen looked at the black dots at the periphery of the outermost circle. Those were the sections reserved for the lowest of society, often considered unclean and untouchable by tradition.

As a guest, Bhimsen could have slept in the guest chambers. But for a priest like him, such a luxurious bed didn't suit him well. He preferred the simpler homes in the outer ring of the city. He left the palace behind and walked through the night to his destination. Riders were already galloping into the night, bearing the message from the king across the kingdom – the five princes had been summoned.

Five Princes

THE royal palace gates were decorated on each side with statues of white elephants standing on their two legs, their trunks joining like an arch. Elephants were not only symbols of might and strength, they also represented royalty and wisdom. The stonework was a masterpiece, something that had taken the combined mastery of many artists to create it. The gate welcomed any visitor or resident, representing the strength and wisdom that lay in the royal palace.

The chariot of the third prince Chandreya passed under the elephant arc, making the prince ponder over the duties of royalties. He often wondered – *could a king be so devoted to his own citizens that he neglected his duty to the world and global peace?* The wheel rolled over the path leading to the palace doors, a little pool on the left and a small flower garden on the right.

Finally, the two white and pristine horses pulling it came to a stop in front of the steps leading to the palace building. It was a gigantic architecture, stretching far on each side. There were seven steps of stone leading to the palace door, each representing one of the seven heavens. The seven layers of upper realms of gods. It was a widespread belief that a man's deeds decide which layer he could go to in his afterlife. The king considered the palace as the uppermost layer in the mortal realm, thus, to reside in the palace, one must come through great deeds.

People were going on with their everyday work in the palace courtyard. Some were taking care of spices being dried in the sun, while others worked with the textiles. Few were busy with keeping the lawn and pond clean from fallen leaves. They bowed to the prince as he descended from his chariot. He offered them blessings but maintained a respectful distance from the lower-class servants. He disliked the rigid customs that enforced such hierarchy, but tradition dictated that he would have to bathe if he touched them, a rule he found tedious but unavoidable.

Chandreya was dressed in white like his name which meant 'moon-like.' Minimal gold and jewellery decorated him, enough to show his position as a prince but not too extravagantly. He walked up the stairs to the palace doors, two guards were standing with spears and shields, and on their waistbelts were sheathed swords. An elephant emblem decorated their banners and shields, and tapestries with elephant patterns woven into them hung on each side of the entrance. They, along with other lower-ranking guards gave him a courteous bow, and he returned them a polite smile. The guards opened the door, leading to a grand chamber. The throne was at the far end of the chamber, but his goals were not at the throne or in that chamber that day.

He paid his respect to the throne with a bow, the ministers and general returned him a bow as he turned left, heading to the waiting chamber. 'Finally, at least he made it, this gives us hope,' murmured one of the ministers.

'Well, it's not like he can enter and see what the summoning is for yet. They all need to gather,' someone else replied.

Another minister added, 'I can't think of the reason why the king would go as far as bringing all princes together. I meant that Prince Chandreya is the best choice without a question, but even the first or second princes would have been enough. No offence to Prince Ritikesh, but we can guess it will be long before he reaches the potential of his elder brothers.'

General Yagnesh cleared his throat and said, 'He is quite a capable man, though not so war-trained like the first, but he has spent the most time in the capital and palace among the five brothers. He knows his way with court and diplomacy. Even Prince Chandreya has been away from the palace now and then, but rarely the youngest prince leaves.'

'My Lord, true it might be, but not all wisdom can be learned from one place, sometimes walking out of the capital gives you knowledge that no books or scrolls can. You, as a warrior know better, no training can match the learning a battlefield gives,' said one of the court members.

Finally, the prime minister of the court added, 'Not if one spends all their time away from the palace, like a certain prince we all know. Last I heard, he was off travelling in the southern hills of the kingdom. He took a boat and rowed alone, not even taking a royal chariot, to avoid leaving his tracks it seems. Gods save his soul.'

'I doubt he will make it in time. Perhaps our King should start the announcement once the four are here. After all, the outcomes are unlikely to change,' said Yagnesh.

Prime minister replied, 'That will not be in the nature of our king, fair chance and justice are important in such a crucial decision. As spoiled as he might be, he is still a prince and will be waited for. Hopefully, he has enough sense to make his way here quickly, wherever he was.'

While the court members chatted among themselves, Chandreya entered the waiting chamber. Many others had gathered there too, waiting to find out what the summoning was truly about. Maids and workers bowed to him, he offered his blessings to them and gave his respect to some of the elders he saw on his way by touching their feet. They all looked drained out, perhaps from waiting on the ailing king, yet the coming of the third prince had given them hope enough to smile. There he was greeted by his youngest brother Ritikesh.

It turned out that Chandreya was the third among the five princes to arrive in the palace that day, which was just a coincidence and had nothing to do with him being the third in order of age. Ritikesh touched his feet and said, 'I would have expected you to be earlier, elder brother.'

Chandreya, being humble and diligent, gave his blessings and hugged his brother, with laughter he said, 'Dear youngest brother, it appears to me that when it comes to attending to father, you surpass all your elder brothers.'

Ritikesh was well dressed in vivid colours and gold like a prince should be or would be. He chuckled, 'I was in the capital city only! Besides, I was beaten to it by our elder brother,' as he gestured towards Sarthak, the Second prince, standing with his minister friends. Chandreya went and touched his feet in respect. Sarthak greeted him with love, he was dressed in green and wore gold, pearl and other jewels.

'Ah, so two more to wait for,' he announced.

Chandreya couldn't understand what he meant, 'Why, elder brother? Can we not go and see father yet?'

'All five princes must enter together, or so was Father's wish,' said Ujjwal as he casually walked into the halls. Even the ministers and guards were slightly surprised to see him reach so early. Being the fourth prince in age, he bowed to his elder brothers and hugged Ritikesh before the youngest one could bend to touch his feet. Although he only had gold earrings, gold bangles on his wrist and some necklaces, he had taken his time to comb well and look presentable.

Sarthak got back to talking with the ministers and such when Chandreya joined Ujjwal with a smile and said, 'I would have thought you would take another few days, given how you keep wandering around the kingdom with no news.'

Ujjwal chuckled and said, 'Maybe it was fate that my paths had brought me close to the capital.'

Ritikesh chuckled, 'Yes brother, that explains why your horse was exhausted when you arrived this morning, am I right?' Ujjwal grinned at him, but they all laughed as he was left with flushed cheeks.

'But seriously, younger brother, you should stay more in the capital and spend some time learning the etiquette of the royal court. You barely have attended any court in years or taken to studies of scrolls and scripts, always wandering off in some corner of the map,' Chandreya said in a soft voice.

Ujjwal rolled his eyes, 'I will think about it.'

To follow their father's word, they were to wait till the first prince arrived. The breeze from big windows was enough to keep them soothed, and soon maids brought drinks as refreshments during the hour of wait. Ritikesh and Chandreya thanked the lovely women. Ujjwal picked up his glass and said with a smile, 'Ah, what do we have here, in the hour of long boring wait, here comes the petals of this palace, carrying such fine drinks. What's more, the soul feels light in the presence of those who wear tuberose,' gesturing at her braids decorated with the flower, he then took a second to think, 'And what seems to be the fragrance of sandalwood.'

The lady giggled and walked away, although she might not have understood half the chattering Ujjwal did. Chandreya put a hand on Ujjwal's shoulder and said politely, 'Brother, is this a good time to be flirting and merry-making, while Father is lying sick?'

Ujjwal smiled and said, 'Dear elder, I understand what you mean – but I believe, a beauty does not diminish in the hour of mourning. Consider a sunrise, it remains beautiful no matter the sorrow in one's heart. As long as I can see it, I will admire it – because joy must be embraced, even in times of grief. Because only then can we smile in the hours of sadness, by admiring things which are made to be beautiful and spread joy.'

He then rubbed the side of his head and said, 'Well, my words made a human smile, someone who is not bound to share our worries. So, I don't see anything wrong in that, no harm done, right?'

Chandreya sighed and smiled as he rubbed his face, 'Dear younger, it seems it is hard to argue with you, given how long and complex your words always are. Yet, I hope you will adhere to some common practices and etiquette.'

Ujjwal grinned and said, 'I will certainly try, elder brother.'

Sarthak and his minister friends watched from a distance as his younger brothers chatted among themselves. One of the ministers whispered to the second prince, 'It is a great relief that he is the fourth, not the eldest son, or else gods only know what he would have done to the kingdom.'

Sarthak replied in a casual voice, 'Yes, although he sure is a smart man, even with all his flattery and sugary words. Besides, it is not like our eldest brother is a better choice in any regard.' His voice turned to a whisper as he uttered the last sentence, although his friends nodded in agreement. All his life as the second prince, he had tried to live up to his name which meant 'significant.' Yet, he always remained in his elder brother's shadow.

*

They had been waiting for a long time by then. The king's deteriorating health had become a news that had spread across the kingdom like a wildfire, and soon, it might reach beyond the borders. Whatever the summon was for, it had filled all their hearts with anxiousness. Sarthak kept a straight and strong face, being the eldest one among the present princes. Yet, he kept tapping his foot now and then, a thousand thoughts flooding his mind. 'Do you know what the summon is all about? I have heard it might be related to the inheritance and choosing the Crown Prince,' his friend whispered to him slowly.

He sighed and whispered back, 'Well, Father said the fate of the kingdom depended on it. So, possibly yes. Although, I don't see why to summon all of us here if truly the fate of our kingdom is at stake. Me or Eldest, even Chandreya would have sufficed. Where is my friend Viryanath anyway?'

'He is busy, my lord. If I may, if it indeed comes to something like the selection of Crown Prince, is the eldest son, not the natural choice?' his friend replied.

'Yes, but who knows what father's thoughts have been of late. However, it must be more important than such matters, if all five princes were summoned together, given his deteriorating health. We must wait to find out,' Sarthak said as he tried to keep his thoughts composed.

Chandreya and Ritikesh had a clear solemn look on their face, hoping that whatever their father was about to say was not worse than the rumours themselves. 'Youngest, since you were the one closest to the palace, had you visited father recently? I am ashamed that his health has gone so bad, and none of us, including me, had any idea,' Chandreya said, his hands crossed over his chest.

Ritikesh had a slightly relaxed posture, as he replied, 'It seems Father kept it hidden to not send a wave of panic through the court and kingdom. Think of it, once news of it reaches some spy or outside of borders, we will have armies marching on us or our allies. Especially when no Crown Prince is there, things can get worse.'

'Indeed, your judgements are correct. I… well, what I meant is, sending a letter to us earlier could have been more helpful than sending it now.'

'Perhaps he miscalculated how bad the disease is. After all, many illnesses do not show their true face until it is too late.'

'Whatever it is he has called us all for, I hope every brother will give their best to fulfil father's desires,' Chandreya said looking at

Ujjwal, who seemed to be gossiping with the maids and servants in the waiting chamber.

Ujjwal tried keeping a cheerful face as he described his travels through the kingdom to maids and other servants in great detail, from mathas (a type of monastery) in the west to hills in the south. They laughed, even if they barely understood most of his long sentences, filled with rhymes and complex words. He was saying, '… And atop the high hills, around a fire, they danced in a circle on that cold night with air too thin to breathe. Oh, a dance it was, and it lasted for hours as if they didn't need to breathe...'

Chandreya gasped when he overheard it, many other eyes were on Ujjwal's revelry too. The third prince thought to himself, *dear brother, that does not suit a prince like you.* Arts like dancing and singing were things for the lowly entertainers, not nobles and royals. The folks at higher layers of society always looked down on such skills, focusing more on law, order, battle and at minimum, trade. Chandreya thought *I hope he learns some royal etiquettes before Father kicks him out.*

Ujjwal lowered his voice to a whisper to say, 'I couldn't hold my desire as I went and asked this lady to teach me, teach me every move she did. And I danced with her and others, becoming one with them, one with the hill and wind.' He playfully swirled his hand in the air, as if gesturing to the maid how he would dance with her if it was a private moment. The maid blushed and giggled, but kept her head low.

Chandreya was deep in thought when Ritikesh asked, 'Does his boasting bother you, elder brother?'

The third prince chuckled and said, 'I wish it did anymore, growing up listening to his tales, I doubt it will unnerve me much. He lives up to his name though, a *bright* source of delight he is. But I wonder what the boy can bring to the court. I have been thinking you know, we are five brothers, five fingers that join to make a fist. Together we are strong, no matter who is crowned among us, the other four must act as pillars to keep the Crown Prince above. I do not need to talk about the might of our eldest brother, crown prince or not, he will stay a warrior. Brother Sarthak is good with reading characters; he will do great in the court. You and I, both of us are good with diplomacy and laws. We will serve Eldest well as his diplomats to foreign lands. While, I wonder what Ujjwal would bring, perhaps we could ask him to take the role of chief reveller, bringing the best singers and dancers from all over the world.'

'I thought you despised such entertainment, dear brother,' Ujjwal came strolling to join them.

'I do, yes, personally. But nobles thrive on such indulgence. Did you manage to bore your audience, finally?' Chandreya chuckled to tease him.

'Well, it seems, I ran out of stories to tell. Can you imagine, me, the one who is called Great Wanderer by others–'

'No one calls you that elder brother, don't make things up,' Ritikesh taunted.

Ujjwal purred and looked at him, 'Youngest, don't! Please, let me have my moment. Anyway, yes, I ran out of stories it seems.'

Ritikesh kept his teasing demeanour as he said, quite loud at that, 'Oh really? Have you already told them about the time you were testing your limits with alcohol, and ran half-clothed through the city while drunk?' Ujjwal's face flushed bright red as he heard the ladies giggling from behind.

He pointed a finger at Ritikesh, but with a playful smile he warned, 'You, I will make you pay for this, youngest,' as he ruffled the youngest prince's hair and walked back to indulge the ladies with his most embarrassing tale. Whether the two princes noticed or not, Ujjwal was struggling to hide the sorrow and weariness, his worry for his father, under the mask of laughter.

Chandreya turned to Ritikesh, 'I worry one day, he will find himself in trouble. But we won't be around to help him out.'

'It's not a big deal, brother, he has not been the one to give a helping hand ever either. Most of the time, well every time our eldest brother was around, he would jump to help me out. But brother Ujjwal, he would stand and watch, but not give a hand ever. I mean no offence or harm to him, but I would rather wait for days till Eldest Brother arrives than have to go rescue brother Ujjwal from some trouble he put himself in,' Ritikesh said with a soft and distant voice.

'I see you admire brother Atikaya. Yes, it is true, whenever any of us was in trouble, he was the first to jump to help. Especially for you, since you are the youngest brother, I guess. I wouldn't say Ujjwal ignored you, though he would always be the one to get others in trouble alongside him,' Chandreya groaned softly. Ritikesh's voice was coming from distant memories, 'Well, he wouldn't help Geetika either, our only sister. Just nudge her now and then, give her a stick to hold onto, but not pull her out of trouble. It doesn't matter; I just hope Brother Atikaya arrives soon.'

Prince Atikaya's chariot moved fast in the direction of the royal palace. Four strong horses pulled the chariot, a charioteer guiding their way as Atikaya sat under the shade. His stature was tall, befitting his name which meant 'Big figure.' His attire was regal, with gold and silver decorating him from head to toe. His sword had gems on its hilt, and many foes it had slayed. In the distant allied kingdoms, when enemies would threaten peace, sometimes Atikaya would go for aid, more to reinforce the position and power of Pandhar than to help. His breath was calm, but it was a calm before the storm. The charioteer knew that his very life depended on getting the prince to the palace in time. He was sweating and making his horses foam from their mouths as the chariot rolled at full speed.

The path was free of mud on that sunny day, lined with dry grass on each side. The chariot rolled forward without any trouble. A few unfortunate peasants almost got run over as they were crossing the road and fell in the path of his chariot. They shrieked as they jumped aside, though the prince didn't bother noticing them. His goal for that day was the palace, and only there his focus was set. As the palace was in sight, he shouted at his charioteer, 'What is taking you so long? Get me there faster.' The frightened charioteer made the horse run at their limits, almost exhausted. Finally, the chariot came to a quick halt in front of the great gates of the palace. Atikaya climbed down, hurried through the gates and passed the threshold to the palace. He didn't even bat an eye at all who were working around the pool and in the garden at that late hour of the day.

He raced up the steps to the palace, nobody dared to stand in his way. He was the First prince after all. As he entered the waiting halls, his four brothers turned to see him, relieved that they could enter the king's chamber now. Sarthak and Chandreya came to touch Atikaya's feet, but he just said, 'It's alright,' as he gently shoved them aside. Ujjwal didn't even bother making an effort, while Ritikesh offered his respect with a bow from where he stood. It was Ritikesh who was most delighted to see him. Although, the minsters and Sarthak sighed in relief too, now that the princes could meet their father. Since all five princes had gathered, the door guards didn't stop Atikaya as he barged into his father's chamber. His brothers followed after him.

The Quest

PRINCESS Geetika, the youngest among the siblings, was rubbing her father's feet on the bed. She was in an elegant saree, her long black hair braided and decorated with flowers that only royals could wear. Yet, her face had grown tired, worry had stolen the youth spirit from her face. All her days she spent tending to her sick father, waiting for her brothers to make haste. She would not have hesitated to take the quest on her head if her father hadn't been so secretive about it. Perhaps because he knew that she wouldn't bother waiting for her brothers if she learned what it was.

As Atikaya entered the chamber, she got up and came to touch his feet. Atikaya stopped – this time he patted her head. 'Have a long and happy life,' he blessed her and walked away to stand near the window. She touched the feet of other princes as they entered one after the other. Ujjwal stopped her midway and gave a hug instead, patting her head. Ritikesh blessed her too, as she hugged him and touched his feet, confused about what suited him best.

Chandreya whispered to Ujjwal, 'You shouldn't be encouraging our sister to follow your path.'

The fourth prince rolled his eyes and said, 'Brother, it's just a tradition. Do you think the love and respect she bears for me will diminish if she doesn't touch my feet?' Chandreya shook his head as if Ujjwal was a hopeless case.

The scholar, *Pandit* Bhimsen, stood with his travel bag. An herbalist was sitting on a wooden stool as he tended the king, wiping his head and administering treatments. As he saw his sons filling the chamber, King Dharmendra joked, 'So, you all have managed to arrive before I passed to the other side!' Geetika scoffed at him as she adjusted his pillow, helping him sit up to talk with his sons.

She said, 'Father, you still have a long time to live, stop saying such nonsense.'

The king groaned softly, 'I hope you all are in good health at least, my love for you would not have lessened if you wanted to rest before the meeting.' The king was looking at Atikaya and Chandreya, who looked tired from their travel.

But the third prince replied politely, 'Dear father, no amount of travel would tire us more than the uncertainty of your health. We can only breath in relief after we have seen you with our own eyes.'

There was a gloom in the room, an aura too depressing to behold. Yet, as his nature was, Ujjwal joked back at his father, 'Ah, I was worried sick, but you look much better than I had imagined, father. Then again, since your blood flows through my veins too, I know for sure, it would not be easy to break a royal's spirit.' Chandreya nudged to silence him, but with a rare smile tugging at his lips before he sighed and looked away.

Dharmendra grunted, but followed up by taunting his spoiled child, 'Had it not been for the loyalty your mother demonstrated, I would have wondered if you truly have my blood in you.' Everyone except Atikaya laughed, and Ujjwal rolled his eyes with embarrassment.

To change the topic, he commented, 'Ah sister, your hair has grown long I see. Perhaps we five brothers shall prepare to greet the host of suitors who will come riding on white horses.' Geetika laughed, it had been ages since she had last laughed perhaps. But soon the gloominess returned, reluctant to allow joy to linger in the room.

The princess lowered her head and looked at her father, though the fourth prince kept grinning, uncaring one might think.

The evening sun was still pouring in through the window, filling the chamber with light and warmth. In that light, it could be seen how terrible the king looked. Ritikesh and Sarthak sat by his legs on the bed, replacing Geetika as they gently rubbed his feet. Chandreya and Ujjwal were on their knees beside the bed, two affectionate sons like children ready to hear stories from their father. Atikaya was standing by the window a little away. Dharmendra grunted as he looked at Geetika and then back to his sons, he coughed and said, 'Well, even if I had a long life to live, sooner or later someone needs to take the throne in my stead.' Chandreya and Ujjwal's eyes stayed low, Sarthak's eyes matched the king's gaze. Ritikesh kept looking from face to face, unsure what to say or do. If anyone had asked him what he saw on Atikaya's face, he might have said *indifference*. The king cleared his throat and announced, 'For that end, I have decided to choose my successor through a quest.'

Atikaya's silence was broken. His voice came down as a roar of thunder from storm clouds, 'A quest? Why is that even necessary? Am I not the firstborn, standing here in flesh and blood, the heir to the throne?' Silence fell in the chamber. They heard each other's breath and Atikaya's fury. The king was still composed, and so was the scholar.

King Dharmendra took a long breath before he replied, 'The firstborn, yes. The heir? That is to be decided.'

Eyes burning with furious surprise, Atikaya spoke again, 'What is there to decide? Do old customs and rules not speak of it already? Do other kingdoms not follow that tradition?'

'The old customs you say! Do you have any knowledge of how many massive wars were fought because of flaws in those customs? Yes, there is a rule that the firstborn should be the first choice as a Crown Prince. Yet, the same rules say that a younger prince can be crowned if the firstborn is deemed unfit for the throne.' The king coughed, but before Atikaya could interrupt him, he continued, 'Now, if you be quiet, I will announce the quest. Mind you, if even a donkey could finish this quest, I would happily make it the next ruler. I hope my own sons can do a better job than that option.' Everyone was silent, but Ujjwal couldn't hold back his chuckle, gaining a few glares from others.

Dharmendra coughed again, Ujjwal composed himself and joined his brothers in their silence as Chandreya nudged him with an elbow. The king surely was struggling to speak. He looked at the herbalist to announce the quest. The herbalist got up from his stool and cleared his throat, looked at the faces of all five princes and announced, 'As per our observations and from suggestions of *Pandit* Bhimsen, we have realised that the king is stricken by a rare kind of disease. It doesn't spread to others, so nothing to worry about. This disease drains away the strength of its victim slowly over time. Since it is a rare kind of malady, such is its cure too, an exceptionally rare one. It –'

'And you want us to bring this cure for you, is that the quest to decide your heir?' Atikaya talked over the herbalist's announcement.

'Right to the throne or not, father, I will go and find this cure for your sake,' said Sarthak as he rubbed his father's feet on his lap.

Clenching his fist, Ritikesh looked up and said, 'Brother, then I will join you too. I am sure my knowledge of herbs and plants will be of great help.'

Chandreya said before Sarthak could respond, 'Shall we first hear what schemes our father has in mind at least? We don't even know what the cure is and where to find it.'

Instead of stopping at his cue, Sarthak smiled at Ritikesh, the youngest prince couldn't read it properly, or he would have noticed the coldness in that smile. Sarthak said to him, 'No need of that, youngest. Let the elders do the hard work. You should attend to father, if harm befalls me or other brothers, you might have to follow behind us. Till then, your service to Father will be much needed.' He looked at the King's face, pale and aged beyond his years.

Ritikesh was about to make his point, but he was silenced by his eldest brother's booming voice. Atikaya spoke from his position, 'By your logic, even you should sit back. I can go alone and find it, wherever in ten directions it is.' Everyone's face turned to the first prince, to his towering figure looked even taller.

The king's voice thundered in that chamber, 'Enough! I will do this, do that! You don't even know what the cure is and where to find it.'

The king coughed again, and Geetika brought water and medicine for him in a chalice. The herbalist continued on his behalf, 'The Royal Blue poppy, a rare flower that only blooms atop the snowy peaks of Dharataj. That is the thing you will need to find. Now, know this, there are many blue poppy flowers in the heights of the snowy mountains. As rare as they might be compared to their other coloured counterparts, they are not the cure. Only the Royal Blue poppy, with its majestic blue that's beautiful in both day and night, can cure this illness. Under a bright moonlight, the three white stripes from its centre on each petal are clearly visible, distinguishing it from other ordinary blue poppies. You have to be careful about what you bring back!'

Everyone was listening intently. Ujjwal asked, 'Is there a smell we can use to distinguish, other than the visual cues? And if it is a flower of the cold heights, what will be the best way to bring it down here to preserve most of its properties?'

The scholar looked at him for a moment, eyes lingering and studying him before he replied, 'A keen observation, young prince. Since its smell is the same as other poppy flowers, visual cues are your only leads. Unfortunately, we don't have any other knowledge of distinguishing it. However, we only need its extract, so you can bring it however you can.' Ujjwal nodded and fell silent.

The king recovered his strength and voice to speak, 'So, each of you can take one person with you, one weapon and minimum supplies for your journey. May the blessings of all gods be upon you. Remember, there is no shame in returning empty-handed. No one in three hundred years has accomplished it. Do your duty with honour and be proud of it.'

Atikaya's eyes widened and other princes gasped at the mention of a flower they had only heard in stories – in tales of battle against demon kings in days long forgotten. It was true that the flower had become part of legends. It no longer appeared in books of medicine but in children's stories. Famous for healing terrible wounds and powerful curses in the wars of olden days, even bringing people back from near death, it hadn't been seen or talked about in centuries. Bhimsen spoke to break the silence, 'Lucky for you, unlike in the stories of old, you don't need to bring it by next sunrise. We have few months at hand, but that is the maximum time you have.' Yet, it was the only cure for their father, and stepping stones to the throne for some. Ujjwal stood up, with a cheerful smile he looked at the king and said, 'Well father, drink well and wait till we bring back the flower then. I need to think of a plan to dare the snowy mountains and I need a drink before that. If you allow, I will take your leave.' Neither the king bothered dismissing him, nor the prince waited for his permission as he walked out humming.

Chandreya rubbed his forehead as he stood up, 'Pardon him, father, you know him well. I will do my best to find this cure and bring it back. You must rest and preserve your strength. But know this, you can rely on your sons in these hours of pain.' He touched the king's feet as Dharmendra blessed him, then he bowed to the herbalist and *Pandit*, walking out of the chamber.

Ritikesh fidgeted with his royal ring, trying to say something when

Sarthak told him, 'My recommendation still stands, Youngest. You will do better by being safe here beside Father, helping him. At least one prince will be there to take the throne if all fails, even if you don't earn it.' Ritikesh lowered his gaze, coming up with words to speak when he held his garb tight in one hand.

He looked up to say, 'I am well–'

'I will not debate with you about this; it's not worth my time. Take it as advice from your elder, or not! I care not,' the second prince cut him off. Without much word, Sarthak bowed to the king and stepped out of the chamber. Ritikesh would have lingered longer, but Atikaya's eyes told him that the eldest prince wanted some time alone. The youngest prince patted his sister on the head, the only sibling younger than him, as he playfully ran out of the room before she could reprimand him.

Atikaya slowly moved from the window, his steps seeming calculated, his eyes carrying a warrior's look, always seeing with tactics. He came to his father's bed and said, 'Father, can I take all my weapons instead of another person?'

'Why? Don't you have friends you can trust, my son?' the king teased him.

'I would rather trust my own hands than trust a weaker individual,' the eldest prince replied with an air of superiority.

The king tried to explain like a father would, 'You have always been the shield and sword to your brothers. I know your mother unknowingly burdened you with a task too important. But you can rely on your younger siblings if you need to, there is nothing shameful or weakness in that.'

Atikaya grunted, 'This has nothing to do with mother. I know I am stronger than them all, you know it too. There would be fewer causalities if I worked alone, with efficiency.'

Dharmendra's eyes lowered, a cheer that he had felt from seeing his sons a moment ago was gone. He spoke, 'Sheer strength and efficiency won't work in this task my son, or else I could have sent a group of soldiers or a general. This is a task that took great heroes to accomplish. I know you are capable, but just like ruling a kingdom, this task has never been one man's job. I would reconsider if I were you, power comes from the unity of many forces working together.'

'Father, I have made up my mind. I am going alone. The only question is, will you allow me to take all my weapons instead, or shall I go with just one as others,' Atikaya's voice was unyielding like a mountain. Knowing that Atikaya wouldn't take anyone along, the king agreed to his conditions. Atikaya bowed and left the chamber.

*

The summon was over, *Pandit* Bhimsen said, 'Your Royal Majesty, I think my work here is done for the time being. I will take your leave and look forward to seeing how the five princes approach this quest.' He gave a courteous bow and left the chamber.

Geetika looked furious though, she almost hissed at her father when she said, 'Did you have to pit them against each other like that? That too while they have to face the dangers of the mountain?'

The king said in a composed voice, 'My sweet child, I did what I had to do. I had to harden my heart to send my sons on this quest. But, do you not trust your brothers?'

Geetika gritted her teeth and said, 'I do. Yet, I don't think it was the best choice to make, at least not as a father.'

Dharmendra slowly replied, 'My daughter, sometimes in life, one has to choose between two conflicting roles. Shall I be a father protecting his sons, or shall I be a king seeking the best heir for the entire kingdom? I gave it a long thought, and then only did I come to this conclusion. I understand, even the wise *pandit* told me it seemed like a harsh test, but it was a necessary test.'

'Well, you should have listened to the wise *pandit* then, father. Because to me, it is not merely a reckless quest, a stupid one at that. If they worked together, they would have achieved it faster,' the princess was not having any of his excuses.

'That might be true, but would they have looked deep into them and found their strengths? Have faith in your brothers, they are capable men.'

'And what if you are wrong? Who pays the price?'

'We all will, as we would have if we put someone incompetent on the throne. You need to look beyond your own family and look at what is best for the kingdom. That is a sacrifice a true royal need to do, the sooner you understand, the better it is.'

Geetika was still fuming, and she would have lashed at him again, had he not needed rest. She took a deep breath to calm herself, bowed to the king and before heading out she said, 'Then pray to all the gods that you are right.'

As Geetika walked out, Dharmendra said from behind, 'We can only wait and see now.'

Counsel of Brothers

ATIKAYA was standing alone as he emerged from the king's chamber. Ritikesh took the opportunity and approached him, 'Eldest brother, since elder brother Sarthak denied my assistance, I will be happy to offer it to you. Father himself allowed us to take one person with us, so you taking me wouldn't be going against the rule.'

Atikaya looked at him as if he said something offending. His voice rang loud and clear when he spoke, 'I am the eldest prince, far superior in wisdom and skills of weapons than you all. I have seen Chandreya's archery, Sarthak's mace, and your policies; I don't think I need to band with you lot.'

Ritikesh swallowed, but spoke in a gentle voice again, 'It is not like that Eldest. I know you are capable of doing it on your own, but time is of the essence. I just want us to find the cure fast so that Father will be healed soon. I have no interest in the crown or throne, not when I have so many capable and deserving elder brothers. But I believe if we work together, we can find it faster than working alone.'

'Ritikesh,' Atikaya said, 'You will only slow me down. That's why I took permission from Father to carry all my ammunition and weapons instead of another person. I trust my strength and skills more than I can rely on you. Strong ones do not rely on the weak, it is always the other way around.' Ritikesh opened his mouth to speak again, but Atikaya's gaze silenced him. His eldest brother said, 'If you are so confident in your skills, why don't you try finding it alone and independently? Or else, go find someone else.' Without waiting for Ritikesh's response, Atikaya walked away on his own.

Chandreya saw his youngest brother standing alone, a little sad-looking. He joined him and said, 'My youngest brother, I too share your vision of finding the cure in haste. Will you lend me your help, so that we can find it soon?' His voice was reassuring as he put his hand on Ritikesh's shoulder.

Sarthak was passing by in the meantime, he commented from a distance, 'Chandreya, don't you see, it is a test? He could have sent us all together, but he chose this. You are stronger than that, if you keep asking for help, you might lose the chance for the crown to the youngest of us all.'

He walked by with laughter, but Chandreya said again, 'Please do not heed his words, he can be a little harsh sometimes.'

'It is fine, maybe Father is trying to test our individual skills after all,' Ritikesh said and stepped back. He continued as he clenched his fists, 'I would like to do it on my own strength.'

Chandreya smiled and said, 'If that is what you wish youngest, I can only give you my blessings and pray for your wellbeing.'

Ritikesh bowed and walked away, although Ujjwal brushed his hair on his way and said, 'You will do good kid, don't worry. Don't listen too much to others.' Ujjwal approached Chandreya while munching some cashew nuts. He said, 'Ask any wise men in your knowledge and they all will agree that I wouldn't be much interested in this competition or quest. However, I too agree that working together is the best option to find the cure for father's disease. If I were to help anyone, it would be you. The other two elders are not of my liking, and Ritikesh is still young for a crown prince.'

Chandreya chuckled and patted Ujjwal's back, 'My dear brother, you shouldn't be talking such things about your own brothers. And I don't see why you underestimate them as such?'

Ujjwal chuckled as they walked, 'You know I speak my heart. But

I don't underestimate them, that's why I am offering my help to you, to give you an advantage. You are wise enough to imagine the consequences if Eldest or Sarthak takes the throne. About Ritikesh, he is smart and high-spirited, but he lacks confidence.'

'I am glad you offered me your help. I think we should plan our journey then,' Chandreya continued, but Ujjwal was smiling at a maid who passed by. Chandreya coughed and said, 'Also, don't get too distracted during the journey.' They laughed and walked towards the throne hall.

Atikaya was chatting with the general about something in the throne room. He was mostly nodding. The ministers and General Yagnesh bowed to Chandreya as he and his brother passed by the throne room. It didn't bother Ujjwal whether anyone bowed to him, he preferred it like that. 'Dear younger brother, why are you not interested in the competition? You are a prince after all, with as much right to the throne as any of us,' Chandreya asked.

'Because it is boring,' said Ujjwal casually, 'Being the Crown Prince I mean. Too many responsibilities. I prefer to be free, travel and meet people.'

Chandreya chuckled, 'Does that include flirting with every woman you meet?'

'The string of words you are looking for is *appreciate their beauty,* don't use such callous words please,' Ujjwal replied playfully. Chandreya laughed too, and then his younger brother said, 'Well, I should sit and think of a suitable path. Hopefully, my years of travel will be of some use,' as they approached the palace doors.

As they came out of the palace, in front of them was a stone path, to its left was the royal garden, filled with marble statues at centres of green patches of grass or flowers. On the other side of the stone path was the pond where some of them used to play in their childhood. Once upon a time, beautiful swans used to swim in that pond.

Sarthak and Ritikesh were also standing at the bottom of the steps when Ujjwal and Chandreya joined. 'Is there anything to talk about, elder brother?' asked Chandreya politely as they approached the two princes, each looking away from the other. Ujjwal munched his second last cashew nut as he playfully made Ritikesh eat the final one.

'Atikaya is talking with General Yagnesh and court members. We shall wait to hear what they say,' Sarthak said, not bothering with formalities of titles.

It didn't take long for Atikaya to come out. He announced from the top of the steps, 'The court members have organised a leisure hour tonight, to offer us good wishes and some relaxation before the travel that lay ahead. Everyone is expected to be present.' He finished saying it as he looked at Ujjwal, who shied away and hid behind Chandreya, knowing that the last sentence was for him. As Atikaya was coming down the steps, one servant got freaked out at his bulky appearance approaching so fast. The poor fellow fell and some of the spices he was carrying got sprayed over at Atikaya's regal shoes. Oh, the fury in Atikaya's eyes would have taken the heart away from even a hardy soldier. The servant was trembling from fear. Atikaya roared, 'How dare you, filth!' as he raised his hand to bring doom upon the man.

The princes and guards looked in fear, it was no mere fear of a prince touching a lower-class servant. Atikaya's might was unchecked in his fury, the servant would not live if he took one hit to his face. Chandreya and Ritikesh's hearts pounded in fear, there was nothing they could do to stop the eldest prince, neither by might nor by right. Even Chandreya froze, unable to act against the mighty Atikaya, his *eldest* brother. To Sarthak, it didn't matter as he had already turned to leave.

Perhaps the poor guy's stars were aligned that day, Atikaya's hand did not fall on him. When Atikaya turned, Ujjwal's fingers were wrapped around his wrist, firm and unyielding if not forceful. Ujjwal smiled casually at his eldest brother and said, 'My dear brother, would you really want to go take a dip in river Neri to purify yourself after touching such a lowly man? I mean, it's not worth it I would say, for a prince of your standard at least.' Atikaya's eyes flickered for a moment before his hand relaxed, making Ujjwal release it. His eyes stayed levelled with Ujjwal's, it had been a while since someone dared stop his hand, and for the first time was it one of his younger brothers. The younger prince didn't let him speak as he strode to the man on the floor and said, 'Get up already, you are having daydreams if you think you will get away with such a crime. I will personally see to it that you are taught a lesson.'

The man stood up, a bit relaxed, but still frightened in the presence of Atikaya. Ujjwal grabbed him by the arm, making everyone gasp in disgust. Without a moment delay, Ujjwal was dragging him away as he said faintly without looking back, 'Don't worry, I forgot to take a bath in the morning, so this will be a good excuse to take one now.' Chandreya gasped and rubbed his face, wondering if it was a wise decision to take such a lawless brother with him, someone lacking social etiquette and boundaries. Atikaya was already in front of the three remaining brothers.

His voice was deep, 'The kid has grown too daring! How did he even dare touch me? It will be in your interest to teach him some manners, and remind him who is the older one!' He was mentioning this to Chandreya, but also reminding all of them to not ever dare stand in his way, because if they tried, they might not get a lucky escape like Ujjwal.

*

Sarthak visited his friend Viryanath, a minister of the court. His house was modest like any other title-holding courtier's. Servants were working around, as the duo walked through a corridor. The windows were stained glass, and flowers were lining the veranda. Viryanath led him to his private office and poured drinks into two glasses. As he sat in the private chamber, the prince said, 'My friend, I have brought news on the successor to the throne. Father has decided to put a quest to determine the Crown Prince.'

'Ah, so he has abandoned the old traditions, I see. That's good for *you,* dear friend.'

'Yet, this quest is to bring back the Royal Blue poppy, a rare flower from the Dharataj mountains. It won't be easy, no one in centuries has seen the flower.'

Viryanath rubbed his beard, 'You must account for the fact that no one has *searched* for it in those years, not with the same passion as you and your brothers will. It will be quite a daunting task though, testing your strength, skill, judgement and wisdom. The king has played well, I see.'

'Yes, that is why I need your help. Once I am on the throne, you will certainly become the Prime Minister of the court,' the prince said with a smirk.

Viryanath chuckled, 'Yes, yes, I am happy to help you.' He offered the prince more alcohol as he continued with a grin, 'But you worry too much. I will not be troubled about your eldest brother yet. He is arrogant, high chance he will take the direct path; a path filled with difficult terrain and other perils that lie in wait.'

Sarthak took a long sip of his drink and said, 'Yes, that shall slow him down. And Ritikesh is the least of my worries. He is smart, but not cunning or confident. Since he spent most of his time in the capital, he might not even dare venture out. But the other two are banding together it seems.'

Viryanath sipped his drink and said, 'Yes, that is concerning.'

He was thoughtful when Sarthak continued, 'It will not surprise me if Father is already betting on Chandreya's victory. His honourable lifestyle, following rules to the line, can make him a big thorn in our way.'

'Yes, he is a trouble, true. But I will worry about him later, his blinded honour can bring his undoing. We need to be more careful with Ujjwal. As much as he pretends to be a fool, he is cunning like a fox. Moreover, he has travelled around the kingdom a lot, and he might already be working on the best path to take. Although, as smart as he might be, he has one clear weakness. If we exploit that and take him out of the story, Chandreya will be stranded alone.'

Sarthak grinned, 'That is why I come to you, my friend, someone I can trust, and someone resourceful.'

'I have already thought of a suitable path and a weapon to take down your brother,' Viryanath raised his glass.

The prince sipped his drink and said, 'Don't make it sound so nefarious my friend, they are still my brothers.' He left a soft laugh as he took his leave.

*

The evening came when the five brothers and other court members gathered to celebrate the homecoming of the five princes and pray for the kingdom's future. It began with light drinks and musicians playing *tabla, sitar* and such. The lighting was warm and colourful; lamps made of coloured glass were burning with dancing flames in them. Beautiful ladies danced at the centre of the throne room, Ujjwal's eyes glued to their bodies as they moved like water. They all watched the fluid and precise movement, taking pleasure in the beautiful performance. The other princes engaged in idle chatter, though Ritikesh was brooding. His keen ears set on Sarthak's conversation with Viryanath, waiting for something unspoken to slip through. Ujjwal teased Ritikesh, 'When you go out there, make sure to meet some lovely ladies, it will do good to your smile.'

The youngest prince rolled his eyes and said, 'Where is that even coming from?'

Ujjwal shrugged, 'Uh, you know, you look quite down today. Did anything happen? Anyone said anything?'

'Well, as usual, all of you thinking of me like some pre-teen. I am a prince too.'

'And who said you were not? That's why I am telling you, find some ladies to make laugh, and everyone will remember who you are. They all know me when I step out of the capital,' Ujjwal grinned.

'Brother, that is not the kind of reputation I seek,' Ritikesh scoffed softly.

'Then find the kind of reputation that suits you, brother. But no one will look up to you with a sad face like that, so cheer up,' Ujjwal smirked, he was about to reach Ritikesh's cheek, but the youngest prince pulled away playfully.

As the final notes of music faded, Atikaya rose with a commanding presence. With a flicker of his hand, the musicians and dancers stepped back, their performance dismissed. Ujjwal gasped as he watched them walk away, wanting more of the delightful performance. 'As the eldest of princes, I have an announcement to make, on behalf of my father,' the eldest prince declared. The room fell silent as all eyes were on him.

'As all of you already know, Father is gravely ill. However, there is hope, a precious and rare cure. We five brothers will set to find it once the sun rises in the east. It will mean that we will step out of our border, and the kingdom will not have any of its princes for a while,' he said with the aura of a leader, a commander, as he looked around the room. He took a deep breath, 'We cannot have anyone other than this council know about it, or else forces from outside will try to harm us and the kingdom. Know this, if anyone dares betray our trust, they will be met with harsh judgement.' He turned to Yagnesh as if asking him to ensure that his will was carried in case someone indeed betrayed the court.

Chandreya looked at Atikaya for permission to speak, when Atikaya nodded, he said, 'My dear lords, as you know, with Father being absent for so long, there will be internal tension in the kingdom. I request you all to ensure that peace is maintained while we are gone. The lower courts must be kept… satisfied, and we must stick to our laws even if Father is not able to administer to them.' There were claps from the council members.

Ujjwal rolled his eyes as if bored or rather, annoyed, while Sarthak whispered to Viryanath, 'Even now he is pulling his charm to win the favour of the court. That's everyone's darling Chandreya for you.'

His friend replied as they all stood up to leave, 'Be thankful that the king didn't make it a popularity contest, with this quest you still have a chance to get the throne.' Sarthak sighed and headed out with his friend. Meanwhile, Chandreya bowed to all the ministers as he headed to rest. Ritikesh was lost in thought when he stared at the empty throne.

Ujjwal nudged him on his way out and said, 'Rest dear brother, we all have a long journey to make.' Ritikesh smiled with a tired face and gave Ujjwal a bow as he too headed to sleep.

When all the dealings and planning with the court concluded, the brothers retired to their chambers to rest. Well, most of them did. One of the princes decided to linger around a little more, paying a visit to the performers. Driven by a curiosity he could not describe, Ujjwal approached the quarters where the performers were resting. 'Pardon me, dear lord of songs,' he spoke to one of the musicians when he ran into him.

'Your Highness, what brings your lordship to us?' the musician bowed politely.

Ujjwal acted shy, averting his eyes as he said in a flustered voice, 'Dear sir, what can I say, I have travelled so far and wide, yet rarely have I seen someone with the skills of dance so fluid as your troupe.

Pray, if I were to request, do you think one of them might show me a little more?'

The musician's eyes widened, but before he could respond, Ujjwal whispered, 'Please, I will pay you all extra for your discretion on this matter.' The prince winked and gestured him towards the door. The musician gulped, whether it was fear or just the charm in the prince's words, he called upon one of their dancers, Rupali, her name meaning beautiful. 'My lady, I must admit, your beauty does justice to your name,' Ujjwal said playfully as he gave her a gentle bow. Rupali turned her face down in shyness as she bowed with a blush on her cheek.

'The prince would like to see your dance it seems,' the musician spoke, but Ujjwal interrupted, 'Please, my lord, admire will be a better word,' adding a giggle.

Then he said with a firm voice, 'No, my lady. What I intend is to learn from your steps, so will you be kind of teach me some of your arts?' Rupali could not deny a prince, as she showed him her steps and the prince followed. He chatted through the dance, using playful words and sometimes sentences too long for her to understand. Yet, even as they laughed, the prince swallowed all the steps he could, memorising each of her steps. In the end, even he needed to retire to sleep, since it was going to be an early morning the next day.

*

The morning came, and the brothers were ready to depart. Atikaya chose his longbow, sword and spear. He was a master with all weapons; he only left his mace behind to travel light. Sarthak had chosen his friend to join him, so he only carried his mace with him. Chandreya chose his longbow, for he was the best archer in the kingdom, even superior to Atikaya. Ujjwal was travelling with him, carrying his sword for any emergencies. Although, he trusted his wit and wisdom over metal weapons. At the end, Ritikesh equipped himself with darts, knives and his skilfully brewed poisons.

One by one they visited their father at their leisure before heading out. Geetika ensured that every brother gave her his word to return. Atikaya patted her on the head before he headed out without much of a reply. Sarthak on the other hand said, 'Dear sister, ensure that Father do not worry too much about us. We are the princes of this kingdom, we will not fail, no matter what challenges lie in front of us.'

Ritikesh kissed her on her brow as he said, 'I cannot promise to bring the flower with me, but I will return for sure.' It was enough for Geetika.

Their father said softly, 'As I said, son, there is no shame in returning empty-handed. But I know in my heart, you will not run away from this challenge, will you?'

'No father, I will prove my worth, to you, to all my brothers,' there was a fire in his eyes. Geetika wasn't sure if she felt proud of it, or unease. When Ritikesh was walking out, Chandreya and Ujjwal arrived, the youngest prince bowing to them before heading away.

Ujjwal said from behind, 'Do not forget about the lovely ladies I spoke up, youngest brother.'

Ritikesh only muttered, 'I will not, brother,' as he vanished from their sight.

Chandreya blessed Geetika as she touched his feet before he headed out after touching his father's feet. Ujjwal smiled at her and placed a flower on her head, pulling her cheeks as he said, 'Keep the old man breathing till we come back, okay?'

She giggled and said, 'I will do my duty, you better do your part, brother.' Even though they both were heavy in heart, they offered each other a smile before parting ways. Finally, the brothers took their separate ways.

Atikaya's Strength

VIRYANATH had predicted well after all, Atikaya decided to take the river and head straight for Dharataj mountain. Rivers were routinely used for transport, given that they could save the trouble of passing through wilderness. River Neri was a calm river – the water was so tranquil that sometimes its flow appeared like oil. The deep parts did not have any jiggered rocks either, ones that could rip boats in two. However, ancient creatures dwelled in its depths, troubling anyone who dared take the path.

Atikaya was no ordinary person though, a proud and strong prince who was also master of all weapons. He had left his beloved mace behind, yet his aim was a close competition to Chandreya's. His sword was sharp and long. His chariot reached the village where river Neri split. 'My Lord, are you sure you wouldn't want to take the roads?' the charioteer asked. He replied as he climbed down, 'The road is difficult ahead, and we may not cross the river in good shape. So, travelling on water seems better.' Being a Prince, it was not difficult to hire a boat and ferryman.

Experienced with the river journey, the ferryman was ready and said, 'Your Highness, if you wish, we can head out immediately.'

It made the prince smile, he replied, 'I much appreciate your eagerness to act without wasting time with negotiations.'

The ferryman bowed and said as he prepared his boat, 'My lord, you are a prince. Whatever your need might be, it must be of utmost importance. I wouldn't waste your precious time.' The prince nodded with approval. Atikaya bowed to offer his prayer to the sacred river, to let him pass swiftly and unhindered, washing his feet in her water before he stepped into the boat.

The ferryman rowed against the water, but it was a smooth journey on that silent and calm river. 'A fine boat you have,' the prince remarked, 'Does it have a name? And what about you, what shall I call you?'

The man politely replied, 'I am Kamesh, and I have named her Smruti.' 'Ah, Memory, that's a sweet name for a boat.' There was not much to talk about, other than life on a boat and things which soon bored Atikaya. The night passed and the next day rolled in, a little bit of wind favouring them now and then. The cycle continued.

Atikaya was napping on the boat one day as a dream took him in. *When his younger brother Sarthak was to be born, he stood by his mother's bed and she said, 'Atikaya, as the elder brother, you will have to protect your sibling. You must get strong to protect them.' He smiled and replied, 'Yes Mother, I will get strong, so strong that I can lift a hill with one hand.' She giggled and ruffled his hair, 'My god, I didn't know I had birthed a hero of ages. Though, it will be enough if you can pick your sibling to put on your shoulders, it will be enough to make me feel relaxed.' Her smile was enough to melt his heart; he smiled and nodded. He kissed her hand and rushed off to play with his friends, or whoever he could drag to play with him.*

He woke up, bending over the edge of the boat he gathered some water in his palms and washed his face. The journey was smooth; the sky was clear with a pleasant breeze. He gasped and looked at the sky, wondering which of the infinite stars was his mother. He softly whispered, as if talking to her, 'It's not that I need to get strong because I have to protect them, rather, I have to protect them because I am strong. I have to protect this kingdom because no one else can.'

Small villages passed by in the distance as they kept a steady pace. The prince was thinking to himself now, *that is why I have to find a flower and end this quest soon. Even though they are my blood, they are neither strong enough for this quest, nor for ruling as a Crown Prince.* His chain of thoughts was disturbed as Kamesh pulled the boat to the river bank, slowly bringing it to a stop. 'Your Highness, this is as far as I can take you. No boat will dare venture further on water.'

Atikaya was surprised, he asked, 'You have only come halfway from where we started, why will you not go all the way?'

Kamesh bowed his head and said with respect, 'Your Highness, pardon me, but the water ahead has become the lair of a demon in crocodile shape. People call it the Makar Asur *(Makar: crocodile, Asur: demon)*. No man dares to take his boat into the waters ahead. Forget boats, even the villagers are scared of using the river for their needs. Even when we requested help from the soldiers, they couldn't do anything against the demon.' His tone made Atikaya believe that it was not some made-up story.

'Then why has this news not reached the capital? Why is the king and court unaware of it?' Atikaya grunted, frustrated.

The ferryman lowered his head and said, 'My lord, this is such a small part of the kingdom that perhaps our voices are lost in the wind. We had requested the king so many times but to no avail.' *Has the court grown so weak and incompetent, or is it mere ignorance,* the prince pondered?

Atikaya gasped and said, 'Demon or not, my path must go on. I cannot stop here.'

Kamesh hesitated, but said, 'My Lord, this boat is all I have. My only means to earn rice and wheat for my family. If the Makar Asur damages my Smruti, my family will go hungry for nights.' Atikaya looked ahead, in the far horizon, Dharataj stood with its black rocks covered with white snow.

He took his time to think, then pulled out a few gold coins from his pouch and handed them to Kamesh, 'Here, take this. You can get a new boat; I will take this one and move forward in my journey.'

Kamesh looked at him in surprise. 'My Lord, that is too big of a price. But then again, this boat had taken so long and effort to build, my heart would not stand parting with her. More importantly, it would take time to build a new boat, if you take her away, I will be left empty for long.' Atikaya considered his options, it was a moment of decision. He grunted, understanding the ferryman's plea, but his need was greater. It was one of the few times that a sacrifice was needed for the greater good. He stood up on the boat, looking tall and mighty.

He placed a hand on Kamesh's shoulder, and with a grunt, he said, 'Listen, man, I can buy this boat from you, or I can throw you off the boat and take it by force. Don't test my patience and don't you dare argue with the First Prince.' His eyes didn't carry malice, but there was no mercy either. It was just a cold stare. The ferryman was trembling; he knew the position he was in. He bowed and took Smruti to the sands, stepping out with a dejected face. The prince handed him the entire pouch of gold coins. Before he could say anything, Atikaya took off with the boat.

*

Villages appeared and vanished along the river bank as he kept rowing. As strong as he might be, rowing was a different skill. It was taking him longer than it would have taken with Kamesh holding the oars. He only stopped now and then to rest and eat, and he ate sparingly only when needed. 'Maybe it would have been faster on the land. But no, the forests and rough terrain would have prevented my chariot anyway. May the blessing of Wind god be with me, till I reach the mountains,' he spoke aloud, if only to keep madness at bay.

He could see trees of different kinds at the bank, especially the *Gulmohar* trees which stood out thanks to their bright red flower. They brought back memories of many summers to him, but he shook his head to stay focused. There was no telling when a demon might appear. He breathed in and continued, the only flower his mind was set on was the Royal Blue poppy.

Three days and nights passed, and there was nothing different, other than the lunar phases. With the little breeze now and then, he got enough rest on the boat. The next morning, he could see villagers looking at him with surprised faces. The water felt deeper too, and slower. He realised that he had ventured into the realm of the demon. However, he couldn't stop yet, he had to keep moving forward.

It was a fine afternoon – the wind was good and the water was static. Atikaya kept rowing now and then to catch speed. A gigantic crocodile leapt at him from the water suddenly. It was not any ordinary crocodile, with black scales like soot, its teeth were razor sharp and menacing, and its eyes were blood red. Such a sudden attack surprised even the warrior prince. With quick reflex honed in battles, his hand swept the oar and landed a hit on the demon's snout. The ash oar shattered into pieces from the impact, barely managing to divert the beast. In its fall, the demon hit the boat flat on its belly, almost toppling him over. He grabbed his spear, delicate woodwork with a sharp iron point, ready to shove it into the crocodile.

The Makar Asur swam around the boat and jumped at him from behind, barely giving him time to react. His spear scratched the demon's scales and got chipped. In a desperate move, he punched its face, throwing it back into the water. Even in its dive, its mighty tail threw Atikaya off the boat, breaking the wooden boat in two as it clashed like a thunderbolt. Atikaya swam as fast as he could towards the bank. The monster was fast, its mouth bared and decorated with rows of sharp pointed teeth. Luckily, he managed to secure footing before it could reach him. The crocodile leapt at him, propelled by its powerful tail.

Atikaya had thrown away his bow and sword to the bank, he grabbed its snout with his bare hands. Those who saw them wrestle in the river made songs and stories about it. Some were certainly exaggerated, yet there was no lie in saying that Atikaya held his ground against a demon. The massive beast tried to roll around, but the prince was firm in not letting it get away. It moved from side to side, but Atikaya kept gripping its snout. It was getting taxing, wrestling a beast of water in a river. While the prince gasped, the demon's limbs and tail splashed water as it struggled.

The prince was thrown off at one point, he steadied his feet immediately and grabbed the beast's snout again, sinking his feet into the sand. This time Makar Asur stood on its hind limbs, supported by its tail, towering over Atikaya as it tried to push him down using its bulk. He used his mass and collided with the demon's belly side, throwing it back into the water. Now he locked its mouth in his arms wrapped tightly around the snout. The monstrous body tried shaking him off, but he poured every last bit of his strength to drag it out of the water halfway through.

The prince tripped on a stone, and the beast got free again. Atikaya grabbed open its snout this time, kicking its underbelly. The demon jerked and lost its balance. Using all his strength, Atikaya opened its mouth wide. The breath was disgusting, its maw looked terrifying. But Atikaya didn't stop until he tore it in two. The demon fell to the water, staining it with red and black, while the exhausted prince collapsed on the river bank.

*

He had no idea how long he had slept, yet he could see a straw roof instead of a sky over his head. He grunted while trying to sit up his wounds were washed and bandaged with clean clothes. There was turmeric and herbs to put on his wounds. 'Where am I?' he groaned as someone came into the hut.

'My Lord, Your Majesty, you saved us, all the villages here. Some of the men brought you to our hut, we have been tending your wounds since the battle,' the man replied politely while keeping his head bowed.

There was a sound coming from outside, a cheerful sound of merry-making it seemed. Atikaya rubbed his head, slowly getting to his feet. The man kept his distance from him, a bit worried but being respectful. The prince said, 'What is that noise?'

'A celebration my prince, for your victory over the demon.'

Atikaya looked around, his sword, bow and quiver lay near him. 'Thank you, for bringing those,' he said and paused, 'For this too,' he pointed at his wounds. In need of some fresh air, he stepped out of the hut. There was a great fire as children danced around it in a circle. Drums and pipes were playing, yet it was all uninteresting to him, or rather savage. He thought, *perhaps Ujjwal would have enjoyed it.*

'Where are you headed my lord?' asked one of the villagers.

'To the snowy mountain, through the teeth of rocks,' he said without looking at anyone in particular.

There was a gasp, and whispers. Someone said again, 'They say there is a terrible creature there, Your Highness. It has no legs or head, but still many men it has devoured.'

'So? Didn't I kill your Makar Asur by myself?' the prince replied as if provoked.

The villagers stepped back, but still, one gathered courage and said, 'My lord, of course, you did. But the crocodile demon never came to the land, so many soldiers did not bother with it. Yet, this creature, a *Kabandha*, lives on land and many warriors have met their end in its hand.'

'Are you questioning my strength?' he stared at the villagers with furious eyes, like a living flame was lighting it up.

'No, no, pardon me, my lord,' said the man with a trembling voice, 'I was just letting you know what lies ahead.'

'It does not matter what lies ahead, I must find what I seek, that is all there is,' the prince said with a firm voice. He looked around the place, then walked back to his tent.

A young woman entered with a bowl of stew and said, 'My lord, please have some food, you must recover your strength.' He nodded and picked up the bowl as the girl placed it on the floor. He tasted a spoonful, immediately spitting it out, and threw the stew on her face.

'How dare you make me taste something so horrible,' he roared. The woman trembled in fear as she bowed her head while sitting on her knees.

'Pardon me, Your Highness,' her voice was stuttering, 'This was all we had today.'

Atikaya spat again on the floor, 'Leave me, I have no need of your food. How do you even call yourselves human while eating such filth!' The woman trembled, but did not dare speak, she gently stood up and left, tears in her eyes.

Only out of formality, she said, 'I wish you a pleasant night, Your Highness.' Atikaya gasped and lay down, struggling to sleep, but his body needed rest, so he forced himself to sleep at last.

The next morning was calm and clear, so he gathered his belongings and tested his weapons. He checked the bowstring and tested the sharpness of his sword. The man whose hut he was sleeping in entered, Atikaya realised he had not even asked for his name. It didn't matter as he was about to leave anyway. The man asked, 'My lord, shall you not rest a little more?'

'I have waited too long already, I can't delay any more,' Atikaya said as he stepped out.

Some men and women approached him, still afraid and trembling, they brought out a bag of rice cakes and one of them said, 'My prince, we do not have the delicacies befitting a royal, but this is our best, if you wish to take it along.' He gasped, but his food was lost to the river already. Even as he found it repulsive, he received the gift without any thanks.

Whatever lay ahead, his only way was to meet it head-on. Thus, began his march to the rocky teeth.

Vishakanya

APART from Atikaya, other princes were taking the same path, moving east. Sarthak and his friend were ahead of the other three. After days of journey, the two friends reached the last village on the north-eastern edge of Pandhar. Sondar was a small village dependent on agriculture and wood from the forest. A vast lake stretched near it, beyond it was the lush and deep forest. Once someone crossed the forest, they could reach the foot of the snowy mountain Dharataj, if they *managed* to cross the lake and the forest that is. The climb from that end was less steep than the side Atikaya had picked.

It seemed the village was preparing for something, a summertime festival from the looks of it. There was quite a lot of movement all over the village in the evening, people carrying wood and decorations. Lamps and torches were lit to make light as they were working through the evenings. Ladies were carrying fruits and water, while the men dealt with heavier loads. The village was so full of life and happenings.

Sarthak greeted the local lord as they reached his home. 'Your Highness, had I known of your arrival, I would have arranged for a carriage,' the lord said in a sugar-coated voice.

Sarthak chuckled, 'Unfortunately, making a great display of our position would be bad for our cause currently.'

He leaned forward as he said to the lord, 'It will be very unwise to disclose our arrival here to anyone, I hope that is clear to you Lord

Nilesh.' The prince's voice reminded the lord of his position. Nilesh only nodded in agreement.

Although to Sarthak's surprise, Viryanath said, 'Well lord, while we hope you will keep your mouth closed, pray tell, did you arrange the thing I had asked of?' Sarthak wasn't sure what the thing was, but he was sure that his friend had been doing dealings without consulting him. He wasn't sure if he should admire him or be cautious.

'Yes, my lord, I have arranged everything as you had asked, though I was confused at first, I understand it a little now perhaps,' the man said.

Viryanath eyed him and grunted, 'Thinking isn't part of your job, lord. Do as you are told and you will keep your head longer. You have been paid already, so keep your head out of where it doesn't belong.'

The man cowered, but said with respect, 'Yes, my lord. Your payment was most generous in these times when folks are not putting enough work - even with all the lashes and whips.'

Sarthak said, 'Then tie them up in the sun till they get their lazy asses moving, we can't go on around with peasants slacking off, the kingdom needs its grains and oil.'

'It will not be the exquisite dining you get in your palace, oh Prince,' said Viryanath as they freshened up.

'Do not worry my friend, it will not be the first time I have spent time away from the palace,' the prince replied. They had ensured the lord would leave them to their devices without much interference. They walked out to the open space in the yard of Lord Nilesh's house.

A man beckoned them to head for dinner on a cot placed in the open air for them. In villages like those, it wasn't uncommon to eat outside on the ground. The cot was arranged for the comfort of the royal and noble. Viryanath took a seat first as food was brought to him, he said, 'Well, Atikaya has chosen a path of physical labour and unspoken threats. I would prefer a path that's safe and smooth, even if it seems longer. Talking of your elder brother, it seems he has made quite some progress.' It wasn't surprising that his deeds had reached far across the kingdom, though none other than the princes and court members knew what a prince was doing that far in the kingdom.

From the where the prince and his friend sat, they could see some of the preparations going on in the distance. People were working around the lord's house too, putting up poles and flowers. The friends sat side by side as they dined, the prince visibly looked unimpressed with the food, yet he knew it wasn't a situation to complain about such a trivial matter. He talked with a mouthful of stew, 'Yes, it seems so.'

'Every ear in the kingdom might have heard his accounts with the beast already.'

'Remember my friend, this quest is to find the flower, not to make a glorious display of strength during the journey.'

'True, I think it's better to work from the shadows in disguise. Drawing too much attention with grand performances will also draw enemies closer. That's why I suggest we abandon our titles once we leave the village since we will be stepping out of the kingdom,' said Viryanath, tearing a *roti* into smaller bits. The rest of the dinner happened in silence, as they enjoyed the beautiful view of the star-filled night sky, occasionally hearing the shouts of joy from a distance as people cheered for their hard work in preparation for the upcoming festival.

People were walking around, and fires were lit here and there as the commoners enjoyed the cold breeze in the summer evening. They kept chatting with each other about their everyday lives, their harvest and such small talk. Most eyes ignored the prince and his friend, or perhaps averted from them deliberately. Only now and then maybe a maiden or young man would steal a glance at them, be it in awe, surprise or a hidden spite.

Sarthak wasn't surprised, given that he could make them do his bidding at will, they would prefer to maintain a respectful distance. But did he truly wield such power? They were just two men, against an entire village if they ended up in any disagreement. Yet, he told himself, it's not him they fear, they fear the consequences of angering or harming him, they fear the throne and palace he belonged to. That *fear* keeps them in check, just like fear had kept him from standing up against his eldest brother ever. He shook the thought away, soon Atikaya wouldn't be a problem, none of his brothers would be.

Once dinner was over and Viryanath had washed his hands, he said softly, 'That reminds me, how far do you think your other brothers are?' He waved his for drinks to be brought, while Sarthak took his moment to think.

The prince replied, 'If my reckoning is correct, given when they left, Chandreya and Ujjwal are about a day or two behind us. I am not sure if Ritikesh is undertaking the quest or he stayed behind.' Their conversation had gotten silent like the night, not wanting any unwanted ears to catch a whiff of it.

'Oh, you reckon? Pray tell, how do you plan to stay ahead if your knowledge of them is limited to calculation instead of facts?' Viryanath eyed him, with a strange and cold look.

Sarthak frowned a little, doing his best to hide it he said, 'Is that not the reason I have brought you along? There is no competition to your resourcefulness my friend.'

Viryanath grinned, perhaps satisfied with the compliment, he said, 'That is true indeed. My spies, or informants if you would like, mentioned that your two brothers would be reaching here tomorrow afternoon or early evening. On the other hand, Ritikesh has been quite secretive about his path, if he is in this quest at all. Perhaps even better than our skills.'

'I see, I am not much bothered with Ritikesh, he isn't a major issue to us even if he was in this quest. We should focus on the other two.'

'That is alright my friend. We will have some time to deal with Ujjwal. But know this, once we are out of the borders, even my spies will not be able to aid us. We need to stop the two princes on their way right here.'

They were handed their drinks and Sarthak asked, 'How do you plan to achieve that?'

Viryanath smiled, 'Well, that is quite simple,' and offered his hand to the serving girl. She bowed and took his hand to kiss his ring. Sarthak was sipping his drink when he noticed her for the first time as if she was just a mist until that moment. Her movement looked so unnaturally precise, not even an unnecessary flinch of muscle. There was more to her, he couldn't help but feel intoxicated by the sensual smell of jasmine flowers decorated on her braid.

Her eyes held him like he was bewitched, his eyes twitching as they browsed her face, her entire self while she stood politely. Her long hair was made into a beautiful braid, her attire delicately covering her body while leaving skin exposed enough to rile up any man's desires. Her curves seemed too perfect to be real, perhaps one of the *apsara* from heaven would be a fitting title for her. Such sensual lips, a part of him almost leapt to taste it. He thought, *such a thing of beauty.* But something was odd, eerie in fact. The bewitching eyes had an inner layer to their gaze, empty and assessing as if seeing through him.

He was sipping his drink, Viryanath waited till he had swallowed his drink and said, 'She is a *vishakanya.' (Vish:* Poison, *Kanya:* maiden) He grinned and put a hand on Sarthak's shoulder, reassuring his friend, 'Don't worry, the drink is just alcohol.'

Sarthak was about to vomit out the drink from fear, he gasped and grunted, 'The lady of venom, *a poison maiden?'*

'Yes, the assassins trained since childhood in the arts of poisons, potions and temptation. Not only are they immune to poisons, but they can also carry poisons and venom in their blood. One bite or kiss can be fatal; your younger brother wouldn't stand a chance.'

The prince still found her beautiful, not in a poetic way, but rather like a sharp dagger to cut down foes. He grinned, though a little struggled grin as if he had other thoughts bothering him, thoughts of what fate awaited his younger brother. Viryanath asked, 'You are thinking about how fast Ujjwal will fall, are you not?'

Sarthak remained silent in agreement, and he hated himself for thinking like that, thinking ill for his own brother. He asked, 'Was the practice not outlawed?'

'My friend, she is a rare relic. It was really hard to get her here,' Viryanath eyed the girl, who stood silently, no expression on her face as if it was trained out of her, only to be used when needed – such a perfect weapon.

Sarthak chuckled, 'Then, all that remains for tomorrow is crossing the lake.'

Viryanath waved his hand to dismiss the girl, but she said in a voice flowing like poison on steel, 'My lord, I understand I am dealing with a high-value target. However, how am I to recognise the right target?'

Viryanath smiled and said, 'Oh you will know him without trouble. He wouldn't be able to resist boasting, and every maiden in the village would know him by the nightfall.' The girl stood without changing her expression, taking detailed notes in her head, standing so still that Sarthak doubted if she breathed. These skills didn't come naturally, they must have been sculpted into her like her beauty, without any regard for the soul inside.

Sarthak emphasized, 'Remember, only one of them is your target. And I don't want to harm them; it is better if you slow them down –'

Viryanath cut him off, 'If needed, put him down, we don't want him to come to bite us in the back later. But be precise, we don't want too much news of it. You may leave now; your payment has been completed if I understand it correctly.'

'Does he carry any weapon? Is there any weakness I could exploit?' Her cold haunting voice was making Sarthak worried about what kind of tools his *friend* had at his disposal, her voice lingering in his mind for a while after the words were spoken.

Viryanath fiddled with his gold ring with sapphire on it, and said mockingly, 'Just a sword perhaps, but you need not worry about it, his weakness is women after all.' She nodded with a deadly silence, absorbing the information. Viryanath rubbed the left side of his face, his finger subconsciously running over a scar. He said in a commanding voice, 'Now, I have paid you to get this job done. It is your job to find relevant information. We have a long day ahead, leave us to our devices.'

'Yes, my lord,' the girl bowed with a graceful yet seductive movement and walked away. For one, Sarthak felt a little unease thinking of how much control his friend had on this living weapon, thankful that they were working together, or so he hoped. Second, something about the girl almost made him pity her, her empty eyes and lifeless lips perhaps. But he couldn't shake off the thought that she was not a woman anymore, she was a weapon forged with many years of effort and torture perhaps, made to kill. Even after she was gone, the fragrance of jasmine lingered, not in an intoxicating manner anymore, more like cold hands trying to strangle his throat. Sarthak felt a chill run down his spine, she was quite a formidable weapon, especially against someone so open like Ujjwal.

Once the girl left, Viryanath turned to Sarthak and said, 'What is this hesitation my friend, do you wish to rule from the throne, or live in fear of when one of your brothers might come back to haunt you?'

'I will be haunted with the thoughts of slaying my own kin if harm befalls of them,' said Sarthak, his mind unsure how far he was ready to go for the throne.

'Do you think Atikaya would have hesitated? No, he would cut down anyone in his path. You need to be ruthless,' Viryanath's voice was like a cold dagger, piercing at his heart and soul.

His friend continued, 'Think of this as a grand game of *pasichi* dear prince. The question is, do you want to be the player moving the pawns, or would you become a pawn itself?' Sarthak felt unsettled with Viryanath's words, how much could he trust his friend in the end. The minister added, 'I came all this way to help you, so you would make me the Prime Minister. Unless you have forgotten your part of the bargain, *friend*, be prepared to dirty your hands a little, though it's not your hand that's getting dirty exactly.' A reminder for Sarthak, that he was already too deep in this game, a rigged game at that.

'Fine, I… we will do what needs to be done. I will let your toy deal with Ujjwal however she sees fit. But in our best interest, we leave this village early tomorrow and cross the lake.'

Viryanath's voice changed to a deducing voice, 'No, we are not taking the lake route.'

'What? Why?' Sarthak asked in confusion.

'A spirit has made its abode in the lake, a *yakshya*. If you wish to cross the lake, you must answer its riddles. Failing to do so will petrify you.'

'So, you are suggesting the long way around? Through the wilderness.'

'Yes, filled with animals and snakes, yet no magical hubris. We will take our time around, but stay assured that Atikaya will not gain much speed with the path he has taken. Leave Ujjwal and Chandreya to our assassin,' Viryanath said in a manner that somehow unsettled

Sarthak. At the mention of the lake, some of the villagers passing by gasped. Sarthak understood that if the villagers didn't dare approach the lake, he had no reason to risk his life with it. As long as Viryanath was making a way, they still had an edge, it was a gamble at the end, a gamble with the hope that Atikaya would get tired in his path before reaching the flower.

He gulped, this quest was important, but killing his own brother was something he was still feeling conflicted about. A group of children ran across the road, shouting with delight as they all prepared for the festivities. It brought back memories for Sarthak. *A game of pasichi,* Viryanath had said, a game of *pasichi* Sarthak was playing with Ujjwal as a child. While other brothers focused on weapon training or reading scripture, the spoiled prince was happy to play mind games with his elder brother.

Sarthak remembered the game, his fingers quickly rolling false dice to tip the game in his favour. Ujjwal had been winning till then, reading through his elder brother's patterns easily. Well, nothing was betted upon, so Sarthak hadn't felt too bad about a little cheating, just a little. He tried to recall, how that game ended, did he win? Ah, no, knowing his incoming defeat, Ujjwal had flipped the board over and ran off. Typical of him, so chaotic. *Did he realise that the dice were false? Perhaps, or perhaps not, it doesn't matter,* Sarthak thought to himself.

Here they were again, playing a far more dangerous game. The younger prince would not see if the dice were rigged until it was too late. *Yet, did he deserve such a cruel fate, just for enjoying his vices, and being a little reckless?* Sarthak couldn't be certain. Viryanath could read the uncertainty on his face, his voice cutting through Sarthak's thoughts like a veil as he said, 'You need to get your priorities straight my friend. A fool's life means nothing compared to your right to the throne.'

Sarthak took a long breath and said, 'And what about Chandreya, what is your plan for him?'

His friend said dismissively, 'He would not go far once Ujjwal is out of the equation. He has spent all his time in the buildings of stones; wilderness is not his strength. Take rest, my friend, we have a long way to travel.' He stood and headed to his chamber. Sarthak looked up at the sky, he had been pulling strings and making plots to prevent someone arrogant like Atikaya from sitting on the throne. Yet, none of his schemes had been this lethal, and he couldn't decide if it was worth it. He also wondered if he was actually the one pulling the string, or if he had become a puppet in the grand game as Viryanath had put it.

Closing his eyes, he imagined a kingdom ruled by Atikaya, his body shivered from the very thought. Though it was no soothing experience to recall the poison maiden, equipped with her beauty and temptation skills. Perhaps it wouldn't be so bad if Ujjwal met his end with such a sensual kiss, a kiss of death.

The prince shook his head from every possible thought and headed straight for sleep. He could think about all these later after he had the throne to himself.

Two Princes

THE sun was hanging low in the western sky as it was late afternoon when Chandreya and Ujjwal walked towards Sondar. A pleasant sound of a river flowing nearby was audible, accompanied by the sound of earthen pots getting filled and the giggle of women. It didn't take a moment for the fourth prince to react as he walked through the clearing of trees, approaching the ladies filling water. One of the ladies was surprised to see him emerge from the trees, and she would have almost dropped her pot. Their eyes met, she blushed and lowered her face to hide her shyness.

Ujjwal smiled and said in a coy voice, 'Dear lady with beauty like that of dawn and voice to rival cuckoo, I heard you singing from afar and all my weariness was lost. Yet, rest I must, and evening is nigh. So, pardon me for asking you this, but can you tell us of any settlement nearby where hospitality is offered to strangers?' Other ladies giggled as they joined her, she was blushing red as she failed to grasp half the flattery Ujjwal did.

She had managed to get the gist of his query and said softly, 'Oh lords from the west, the people in our village are very hospital. You might need to just ask politely, and plainly.' Her friends laughed and left with her, leaving Ujjwal smiling as he placed a hand on his chest like she had shot right through his heart, making them laugh even more.

Chandreya shook his head as if he had lost hope for his younger brother when he joined him. 'Why must you flatter every woman you meet?'

'Oh, dear elder, what a waste of life it will be if I, a prince with a charming attitude and so much free time at hand, were not to use it for sharing a giggle with beautiful women,' said Ujjwal as they headed to the village.

'Do you realise that half of your talk is incomprehensible to others?'

They both laughed as they entered the premises of Sondar.

Ujjwal hid his sword under his garment and said, 'Let's not scare them with sharp objects, shall we?' Chandreya followed his lead, slinging his bow on his shoulder like a hunter rather than on his back like a warrior. Houses in Sondar were typical, with straw roofs and mud walls. The sweet aroma of delicious food was filling the air. Ujjwal savoured the smell and said, 'Oh, this makes me even more hungry. I would have had so many meals by now if I was at home.'

His brother teased him, 'Perhaps this is your punishment for making Mother run around to feed you when you were a kid.'

'Do you think Mother would have approved of this quest?' Ujjwal asked with curiosity as he played with a branch he had randomly picked up on their way.

Chandreya said with a matter-of-fact voice, 'I don't think so, not that it matters. A king's words are final; she wouldn't have been able to change it anyway.'

The fourth prince argued, 'Not as a queen, but as a wife and mother she certainly would have made him rethink his decision.'

'That would have been so disrespectful of her, to raise voice against her husband like that,' Chandreya was speaking in the voice of the elders and men of tradition.

'Yet, Geetika sure is doing it in her stead. Seems like mother left her image in Geetika, in her last child.'

'I would say that you have played some parts in corrupting her. Still, she sure will make a good mother, a good queen.'

'Why? Why can't she be something else? Why must she become a queen and not something of her own desire?'

Chandreya looked at Ujjwal as if he had asked something obvious as he answered, 'Well, she is a princess.'

The younger prince wasn't convinced by such a thoughtless answer, so he continued, 'I understand elder brother, but why shall she be losing her freedom because of her birth circumstances? Why can't she choose whom she wants to share her life with?'

Chandreya grunted with frustration, playing with the ring on his finger as he said, 'What do you mean? She is a princess... a life people will sell their souls for… just for the honour of being one. Besides, she already gets to choose who she will marry, like every princess does. We have a ceremony for that, right? When princesses come to age, they get to choose their husband from a long list of suitors.'

'Exactly!' Ujjwal said with a voice ready to debate, 'From princes chosen by… by… by the society. Is it truly freedom? Why can't she choose someone she loves, instead of being married off to a life that she may not even be happy about.'

Chandreya was growing exasperated as he said, 'That is her duty as a princess, to become a queen and continue the royal bloodline. Besides, it is a necessity to honour alliances through marriage, or else bloody wars will commence.'

Ujjwal said almost like testing his limits, 'A duty bestowed upon her by people she doesn't even know.'

'Ujjwal, laws and rules were made to run a stable society! It is not our place to challenge that. Besides, why are you even telling *me* all this? There is nothing to be gained from this pointless discussion, nothing will change according to your will.'

'Well, dear brother, you will be the future king, so I am trying to fill you with my madness so that you might change the rules once you have the throne. Then our lovely sister might get to marry someone of her choice,' Ujjwal said with a playful yet unyielding voice.

Chandreya tried to chuckle, 'My little brother, what makes you so confident that I will be the next king?'

Ujjwal only said casually, as if seriousness was not his skill, 'Since I am helping you brother, I must have confidence in me.'

Chandreya wondered if it was confidence or arrogance, he pressed on, 'Why don't you bring this up later to all the brothers together. We may think on it together, irrespective of who takes the throne.'

Ujjwal strolled ahead as he said, 'Alright if you say so.'

'Ujjwal,' Chandreya's voice was firm enough to make the younger prince turn around and look at him. The third prince continued, 'One thing I must make clear. Even if I were to take the throne, I would not turn to a tyrant bending the rules to my will. They exist for a reason, and I respect them. I will not cross the line to fiddle with them, nor will I allow anyone, even my kin, to fool around with them.' His voice was like a rock standing still, that no power could move. Ujjwal didn't utter a word, though his gaze was like a river that would cut down even the biggest of boulders. He only smiled and headed forward.

They were starving for a day, and would not be getting any well-cooked food for quite some time. Ujjwal suggested, 'Dear brother, shall we find a shelter for the night then.'

Chandreya said, 'Well, I don't think princes should be sleeping in the huts of farmers, if that is what you are recommending.'

Ujjwal sighed from tiredness as he pointed at one of the nearest houses, 'That looks big. Perhaps it belongs to some merchant. That shouldn't be too unbecoming of princes like us to spend a night there, will it?'

Chandreya turned his face away, without arguing. A man was entering the house, and Ujjwal walked casually to him and said, 'Dear Sir. We are travellers from the capital, traders in the profession. I am Murli and that is my friend Shankh. As it happens, the evening has arrived and we will need a place to rest. Will you, good sir, let us know where might guests like us be welcome?' as he greeted with hands joined and a courteous bow.

'My dear fellow, Murli was it? I am Sashidhar, and the village is filled with joy in preparation for the coming festival, you may find hospitality in any house. Feel comfortable to stay in my humble house,' he said as he reciprocated the greeting.

Chandreya joined and said, 'Thank you for the offer, but we would prefer to stay in the house of the village chief.'

Worried that Sashidhar might get offended, Ujjwal immediately said, 'My sir, what my broth – my friend Shankh wants to say is that we will not like to trouble you as you prepare for the festivities. All we need is a roof over our heads and some food to eat. If a kind gentleman like you were to show us to it, we won't mind sleeping in a storage room.'

Sashidhar chuckled, 'You ask me to be kind, yet ask me to let you sleep in a storage room. Isn't that contradictory? In any case, in villages like this, houses are joined. Though I might not have two rooms to spare, I could ask my brother if he has a room for one of you to use.'

Ujjwal bowed and asked, 'So, shall we wait here for your brother's answer?' Sashidhar nodded and walked into his house to ask for his brother's consent.

Chandreya frowned as if regretting bringing Ujjwal along, as he said, 'Why must the first thing you do when you enter this village be lying? We could have just paid for a better suiting accommodation or told them who we are to secure one, instead of sleeping in this, gods know what kind of man's house. I hope not all your honour is lost.'

The younger prince breathed softly in his wait, as he patiently said, 'Dear elder, we will be crossing the border. If some enemy finds it out, we will be easy targets, to blackmail the throne at best. Secrecy is a weapon when wielded well. Besides, look around yourself, don't you see a humble village lost in its preparation for the festivals. Would you find it honourable to impose authority on these people, make them run around in panic to make us comfortable, abandoning their hard-earned joy? A guest must be treated well, even more, if they happen to be royals. Let them enjoy their moment, instead of burdening them with a duty to us.'

'And is it right to just walk in and sleep in someone's house for free?'

'Who said it was free? I will happily offer my service to pay for the generosity shown to us.'

'What services do you speak of brother? We are princes, not some blacksmiths or cobblers! Let us not forget the gift the divine has given us.'

'Well, I would not let the future king blacken his hand. I never said we would pay, I said I would pay with my service, and I will take the load for your part too. I am a hopeless case, after all, nothing much will change, will it?' Ujjwal gave a genuine smile.

'Are you really going to be comfortable in a bed not made of soft feathers, little brother?' Chandreya reminded him of his vices.

Ujjwal chuckled in a carefree manner, 'Brother, we will be soon sleeping on mud and whatnot, this will be far more comfortable for me.' His voice died down as they saw Sashidhar coming out, though for once Chandreya smiled and looked at his younger brother with admiration and pride.

'Welcome dear friends, come inside and get refreshed,' Sashidhar led them in. It was a fairly big household for a village, old people were sitting on cots, while children ran around. The wives and daughters were busy preparing food in the kitchen.

'It smells so good; is it butter and garlic?' Ujjwal asked as Sashidhar showed them their rooms.

'You have a good nose, my friend, I hope you will enjoy the taste too.'

'As the saying goes, everything tastes heavenly to a hungry stomach.'

They both laughed. Sashidhar mentioned in passing, 'Been a while since so many folks from the west crossed through our village.'

Ujjwal's interest piqued as he enquired, 'Pray tell, who else has crossed these lands recently?'

'I wouldn't know the details, but they looked like nobles, perhaps a royal. One of them had a sapphire ring,' Sashidhar said casually, not hiding anything. Ujjwal nodded, glad that his brother had stuck to secrecy too. The dinner was still a while when they sat and chatted lightly about the village and festivities.

Lamps were lit, their light looking lively in that summer breeze. Chandreya was looking up at the starry sky when Sashidhar asked him, 'So, Shankh, what goods do you trade?'

The prince would not lie, out of principle, Ujjwal took the lead and replied, 'Oh, nothing fancy, some spices mostly. We are seeking good trade routes in and out of the kingdom, to alleviate the economic burden our kingdom is under currently.'

The prince yawned and stretched as he said, 'My lord, I forgot to ask, is there any way I could lend a hand with something, to thank your generosity?'

'Oh, please, you are my guest. It is my duty to aid you,' his host returned.

'True, but in the part of the kingdom where I grew up, we have a custom to return help for help, so please offer me any duty you may have,' the prince lied as if it was as natural as blinking to him, keeping a pleasant smile on his lips.

He was sent to fetch water from the well, pulling bucket after bucket of water for the washes after dinner. When he was done and came for the dinner, he grinned and said, 'Now, I am famished. Pardon me if I overeat, though I will try to control it since we have to wake up early.' The others in the dinner hall laughed. He washed his soiled hand, making Chandreya wonder if he could ever understand his younger brother. *Perhaps not.* The ladies were serving and waiting for the men. Ujjwal grunted but didn't push his chaotic ideologies too much, Chandreya looked at him with more gentle eyes than before. Perhaps he was finally able to teach his younger brother some manners.

It was not a grand meal but a decently cooked curry alongside some rice and lentils. They offered their prayers to the goddess of food and wealth, enjoying the meal silently. The princes savoured the taste; they had no idea what they would have to eat once they ventured into the wilderness. When the dinner was over, the princes washed their hands, thanked the ladies for their service and bid goodnight to others in the household. Sashidhar asked, 'Will you be needing anything more?'

Chandreya replied politely, 'No, lord, we already had the pleasure of dining with you. We need nothing more. We wish to depart early, so we will be grateful if our rest is undisturbed.'

Ujjwal said suddenly, 'Yes, that part is non-negotiable, please, no disturbance when we go to bed. But,' he paused, then said, 'The village seems to be preparing with full strength for the festivities. I wonder if we could have a little pleasure of seeing the preparations.'

'Yes, why not? Please feel free to take a walk. Although you might only meet drunkards at this hour. Even the children have gone home after running around all evening,' Sashidhar remarked.

Ujjwal chuckled, 'Dear sir, that is fine with us. After all, you hear a man's true self when he is drunk.' Chandreya gasped, not wanting to get involved in his brother's indulgences, turning to head for his room. Ujjwal was quick like a cat to hold him by his shoulder, a thin line of blade he was walking on, touching his *elder* brother so casually. 'Brother, come with me, it might be the last time we get to enjoy this festival preparation in a village,' he mumbled as he pushed Chandreya out of the house gently.

Drunken Banter

THE two brothers walked the streets together, looking around at the decorations put on throughout Sondar. Few women were returning to their homes after their part in the preparations was over. 'Good evening, ladies,' Ujjwal said with a smile. They hid their faces in a veil and bowed, walking away in a hurry. 'I just wanted to ask for direction,' Ujjwal said to himself with disappointment.

'This might be the place where your charm doesn't work after all,' Chandreya taunted him, and Ujjwal chucked.

After a little roaming around and seeing the beautifully decorated pillars and stages, they came to a place where men sat on jute cots and drank alcohol. They were laughing and gossiping, making Chandreya turn in disgust to leave. Ujjwal stood in his way and casually said, 'Brother, we still have time.'

'No, we are heading back. Ujjwal, I am not going to stoop low enough to go sit and chat with drunkards. Take my advice and avoid them, if you have any honour left. It is unbecoming of a prince to get entangled with such losers,' Chandreya's voice was firm, a strict command.

He stepped aside to leave, but Ujjwal grabbed his wrist firmly, not letting the prince walk away. He said, 'It is also unbecoming of a prince to abandon his citizens to their suffering instead of hearing them out!' Chandreya looked into his younger brother's eyes, something was different, it was not the playful and silly man he had known all his life.

His voice softened, 'What do you mean?'

Ujjwal replied without releasing his wrist, 'Nobles and rich drink to celebrate, to enjoy. The poor, they drink to forget... forget their sorrows, the very sorrows they suffer through because their king and royals abandoned them.'

Before the conversation could go further, two men came to greet them after overhearing their argument. One of them said, 'Are you travellers, my friends? I know when I see someone not from the village.' His breath was reeking of alcohol even from a pace away.

'Yes, we are traders, though we hold nothing to trade at this moment,' Ujjwal replied quickly as if to prevent his elder brother from saying anything rash.

The other man grunted as if trying to form words in his mouth, then he said, 'Come then, why don't you join us for a drink?' Ujjwal placed a hand on Chandreya's shoulder, giving him a 'it is alright' look as he gently made his brother turn around.

Ujjwal and Chandreya sat on opposite beds, there were two more men around them. One man placed six earthen cups for them and brought out a vial full of alcohol. 'What shall we drink for now, eh?' he asked his friends.

Ujjwal answered as if a part of the group already, 'For a day well spent.'

'Yes, that is a good thing to drink to,' the man poured into everyone's glass. They introduced themselves, and Ujjwal made a false introduction for himself and his brother. On his right was Ketan, and on the left was Vijay. On the right of Chandreya sat Mrudul and on the left was Adil. Ujjwal eyed Chandreya to take a few sips out of courtesy, and the prince pretended to sip his drink.

The younger prince asked the group in a friendly voice, 'How have been things of late for you dear fellows, any good harvest lately?'

Vijay took a long sip and replied, 'What can I say, the last flood came out of nowhere, ruined half my crops, and some of our cattle got lost too. Things have been hard since that time. The king doesn't care about what happens to these lands. Bless his soul, yet, he never bothered with seeing if people starve here in the winter.' His voice was burdened with despair.

Chandreya talked this time, and he said, 'My dear friends, the king is sick, or so I have learned when I was in the capital. A good king would never abandon his subjects while he still has strength.'

Mrudul coughed beside him and said, 'Yes, a great king he is, sick too might be, but that is no excuse for pissing on villagers like us, brother,' as he stared straight into Chandreya's eyes. The other three village drunkards agreed by tapping their thighs. 'Tell me, brother,' Mrudul continued, 'If I were to fall sick and fail to make a good harvest to pay my taxes, do you think I will be spared for being a good man? No, I will be awarded with twenty bloody whips from our local lord. Now, you say the king is sick, so we shall just get along with it. Why can't he, the Lord of the kingdom, put someone in charge to handle things when he falls sick? No Crown Prince or Ministers were available to hear our miseries. Forget that, no emissary came to hear our plea either.' He took a long gulp to finish his cup and poured again almost half of it falling outside the cup.

An owl flew overhead, making the drunk folks gasp and join their hands as they said, 'Oh Goddess of Wealth, bless our houses with riches that the nobles will be jealous of.' The owl flew away without ever acknowledging them, so they got back to their drinks.

Ketan grabbed the vial and filled his and Ujjwal's cups. The prince was barely sipping but made sure his cup looked empty every round. As Ketan drank his alcohol, he said, 'It is the pearls, that's all they care about. Their pearl and marble! Everything else is just unimportant to them. They keep asking for more mustard when we barely get time for grain and cereals. The local lord, that brute Nilesh, keeps harassing us with taxes while he hoards all the lands, barely giving us any work. Even when we want to cultivate something, we have to take a loan from him at prices that will take us seven lives to pay back. That bastard would sometimes then ruin our crops just to mess with our lives.' There was sorrow in his voice.

'It is a mess, sometimes when we do get a good yield of rice and wheat, it lies around till pest claim it because the folks at the capital are too busy with their pearl business. They wouldn't care about what we need or want. They give free rein to local lords to whatever they want with us,' Vijay added.

Ujjwal looked at his elder brother, who responded by saying, 'I see, that is completely understandable. But, look at it this way, these trades bring money and keep our economy stable. Food and such things can also be exported when we have a surplus, or imported when we have a deficit.'

Ketan groaned, 'Bloody merchants, there you go with your phoney words.'

Ujjwal laughed in a drunk manner to calm the atmosphere and said, 'Alright my friend, tell us your side of the story too.'

Vijay grabbed the bottle while Ketan continued, 'Very well then, hear me out, you lot. Let us buy your words, Mr. Trader, for a moment. But what happens when that moment passes and war or famine dances in and around our borders? Do you think people will eat the pearl and gold? No, we will need food, and when famine or war visits this world, not many kingdoms will be so generous as to send us food. Yes, your pearl and marble make you city folks rich, make the west of the kingdom important. Yet, you can't just forget the eastern villages and the vast source of food that we are.'

Before Chandreya could speak anything, Ujjwal interrupted, 'Well dear fellas, when we return to the capital, we sure will try to put a word in the king's ear. Heard they are finally choosing the Crown

Prince.'

'They better choose a goddamn good one, someone with a heart for us village folks too,' Adil said as he broke his silence. Vijay was still busy pouring more alcohol into his cup, Ujjwal took the chance and accidentally nudged him. The earthen bottle of alcohol hit the ground and shattered, spilling over all its content.

His fellows shouted, 'My dear gods!' 'What have you done?'

Poor Vijay was too surprised to react to their comments as he stared at the floor and the shattered bottle. 'It is alright, no need to make a scene you nice folks,' Ujjwal tried to talk them down, 'I think that's all we had to talk about after all.'

Chandreya was about to get up when he said, 'Yes, dear men, it was great learning about your village and its... uhm... its importance to the kingdom. But I regret that we must rest soon.'

Adil placed a hand on his thigh to keep him sitting. 'Oh, my friend, worry not, you will have all the night to rest. Let us drink another round.' He looked at the drink seller and shouted at him, 'Send some *mahua*, my friend.'

Chandreya wasn't in the mood to talk or drink more, Ujjwal said, 'I will join you in his stead, friends. Let me show my friend to his chamber.' At that moment a beautiful girl in a saree, covered from toe to neck, brought a new bottle filled with *mahua.*

Ujjwal looked at her and said, 'All this time I thought the star-filled night sky was the most beautiful thing I would see today, and here I stand corrected as I stare at your eyes.' The village folks around him giggled as the lady shied away after handing over the bottle.

Mrudul said to Ujjwal, 'My dear fellow, do you plan on settling down here? But let me tell you, village girls are nothing like your city girls. Hard to win, but they love fiercely.'

The prince replied, 'Is that not what makes them more beautiful, that mystery-shrouded eyes, those barely visible skin?' They all laughed again, except for the third prince. Chandreya could not bear any more of it, he stood up to leave. Ujjwal got up too, turning to the four he said, 'I will be back in a moment my friends.' He grabbed the bottle and pretended to drink, spilling quite a lot in his imitation of a shaky hand.

He joined his elder brother on his walk, who sighed and said, 'Ujjwal, sitting with drunkards and making remarks about women of this village is still a degrading activity at the end. I see where your heart lies, but there must be better ways to know their pain.'

'Do you expect them to open their hearts to us, to royals they think so bitterly of, if you go around announcing who you are? No, brother, we need to get dirty to their level to make them talk,' Ujjwal said with a firm belief in his heart, 'It hurts me too, to act so blatant and vulgar, but that is what we need to gain their trust, to get the permission to see the deepest scars in their hearts.'

Chandreya hissed, 'Brother, I got your point. If I become the Crown Prince, I will keep an ear for their troubles. If not, I will still make their case at the royal court. But there is no need for me to spend a single second more with such jobless hooligans.'

Ujjwal's eyes narrowed, from a calm and carefree breathing, it changed to a cold and composed one. He said, 'I don't think you got my point brother. There are hundreds of such villages, so many people abandoned by us... by you. They, our citizens, suffer because we are too busy maintaining international trade and satisfying lesser lords. Is it not our obligation to make their lives better? Because hear me out oh brother, if we keep turning a blind eye to them and their needs, their resentment will keep festering. It will reach a point where they will take weapons in hand and we will have to deal with civil unrest, or worse, terrorism. What would you do then? Crush them like brother Atikaya would? The best solution is to make our citizens happy, to the last village so that we won't have to see such a dark day in our time.'

Chandreya's eyes widened as he lowered his gaze, he uttered, 'Then what will you have me do? Send riders to every village asking for their wellbeing? If we try to pick every issue from every village, what will happen to the kingdom's economy? Don't forget the kingdom's health, regional peace as its extension, depends on a healthy and growing economy?'

'Wrong! A kingdom is only as strong as its weakest village. Don't forget brother, in the ancient text of Statecraft the scholars have placed Welfare of the People as the second point under the Duties of Kings, while Economic Management comes fourth,' Ujjwal's voice resonated.

Chandreya gasped and turned away, 'I will do what I can if that calms your heart. I will retire now. You may spend time with them if you desire so.'

'Good. Fret not brother, I won't be late in the morning,' said Ujjwal as he started stepping back, without taking his eyes off of his elder brother.

Chandreya said, 'I am more worried about you getting carried away too far.'

'It will take more than four drunkards to make me pass out,' Ujjwal paused and said, 'Though I hope four drunkards were enough to sober you up.' He didn't wait for a reply as he turned and walked towards the group drinking and laughing.

The third prince stood there for a moment, his mind still not able to accept Ujjwal's behaviour, not able to tolerate his harsh attitude. He was still the younger prince and should show respect, yet he didn't lack logic. *Remembering the first few pages of a book with five hundred pages is not a display of wisdom, true wisdom is displayed through virtue and respect,* Chandreya thought while gritting his teeth, yet it was his brother in concern, he would have to keep an eye on the young prince. There was much for the fourth prince to learn, though Chandreya doubted if he had the skills to teach his younger brother.

Ujjwal returned and grabbed the bottle himself, pouring it into everyone's cups while making sure he spilt most of it outside. 'Cheers again, friends,' he said, 'Let us say, if tomorrow I were to return to the capital, if the king were to ask me about what news or request, I have brought, what would you like me to tell?' There was a moment of silence.

Then Mrudul, unable to sit straight anymore, pointed his finger at Ujjwal as he said, 'That is a lot of ifs, still… Tell that… Bearded crook, that we want to be paid for our rice and cereals. Tell him to not let it rot, either build us a storage or take it to the capital and store it there.'

Ujjwal nodded and said, 'That sounds reasonable to me.' He looked from man to man.

Vijay said this time, 'Yes that, and about the damn flood. Every time it rains a little heavier than usual, we get flooded. Tell him to do something about the river.'

Ujjwal thought for a moment and said, 'I am not sure what can be done, but I will pass it on to them for sure. I am grateful for this chat and for sharing things with me. If I may ask, will any of you know some tricks or paths to trek up the mountains safely?' They all looked at his face, studying him silently.

Ketan burst out, 'Have you gone mad? Why would you want that? Are we drinking the same thing?'

Ujjwal chuckled and said, 'Pilgrimage to the mountains apparently cleans one soul.'

'Oh yes, you rich crooks need that a lot. Hmmm…' Mrudul joked. Ujjwal joined with a burst of laughter.

Silence fell, and Ujjwal kept his gaze on the four, still pressing for an answer. Adil gasped and said, 'Fine, if you have really gone so mad, I will tell you where to find the information. There is a man, the old piper, Sarat.'

Ketan added, 'Jolly fellow actually, survived the damn mountain all alone once.'

'Yes, you shall find him in the hut near the big fig tree, you can't miss the tree even when drunk,' Vijay said with a comical laugh.

Ujjwal chuckled, 'Oh, no problem if I finish this then,' as he poured the bottle on his face, emptying it. He said in a playful voice, 'Thank you, my friends, I wish you a good night and perhaps you should head back too, or else your wives might get worried if you got any.'

They laughed with him, finally the prince stood up and walked back to the village road, heading for the old piper.

The Old Piper

UJJWAL walked to the fig tree, it was quite an isolated place to live, even in a village. There was a mud hut with a straw roof like every other house in that village. Like many other houses, a man was sitting outside on a jute-woven cot. Ujjwal approached slowly, leaning forward in a respectful gesture, he said, 'My dear jolly sir, will you happen to be the famous piper Sarat?'

The man placed down his alcohol flask and grunted, 'Yes, I am Sarat, not so famous as a piper though. I am just famous for the lucky escape I made from that damned mountain one time.'

Ujjwal stood by the cot and said, 'My good sir, lucky you must be, and I am lucky to meet you. May I dare ask you for kind suggestions about the best roads to take, if I were ever to climb the mountain? Perhaps tell me the tale of yours in that manner.'

Sarat took a long sip and laughed, 'Go up the mountain? What mad dog has bitten you, young man? From your hair and look, I would have taken you for a nobleman, surprised why a noble would want to hear my tale. But the way you talk, I assume you are another drunkard visiting this village?' The prince only chuckled, not denying or agreeing to the claims. The piper continued, 'What use is the mountain to you? Besides, even with all the alcohol in you, you would laugh at my tale, such a fiction it sounds.'

'Nobles would indeed have no business up the mountain, nor would they be interested in your tale,' Ujjwal chuckled, 'But my dear fellow, let me assure you, I won't even need a single drink to believe in your story. I have come all the way to hear it; I am a collector of lore and tales after all. So, please tell me the adventures you have taken.'

A black cat passed by, Sarat's eyes trailed the beast, he was silent till the cat was gone. He softly said, as if the cat could overhear, 'Some say cats and tigers lived together before they had a fallout, some say cats hide their poop to leave no trace for the tiger to come after them. Well, doesn't matter, I wouldn't trust a cat in my life.'

Ujjwal wasn't sure what it was about, so he just grinned, giving the man assurance that he was still listening. Sarat gestured for him to take a sit, and Ujjwal gently sat on the cot. Sarat grunted and continued, 'It is a story from the time I still had some strength in me. But, to be brutally honest with you my friend, I wasn't in much better shape than today in any manner. Of course, my pipes were more melodious back then.' He coughed a little, Ujjwal looked around for water, but the man only had alcohol for him. After taking a sip, he tried to remember the story while Ujjwal waited patiently.

'Oh yes, I remember, it was autumn then,' the storyteller continued his tale, 'Just after the monsoon had passed. We were a part of this marriage procession. Unlike city folks like you, we don't get horses and *palinki* and such, it was all through bullock carts. I was the piper, of course, playing a *mohuri* alongside the drums, *shehnai and bigul.* It was a cheerful procession; everyone filled with merriment and in high spirits. The groom and bride were sitting on the bullock cart; newlywed lovers lost in their dreams as we travelled through the forest. As I said, the monsoon had recently passed, the soil was wet and we had to travel slowly. The evening was nigh, but we were travelling in a group, so we kept moving forward.'

'If I may interject, how does this relate to the mountain? I mean, aren't the marriages usually between villages?' Ujjwal carefully asked.

The man sighed, 'Oh, no one would want to go through the lake, the other path was too long. So, some madman suggested going north and passing close to the mountain. There were not many bandits back then, as many as now they are. Pesky rascals, looting and plundering our poor folks. But the king would rarely send any soldiers to deal with it, since it's a problem from *outside* the kingdom's border.' The man huffed and continued, 'And even when they arrive, they can't do anything to the bandits!'

Realising that the story had taken an unexpected and unwanted turn, Ujjwal coughed and said, 'Ah I see. So, were you attacked by some bandits during the procession? Or some landslide happened from the mountain?'

The man looked at him, not accusingly, just lost in thought as he recollected his memories. Ujjwal stared around the sleeping village, barely any flames dancing on torches or braziers. Sarat looked up at the sky with a sigh and said, 'No.' There was a dramatic pause, the man looked around, perhaps for the cat. He slowly said, 'All of a sudden it came at us, out of the woods. A regal beast it was, the royal of the forest, a tiger.' The man stopped to take a long sip as Ujjwal watched him lazily, savouring his enthusiasm to tell his accounts.

Sarat gasped in a theatrical horrified expression, 'As I had told you, I was not in my best shape. They all, every one of them, ran away at the first sight of the beast. Not as fast as them, I was the one left behind. It would be a lie if I said I wasn't afraid. I got so frightened when the tiger came at me that I passed out.' Ujjwal was about to laugh, but the man didn't, so he held back his laughter.

The man looked at the north, where the Polestar guides the way. A symbol of hope it was, there were tales of a prince who was given a place in the heavens as a star by the God with eyes like that of a lotus, after he meditated for years devotedly. There were still many hours before the Seven Sages, the seven stars in sickle shape would point north and the polestar would rise. Yet, maybe just the thought was enough to remind the old man of hope.

Then Sarat said, 'The next time I opened my eyes, I was lying in a cave, on a cold floor with stones all around me. There was more to the cave, it was full of bones, skulls… and jewellery.' His eyes widened, and Ujjwal kept his composure, pretending to be excited at the notion of a hoard of jewellery. 'So, you see, I wasn't dead, of course… or else I wouldn't be telling this story,' Sarat laughed a soft laugh, Ujjwal joining him.

The piper continued, 'Thank the gods in heaven, I was still breathing and could move my limbs. But I didn't know where the damned beast was. I could tell that I had been unconscious the whole night, there was a faint light of dawn pouring in from the cave mouth. I searched around with my hand, just bones and stones, sometimes a gold earring or necklace. I wasn't sure where the beast was.'

Sarat looked at his palms as if he could still feel the gold in his hand. He sighed again as he dropped his hand, then looked at Ujjwal and said, 'At first, I thought of escaping and crawled to the cave entrance. There I saw it, the tiger was facing east, rubbing its paw every now and then as it looked at the rising sun. I stepped back and hurried to find a different exit. The cave ran deep and long, I kept walking without an end, it forked now and then.'

He used his hand gestures to show the caves were forking and going up. Then he returned to his story, 'That is when it dawned on me that the dawn would pass soon. The beast would return to devour me.' Sarat paused to clear his throat with alcohol.

The prince waited with anticipation till he continued, 'So, I am going to tell you what I did then. I gathered my wit and courage; I took my towel and grabbed as much of the jewellery as I could. I still had my musical pipe, my *mohuri,* tied up on my waist. I walked silently to the entrance. I was careful enough to not even make a breathing sound.' Ujjwal leaned in, as if preparing for the big reveal, to encourage the man to continue his long tale till he mentioned the mountain path.

The man looked at him, with eyes filled with pride for his great deed. He said, 'I got as close to the tiger as I could, it was still praying to the morning sun or whatever it was doing with rubbing its paws. I played my pipe right near its ear as I stood behind it. It was loud and sudden, even the king of the jungle was startled. It jumped and bolted away in a straight direction.'

Ujjwal put one leg over the other, titling, showing a curious expression to let Sarat expand more on this part. 'I rushed down too,' he continued his tale with gestures of hands, 'In the opposite direction, not knowing where I might end up.'

'Did you find any path?' Ujjwal asked, getting a bit desperate for the information.

Sarat went on, 'I slipped, fell, rolled, but I kept moving down. I fell flat on a stone. When I looked down, it was like steps made of stones, one after the other. Yes, it was, stone after stone arranged just to step on. I climbed down as fast as I could and reached the forests at the foot of the mountains. It was terrible though; I could barely save any gold from those bloody bandits.'

Ujjwal said in a sympathetic gesture, 'Oh, damn those bandits. I see why you must live with so little to yourself –'

'Oh you, folks from the city wouldn't know the pain of living alongside bandits. Even if they don't dare enter the villages, going anywhere becomes a danger to life. They take away the children and women if we don't have enough gold to pay off. But the king wouldn't bother doing anything about it! Matters outside the borders are not theirs to care about! Out of the borders my foot,' Sarat started talking with frustration.

The prince tried to console him, 'My friend, let me assure you, I will make sure the king hears of this matter and –'

'Like hell, he will do anything! The soldiers he had sent ran off after getting raided. Don't you see, these bandits grow up and train in the forests, their tactics are well developed for such fights.'

'Oh, is that so? Would you know why our trained soldiers fail to capture these fiends?' the prince asked with a curious voice.

'They know the forest, they hide, then hit and run away. Your soldiers trained for the battlefield won't last a day against them. Even if the soldiers won a few battles, it won't matter,' Sarat's voice was filled with sadness while Ujjwal listened patiently, absorbing every word.

'Why?' the prince asked to gain a deeper understanding of the issue.

'Why? Haven't you looked around? People are angry, and unhappy, with all the taxes and local lords harassing them, people are at an edge. It becomes easy for the bandits to recruit more, with a promise of justice or revenge if not money or family. You can keep cutting them down, but they will keep coming back like weed. They say that the eldest prince is a great warrior, perhaps he could save us, but gods know if he would even bother visiting villages like these,' said Sarat with visible anger on his face. There was truth in his words, wisdom too, it's always easy to push ideologies on people who are unsatisfied with their lives, easy to spread anarchy in a population that has lost in the law and order that is supposed to protect and govern them.

Ujjwal took a moment to think, then said, 'You know, I have chatted with some of those princes. I will try to convince at least one of them to take care of the bandits in some way or other. I give my word to you.' The prince clasped Sarat's hands in both hands. He then continued, 'Will you be able to tell me where may I find these steps if I were to look for them? I trust every word you say, let me assure you. But I need to know because I plan to visit the mountain, even if everyone considers it madness.' Ujjwal leaned closer as he said the last part, trying to imply to the man that they were in the same boat when it came to how people saw them.

Sarat scratched his head for a moment or two, then answered, 'All I can remember was this temple or shrine-like entrance, hidden within the woods. It was very close to where the bandits were camping, that much I am certain. That is why they caught me as soon as I came out of the mountains. I don't recall a lot you see; I was in a great hurry to find my way home and I was scared to my bones. I was running with my life.'

'Yes, yes, I completely understand that,' said Ujjwal. There was nothing more he could have obtained from the old piper, so the prince decided it was time to rest. 'Thank you, my dear sir, and I will leave you to your own sweet dreams. I will not forget the words I have given you,' he said and headed back to his room.

*

Chandreya had already gotten to his bed, ready to fall asleep when he heard a gentle knock on the door. He sighed, thinking it might be his younger brother who had come back to disturb him. He went to the door and softly said, 'Yes?' as he stood by it.

'I have brought some *kheer,* a pudding, my lord,' a pleasant feminine voice answered. He was a bit surprised but opened the door to greet her. His room was filled with the sweet and sensual aroma of jasmine.

Katyaki wasn't dressed too luxurious or fancy for a village woman, yet she had an intoxicating and seductive look with her saree barely wrapped around her body. 'I am sorry, I am just a guest, not any lords of this house,' Chandreya said while trying to keep his eyes diverted from her scandalous body. Perhaps that is why he couldn't sense the coldness that warped the air around Katyaki.

'Oh, please, it is just a gentle token. Something sweet after dinner,' she said with an innocent yet alluring smile, filled with playfulness. The prince rubbed his head and hesitated, he had enough to feel indebted to Sashidhar, yet he didn't feel right to deny a gift.

He reached out with his hand to accept the grail and said, 'Thank you, my lady, please send my regards to lord Sashidhar.'

It was clear to Katyaki that this was not her target. A *vishakanya* didn't use the same art of killing as regular assassins. They didn't apply poison to weapons or add venom to food or drinks before making the move. Since they could store poison in the body, their preferred method was adding it right before the action. It avoided the risk of accidental mixing up or unnecessary deaths. She took a deep breath and handed over the grail filled with *kheer*. She simply bowed courteously and said, 'Have a pleasant night my lord.' Her eyes were dead and her voice had chill like that of a grave, yet Chandreya was too tired and already heading in to notice her true face.

As the prince closed the door and went to sleep, she turned away. There was no point in carrying out the weight of an undeserved and unwanted death. She wasn't paid to kill this prince, she was a professional, not a fool to go around slaughtering random people to get into trouble. She walked away from the third prince's chamber, to find her real target, Prince Ujjwal.

Kiss of Death

UJJWAL returned to his chamber while humming to the tunes of a peasant song he had learned during one of his travels. His head was feeling slightly heavy by that hour, even though he had only drunk minimally. 'Been a while since I have been this tired, I hope elder brother wakes me up in the morning… shouldn't have boasted about getting up early, *na' ah…*' he gasped as he closed his door. Someone stopped it right before it closed.

'Pardon my intrusion, my lord,' a soft voice of some lady came from outside, followed by a mesmerizing scent of jasmine filling his room. The prince turned around and opened the door – in front of him stood a beauty that could only be described in poetry. Her eyes held his gaze spellbound, though he couldn't help but trace his eyes along her slender body, her smooth waist revealed from a seductively worn saree. He gulped and looked at her lips as she said in a coy voice, 'Just to sweeten your taste before your sleep, I brought you some sweet rice pudding.' She brought forth a grail filled with delicious-looking *kheer*, for a moment reminding him of his childhood. His mouth felt filled with a desire to taste, and he stepped back with brows raised, though still holding onto the door for support as he struggled to stand straight.

He had been completely silent since he saw her, not uttering a single word until she spoke. He smoothly replied, 'Lord Sashidhar has truly a great eye for beauty if he sent a heavenly beauty for such a service.'

'Indeed, he does, and there is no comparison to the delicacies we make in this village, my lord…' she said as she held him with her gaze, getting closer to make him inhale the arousing scent of her flowers as she breathed the alcohol in his breath. He finally stepped back without saying a single word, letting her walk in as he gestured towards a wooden stool near his bed.

She walked in gracefully, her walk smooth and alluring. She heard the door close, and she smirked, *must be hard for a prince to not just walk up to me,* she thought to herself. She adjusted her braid to one side, revealing a little more skin on her back to distract him as she brought the grail to her lips. Her saliva, mixed with potent poison, transferred to the dessert immediately.

Her body was a weapon itself; a weapon forged through hours of training and torment since she was a child. It saves the trouble of carrying iron and vials, no one would ever doubt the harmless woman without a blade or such. It made her job easier, making people let their guards down. Her smell, posture and subtle movement left no space for someone to doubt her true intentions. With her charm, she could put the poisoned grail at someone's lips and they would gladly drink it all for that false promise of passion. But that night, as she was to find out, it had failed to tempt the prince.

He was right behind her, his callous hand tenderly holding her smooth hand, not letting her put the grail down. She could feel his breath on her nape, as he whispered, 'You see, I just had quite a lot of drink, and as far as I reckon, milk and alcohol don't mix well. For your kind effort, why don't you enjoy it for yourself?' Without letting her speak, he raised the grail in her hand, tilting it to make her gulp every drop. It was not going to kill her, yet it was not how she had planned things. Being an assassin always meant improvising to suit any unusual happenings.

She emptied the grail and put it back on the stool, keeping as much pudding as she could in her mouth. She turned playfully in a flash and stared at the drunken prince's eyes. She felt his other hand suddenly tracing from her shoulder to her wrist. She leaned in to kiss him, and his face moved out of her reach. Whether it was drunkenness or playful gesture, she wasn't sure, not that it mattered, he would fall for her soft lips sooner or later. Before she could do anything, he grabbed both her wrists in one hand, his other hand softly placed on her waist as he led her to bed.

She kept the pudding in her mouth, even as she softly groaned with her mouth closed, trying to arouse the prince. He lifted her wrists above her head and slowly made her lie on the bed, keeping his face out of her reach, a playful grin on his lips. Looking at her eyes, his hand moved from her waist upward as he straddled her on the bed. She couldn't even flinch when he tied her wrist to the bedpost with his *uttariya,* quickly getting down from the bed to take a seat on the stool.

Katyaki couldn't speak while her mouth was filled, her eyes widened as she realised her struggling hands wouldn't come free anytime soon. She looked at his face, any sign of desire was absent. He watched, just stared at her blankly, as if waiting… waiting for her to speak. She had to gulp down all the dessert herself, she stared at him venomously, but kept her voice soft as she said, 'What will the lord want to do with a woman tied up on his bed?'

Ujjwal's voice was firm, 'To converse like a gentleman.' He waited, but she couldn't come up with words. He continued, 'Who sent you?'

She kept her voice professional, staying in the role she was playing, 'I am not getting what –'

'Dear lady, with respect, this play is over. I had been quite strict when I told Lord Sashidhar to ensure we were not disturbed in the night. Yet, here you are. So, I am sure it was not him who sent you,' Ujjwal's voice was filled with command and authority.

Katyaki's inner voice screamed at her, this couldn't be the same drunk man from a moment ago. 'I cannot reveal the names of my –'

She was interrupted when he pulled his sword out, 'Was it one of my brothers? Who? Ritikesh or Sarthak?'

'You can't just threaten me!'

'Why not? Are you going to scream, assassin?'

She knew screaming was not her option. 'Forget it, it doesn't matter right now. Tell me what was the task given to you?' Ujjwal's voice was like a blade ready to cut into her heart. There was fury in his eyes, yet he playfully placed the tip of his sword under her chin, lifting it to make her look him in the eyes. She ran many thoughts through her mind, searching for lies and tricks to turn the tables.

Yet, with her hands tied up and a man pointing a sword at her, she didn't have many options. Grinding her teeth, she moved her face away from the sword as she matched his eyes. She gave him the truth in a sarcastic voice, 'To poison you.'

Ujjwal didn't move from his seat, he just glanced at the door and said, 'And am I to believe that you just do what's told to you?' He stood up, and she could guess that he was talking about his elder brother.

She hissed from the bed, 'Your brother is sleeping peacefully and safe, don't worry. Professionals don't go after someone if they are not the target.'

Ujjwal relaxed, he lowered the sword and his demeanour changed to a playful one as he softly said, 'Oh my, I feel flattered and honoured that someone bothered sending an assassin after me. But perhaps they painted a false image of me to you, I won't blame them though. I have put a lot of effort into keeping this illusion intact, can't have myself dragged into royal affairs after all.'

Katyaki looked away from him as he grinned, 'You were supposed to be an easy job for me I was told. How did you even guess I was an assassin? I mean, just bringing some pudding doesn't make someone a killer, especially if it's for some charmer like you.'

Ujjwal smiled to himself, 'You see, I have been talking to women in this village, rarely any of them reply, forget about starting the conversation from their side. I have been keeping an eye on people around, and one this for sure, your attire and attitude are too bold for a young lady from a village. That sharp tongue and enticing body became your undoing. Your weapon gave yourself away, oh temptress.'

Katyaki narrowed her eyes as she stared at him. 'I must admit,' she said, 'You were smarter and more vigilant than my usual targets, mostly spoiled noble lords of your kind.' There was a moment of silence.

'Thank you for the compliment, rare to get those for someone like me,' the prince said as a taunt. He looked at the empty grail, his eyes filled with questions. His voice was playful and casual as he asked, 'So, what was the plan? Were you to drug me with the pudding? Kill me afterwards or what?' The assassin looked into his eyes, and she tried to free her hands. Neither she could do it, nor the prince showed any interest in freeing her. Keeping talking was the only option she had in her situation.

'That pudding was the poison,' she hissed like an angry cobra. Ujjwal's eyes were filled with questions as they wandered on her, studying her, searching for answers. She regretted speaking so much, cursing herself internally.

She felt cornered when he asked, 'How are you still alright then?' It was more of a verification than a question, he already had the answer, or an educated guess. There was only one possibility.

Ujjwal waited for her to answer. Her voice felt distant, as she uttered slowly, 'I am a vishakanya, a poison maiden.' Ujjwal walked up to the door, just standing there thoughtful. The air around him felt so cold, a rage boiling through his blood, a rage not pointed at her.

His voice was tender, yet filled with fury, as he said, 'So, such practices are still alive in this time!' He closed his eyes as he recalled all the kids he had seen throughout his life, children running around with great joy as they chased butterflies and dragonflies, or ran from angry gardeners from whom they had stolen mangoes and such. With his fist clenched hard, he thought, '*Such vile practice of stealing children and feeding them with poison to create the ultimate assassins.*'

He raised his fist to smash on the wall but dropped it after a deep gasp. 'And why do you feel so bothered by it, oh princeling?' Katyaki said while walking a fine line between being polite and taunting him. Though more importantly she was confused by his reaction, she added, 'Do the royals and nobles not benefit from such weapons?'

'Of course, it bothers me. How can a kingdom or world be just and fair, if children can't live full life, a life of their own where they are free to choose their destiny? There are many ways to sabotage and wage war, but taking away the freedom of children, not letting you have the freedom to become a woman of your choice, is not one of them,' said the prince while facing his back, but she could feel he was fuming with anger.

Katyaki wasn't sure how to put it in words, she tried to be polite and calm as she asked, 'And are you going to do something to change that, prince?'

Ujjwal turned around to look at her, he said, 'I can't do anything.' Yet, there was hope in his eyes and smile as he continued, 'But my brother can, once I help him be the Crown Prince.' Ujjwal stood against the wall, more relaxed now.

Katyaki decided to ask him, 'And, what do you plan to do with me, now that I am stuck here?' her heart desperate to see through his illusion of kindness.

The prince rubbed his chin, calculating all the possibilities, he replied, 'You are dangerous to set free, but I don't want you tied up all night –'

'Oh please, you don't need to pretend like you seek no pleasure in life, *prince.* You too are a human after all,' she said in a mix of invitation and hissing, wanting to prove herself that even after all the big talks, he was as rotten as any spoiled royal or noble. There was still a chance for her, all she needed was to bite or kiss him once, one chance to poison him.

Ujjwal kept his gaze on her, 'Out of personal principle, I have never touched a woman if she has not liked it.'

The assassin frowned, her eyebrows rose in a disbelieving look as she hissed softly, 'How did I end up here then, will you tell me?'

The prince rubbed his forehead as he said with a grin, 'Of course, our earlier encounter was different, it was a survival move against an enemy. But we are over that now, so you should stop pretending like you want my touch. The more appropriate question will be, what will you do once I set you *free?'*

She wasn't a stranger to men's gaze, yet Ujjwal's stare made her uneasy, made her feel vulnerable. She groaned, 'What am I supposed to do other than the job given to me? I have no option but to kill or harm you.'

Ujjwal rubbed his face like dealing with a stubborn child, someone like him. His gaze turned intense, 'So, you will follow the order someone *shoved down* your throat, for whatever money or reputation, irrespective of how it might lead to your *own doom?* Would you never sit and think, or resist the profession that was *pushed down* on you?'

That moment she realised what made her nervous about his gaze. His eyes were baring her, not to her skin, but through her skin. He was stripping her to her soul with his look. Even as a temptress, never in her life had she felt so uncovered and bared. It was the first time she met someone who didn't see her as a weapon, someone who saw her as a human with a soul because he was looking straight at her soul.

Unable to hold her emotions, she cried out at him, 'What do you even know about me to say what I shall do or not? Every breath I took was to kill; every word and move was to charm and murder. The only thing I was taught was to assassinate. Even when my throat was dry with thirst, I had to drink poison after poison instead of a single drop of water. I had to sleep on my own vomit and blood!' The rage in her voice made the air boil, Ujjwal's heart sunk from hearing her anger, he could only lower his eyes. She didn't stop, as she hissed like a venomous cobra, 'Since the world has bestowed this fate upon me, and there is nothing else I can do, I will take as many lives as I can even if it leads me to a bitter end!'

Ujjwal rubbed his temple and chose his words carefully, he smiled, not in pity but in a soothingly sad way, 'And gain what? Just to prove that you are exactly what the world says you are. Do you think that will make you free?'

Her heart was filled with desire to punch, bite or scratch him, only if her hands weren't tied. He made her feel so weak and angry at that moment. Yet, so relieved and comfortable, like someone who understood her pain and shared the burden of an imposed fate. Even with her hands restrained, she felt safer or freer than ever in her life. She scoffed at him, 'Killing is the only thing I am free to do! What can I even do to stand against this fate… this curse?'

'Everything else,' Ujjwal said without wasting a breath, 'Anything other than paid assassination. As long as you do anything other than that, you are rejecting the fate forced upon you. You can only be truly free if you choose your own path, instead of walking that path laid out for you.'

'And then what? How long will it keep me alive? As if fate won't come to claim me after all,' she groaned, not ready to accept her helplessness.

'Are you not an assassin, a trained killer? Grab that fate by its throat and rip it apart. I would choose to die of my free will than live as a slave to fate any day,' the prince's voice resonated against her heart.

Katyaki stared at him, but she wasn't allowed to talk. Ujjwal said in a soft and warm voice, 'It is true, I will never understand the life and pain you went through. But know this, this life of a prince, I would have given it away in exchange for freedom to travel and do some carpentry or pottery.' He chuckled, then continued, 'Yet, as I travelled around and met people, I realised that though the position of a prince is tiresome, one can use it to help others. I may not be able to break the curse of this world, but I will put every last strength I have and work hard to make even the smallest of change possible.'

She made a mocking laugh, and just to verify the truth of his words, she taunted, 'Give up your princely life? People will die or kill to be born in a noble family; royal family is a different beast.'

The prince smiled at her taunt, and in a kind voice, he said, 'That is why I am helping my brother become the Crown Prince, instead of running in that race myself. You are correct to say that a royal life comes with privileges. Yet, there are many constraints and restrictions that I cannot handle, nor can I be burdened by the load of responsibilities. But my brother is stronger than me, once we win this quest, he will take the burden on his shoulder like great warriors of old lifted hills with their bare hand.' His back pressed against the wall as the moon and stars moved in the night sky. He closed his eyes in thought.

Perhaps you are not like the others, perhaps there is nobility and humility in you after all, Katyaki thought to herself as she scanned the prince with her trained eyes. Her breath became calm, and her mind felt clear. She held her emotions together as she offered, 'I will help you. I will help with your journey.'

He looked at her in surprise and confusion. His lips pursed together, he asked, 'Why? And if it is not rude to ask, how?'

She smiled coyly, a genuine smile after a long time in her life, 'Your kingdom considers us illegal and won't tolerate training of assassins in plain sight. So, I was trained beyond the borders of your land, and it just happens that I overheard of some lakes and forests and mountains.'

'Why?'

'You said to choose my path! I am choosing now. To help someone who can break the curse.'

Ujjwal scratched his hair, 'And why shall I trust someone who tried to kill me once?'

She replied as her eyes darted aside a little, 'You are too skilled for me it seems; I must admit. Even if I were to try again, I would fail for sure. And if it happens, feel free to kill me, instead of making me feel... like... saf – Hopeful.'

He looked at her, a bit hesitant still, as he said, 'You could be free to do anything, why would you choose to come with us?'

She could read his hesitation. She was an assassin at the end of the day – a weapon. But he was different than others, wasn't he? She said, 'After speaking such words of boldness if you don't give me the chance to taste freedom, why would anyone give me that chance? Why would the people who always thought of me as a weapon or threat would want to grant me a chance to choose my path? So, let me help you, if there was any weight to your words of enlightenment, princeling. Show me oh prince, what true freedom is... Please, set me free.'

The prince was thoughtful, his eyes lingering on her hands and then on her eyes that seemed like they genuinely sought freedom. It was a good offer, since he had never been to the eastern part of the kingdom so much, not this far at all. Had it been only him, he wouldn't have been too concerned. Since he was with Chandreya, his thoughts kept oscillating between trusting her versus playing it safe.

He needed every advantage he could muster compared to his brothers if he had to succeed in making Chandreya the Crown Prince.

Seeing him lost in thought, Katyaki tilted her head and said in a challenging voice, 'Or are you really scared of me being around oh prince? Perhaps you are not so immune to my charms.'

Ujjwal smirked, 'I see. Well, your challenge is accepted, thank you for your offer though. However, let me be very clear, if you try to harm my brother, you won't have another chance.'

'Words have value in my profession. Though it is more of a personal choice, you have my word,' the poison maiden replied.

He decided to take the risk anyway; it was his way after all. He set her hands free as he said, 'We plan to leave at early dawn before the sun god has blessed this world with his first light. Meet us near the old banyan tree.' His hand brushed against hers for a split second, and a shiver went down her spine. It felt strange, a touch so delicate and tender, yet so free of desire or control.

She stood up in a flash, almost making him jerk back, but she had a genuine playful smile as she bowed, 'As you command, Your Highness.' Without waiting for his response, she headed out into the night, to find some rest. The prince sighed and went to sleep.

Ritikesh's Resolve

RITIKESH was in Kundal village when Sarthak and Viryanath left Sondar. The youngest prince decided to keep his identity hidden and assumed the face of an herbalist. He had honed skills of herbs and poison through hard work, though he rarely got to use them. Even his brothers weren't well aware of his skills. He would head to Sondar the next morning, perhaps reaching around the time Chandreya and Ujjwal would be leaving. He needed to keep some distance while staying close enough to not lose track of his brothers.

Kundal was another typical village, with not much life going on. When Ritikesh arrived, the people there too were busy with preparation for the upcoming festival. A great festival of joy it was considered, a festival of two lovers meeting after great ordeals. No ordinary lovers were these – the Destroyer, the god of gods and Lord of the three realms had found his love, goddess of strength and war, the Lady of purity, on this day. People celebrated the day with their hearts seeking a less harsh summer. Children were running with joy as they saw the carnivals appearing, bringing their swings and sweets. The smell of jaggery and *jalebi* was thick in the air.

Ritikesh learned soon that his brothers had been quite secretive about their journey, though he had beaten them in that game quite well. No one would notice him as a prince, not that anyone did before anyway. He was mostly been seen as the youngest son, even as a prince he barely had much authority when his brothers were around. It didn't matter; he had this chance to prove his worth. If his father had thought any less of him, he would have stopped him from joining this quest, to begin with.

Since his father had faith in him, he could go on fighting. He decided to eat at a farmer's house, better than revealing news of his arrival to any Lords of the village. He thanked the farmer for a fresh and warm dinner, though he mixed some of his own spices and herbs for a better taste. The farmer seemed poor, and he couldn't have asked much of him, so he accepted the offer to sleep in the barn. It was good, because rarely would anyone come after a man so poor that he slept in barns. Who would suspect him of being a royal in that state?

He managed to find a space in the barn to sleep in, stinking of buffalos and bulls. He lay on the haystack as he looked at the stars through a window. He had arranged the hay to keep himself comfortable, after following some of the tips Ujjwal had uttered in one of his travel tales where the fourth prince had to spend his night at a local lord's barn. He wondered how fair his brothers were doing. His thoughts wandered off to his sweet sister, he hoped she was not overstressed from the quest. She must have been the most heartbroken of all the siblings, watching her brothers being pitted against each other.

He thought of his mother. She tried to be a fair mother, yet there were times he got favoured as the youngest son. Only if he had the skills of herbs in those days like today, perhaps… he could have saved her. Then again, some of the greatest herbalists were looking after her, if they couldn't succeed, how could he have. This time, it would be different though, they knew what they needed to save their father. Deep down, Ritikesh was sure one of his brothers would manage it, perhaps the mighty Atikaya or hopefully Chandreya would achieve it.

Sarthak shouldn't succeed at any cost. It was for that reason that Ritikesh was keeping a close eye on him and Viryanath. He was going to prove to his elder brother – who always talked down to him – and to everyone that he was capable and a force to be reckoned with. He went through the toxins he had spent so much time preparing. One vial was enough to sicken a small part of a village. The question he had in front of him was how to best use it. Memories haunted him, Ujjwal pushing him off a branch into the pond when he was unsure about the jump. Maybe he would have jumped, even if Ujjwal hadn't pushed him, though at that time, he was half thinking of climbing down from the tree instead. Atikaya and Sarthak swam to rescue him, not that he needed rescuing, he was just a little unsure about the earlier jump. They were always there when any trouble came to him, always pulling him out of it even before he needed to react. Yet, somehow, somewhere along the path of growing up, his elder brothers had gotten distant from him.

Atikaya rarely looked at him, only as if out of pity for his timidness. He didn't go to fight battles like Atikaya, staying back in the capital to help with court and royal affairs. Perhaps that is why his eldest brother couldn't accept him as kin; he was all about strength after all. Sarthak was a different case though, he was a political man. Quite often the second prince visited the courts of noble lords, bringing back news to the royal court. They shared debates and information many times during their father's court. Then why… Sarthak never acknowledged his intellect, always shutting him up during debates as if his points didn't matter. Did being the youngest one mean he wasn't allowed to hold and express opinions?

The prince was startled by a noise down the street. The apparent quarrel wasn't his trouble, but a sleepless night would be. He stood up and dusted off the hay from his attire. Perhaps it was some poor folk fighting around for money or such. He decided it was better off to shut them up by offering some money. He walked down the street to meet the people causing the ruckus.

A man crouched in front of a hut while wearing a torn *lungi* on his waist. He was blocking his face with his hand as a woman kept hitting him with a *jhadu*, a broom made of coconut leaves or grass. 'Why are you two so loud at this hour?' Ritikesh said in a formal but polite voice.

They turned to him, and the woman said, 'That is none of your concern. My husband is my business; I will deal with him however it suits me.' There was another smack on the man, even making Ritikesh flinch back.

The prince gathered his composure and said, 'Please if it is something I could help with, I will gladly help you in exchange for a little quiet.'

The woman stopped and held the broom to her waist, the man stopped shivering. The wife looked at him and said, 'Oh will you now? Will you be getting us back the money he gambled away!'

Ritikesh gulped, maybe it was not a good idea to get involved with other's affairs. He placed his hand on his gold pouch, if it was related to gambling and loss of money, perhaps he could break their fight with some money. He slowly approached and took out some gold, shining in the dim light of torches. He said, 'I could pay off whatever he has lost if that makes you happy?'

The woman howled as if utterly baffled, 'Dear gods, you are just like them, his brothers who spoiled him with all the money. What do you think he will do with that money? Take it and gamble away tomorrow evening itself! No, thank you, you can keep your golds my lord, wherever you are from. We work honestly and earn our share here.'

She hit her husband again; the man still crouched on the floor. Ritikesh wasn't sure what to do, most of the cases in the royal court could be solved with fair monetary compensation or an equal share of whatever was in dispute. He took a moment to think about what his brothers would have done.

Atikaya would have beaten the man himself perhaps, and Sarthak would have used his resources to get the money out of the winner. Chandreya would have walked away at the very mention of gambling, Ujjwal would have perhaps said something unnecessarily long that was inappropriate for the situation, or maybe uttered some words of brilliance, he was nigh unpredictable after all. But he was not them, he was the youngest prince, and he couldn't do what others did. He looked into himself and said, 'Tell me what truly causes you pain, my lady, would his brothers not pay off the money he has lost if they used to spoil him so much?'

'Don't you see that is the problem, oh lord?' the woman stopped, perhaps tired now. She said with a sad face, 'They used to give him all the things he asked for since childhood, showering him with their hard-earned money. But they grew up and got families, and so did he. No way they could have supported him anymore, but being a lazy ass he was, he couldn't get much job done. Treating him like a weakling or wimp, they kept feeding him till he was a grown-up, acting like some affectionate brothers they were. Like a fat load of good that did. And when it matters, they are all gone!'

She paused to catch her breath, but before Ritikesh could speak, she continued, 'Only if his brothers hadn't spoiled him, perhaps taught him some life skills or been a little harsh when he was slacking his ass off. Now he has debts to pay, no job at hand and when I got some money arranged, he went away to gamble it.'

The man tried to speak, 'I was trying to get it double –'

She silenced him with a hit from the broom. Ritikesh was about to say something, but then the mighty wave of realisation hit him. Had he not been in a similar boat, guided by his brothers all his life till they all turned away?

Had he not been the favourite all the time? Had he not spent all his life at the capital, dealing with royal affairs after affairs? Then why did he feel so helpless to help out that couple? A cool breeze washed past his face, a relief on that summer night. He gasped long and said, 'My lady, I see that money would be not of much help here. But if you may, can you tell me why can he not find any jobs?'

She groaned again, 'You must be from the cities if you don't know how hard we have it in villages. The local lords would hold onto the lands, only letting a select few to work on their fields. There is not much one could learn either since everyone keeps their jobs their family's secret.'

Ritikesh thought for a moment, he was a prince after all, and he should be able to find some solution for his citizens. He pulled out some of his herbs and said, 'There is not much I can teach in a few hours, but here are some medicines. You could find them around the village too. Maybe you and your husband could sell some of these mixtures to get some money. I will try and talk to one of the lords or someone to help find your husband a job. I can only try at this moment, but I will try my best.'

He gestured the pouches filled with different herbs at her. She was hesitant, he sighed and said, 'I am from the capital, travelling for a reason. These are of not much use to me; I could find more anyway. They are nothing suspicious either, you can get it verified by your herbalist here.'

She looked down at her husband, seeing his sorry state, she finally reached out and took the pouches. 'Thank you, my lord, may the gods bless you,' the man muttered from the ground.

Ritikesh got to one of his knees to be at the level of the man. He tried his best to make a royal intimidating voice, 'Hear me out, I know where you live now. If I am ever crossing by this village and come across your gambling addiction, instead of broom you will receive whips on your back. I am trying to help you out here, but you need to accept the help and make use of it!'

The man nodded while his hands trembled, clearly the effect of alcohol. Ritikesh sighed and stood up, recommending some mixture of herbs to help him slowly get over his addiction. The woman gave him many thanks as he walked back to his hay bed, dragging her husband inside. That was not something that would have happened in the capital or one of the cities. Villages were truly different, with their own tales and problems.

The night felt light, morning came soon for the youngest prince. He kept thinking back to the couple. It was such a rare case for him, so different than usual land disputes or trade conflicts they dealt with at the royal court. Had he not travelled to these remote villages, he could have never learned of their problems, and most importantly, how to resolve them.

'Maybe I understand your travel addiction a little more, brother Ujjwal, perhaps I can understand you a little better now,' he muttered to himself as he made his way to one of the local merchants.

Even though he didn't want to reveal his identity, he used his royal ring to use his authority to get the merchant to agree to his terms. After a little word of authority from the prince, the merchant was obliged to give the drunken man some sort of basic work to start with, as long as his addiction didn't cause any issues. Ritikesh was content with the deal, he felt like he had achieved something, something by himself.

That reminded him of the times at his father's court. Perhaps he could have resolved issues of the citizens in his ways if he was allowed to speak up, to put his thoughts on the table. *Who was it that always talked me down?* He said to himself as he recalled his arguments and debates with the second prince. He looked up at the sky, it was a clear day ahead, a long day to travel to Sondar. Then he had a couple of choices, either to find a way of his own to seek the Royal Blue poppy or follow one of his brothers.

'I need to prove myself, no, I *will* prove myself this time. I have skills of my own, brother,' he said to the sky as if asking the winds to carry his message, his warning. A humiliation, a desperation, a dark thought took hold of his mind. The desire to prove his worth to those who had insulted or looked down on him became his drive. The youngest prince looked at his hands, they were not skilled in warfare like Atikaya, and he wouldn't be able to challenge the first prince. But he had wits like Sarthak and Ujjwal, though he felt no enmity to the fourth prince. He ran his fingers over the vial of toxins he was left with, immediately withdrawing his hands. Perhaps there are other ways to poison people, one that doesn't affect the body, but the mind. He decided to follow his elder brother and prove his skills personally.

Teeth of Rocks

AFTER a hectic journey towards the North, Atikaya stepped out of the kingdom's boundary, venturing into the rocky region lying beyond. It was a sight to behold for some, while for others it was eerie. Rocks pointing upward, column upon column of those spiked rocks everywhere. They were towering, appearing like thousands of rocky teeth. That barren land was not just famous for those grey rock spikes, something else made it more infamous. It was the dwelling ground for a creepy creature, a *Kabandha.* It was a monster with no head, a mouth on its abdomen and eyes on what's supposed to be its chest. Its limbs were small and clawed. Rocks were its major diet, but birds or beasts fell prey to it now and then too. Humans were rare in its dishes, but it never shied away from them, they were more of a delicacy to it.

The confrontation with Makar Asur in Neri was intense. Though, Atikaya had managed to be left with enough food for the journey, his sword, bow and arrow intact. There had been no time to get his chipped spear repaired, so he left it behind. The bow was a masterpiece of woodwork, while he had got his sword blessed in the temple of the God of Destruction, the Lord of three realms. It was a mere blessing instead of some enchantment like in the olden days, yet the idea of a blessing was enough to give hope. More than any weapon or enchantment, he had faith in his own strength. He had wrestled beasts in the arena, mighty tigers and bulls at that.

He walked for hours in the direction of the snowy mountain, its gigantic figure looming in the distance. It reminded him of himself, tall, mighty, and unyielding. Afternoon came and clouds were stained with pink sunlight soon. He stopped to eat and rest through the night, and there had been no sign of any demons or creatures. His valour was famous from his kingdom to the entire land. It had started itching in his mind that a great warrior like him was to pass through those lands without defeating the *Kabandha.*

Many warriors it had devoured, or so was told to him by the villagers. What kind of strong prince was he, if he couldn't defeat such a demon? How was he supposed to keep the kingdom safe, if he lacked the strength to surpass one enemy? These were the thoughts eating his mind from the inside. He took a long breath and turned his face to the south as if looking back at his home. The eldest prince said, 'Is that what has become of your kingdom, oh father of mine? Your military strength dwindling, its soldiers running away from threats that devour your citizens. Demons or not, it should have been their duty to protect, yet they would not, fear is no excuse for such weakness.'

He said to the barren stretch in front of him, 'Long have I fought armies of men, crushed my enemies at the land of others even. Yet, why do I fail to find this monster at the border of my own kingdom, why shall I not be the one whose strength brings an end to its terror!' Soon, his arrogance taunted him, wanting him to be part of songs and tales about how he conquered the wretched creature. His voice echoed through the rocks, 'How dare they challenge my might, to even think that I need to be scared of some coward demon! I would show the villagers, and everyone in the kingdom… no, in the world itself, Atikaya is not going to bend even in front of demons of old.' The words of caution from the fair villagers had become the fuel for his fire of ego.

The next morning, after freshening up for the day's travel, he roared into the silent air, 'Oh *Kabandha,* headless fiend of these rocky teeth, I challenge you to come forth and battle me.' His declaration was replied with emptiness. No demon came, the day passed on as usual, apart from a little drizzle in the afternoon. There were no stars in the sky that night, a host of clouds covering everywhere. The next day also passed without any glorious battle, though the sky was clear with a bright sun. The prince was getting irritated with each day; every day he spent in search of the demon was a day he could have moved closer to the mountain. By his reckoning, he would have reached to deep forest's edge by then. Yet, something in him could not make him turn away from the thought of that demon.

Someone else would have thanked heaven and celebrated when the demon wasn't blocking their path. However, Atikaya was filled with a desire for heroics now. With every passing day, his zeal to slay the demon increased. It had gone so far that his eyes were set on defeating the infamous *Kabandha,* putting his true mission as a second priority. He said to his father, though he wasn't there to hear, 'Oh dear father, what a fool you were to set us on this pointless competition. Was there ever a question, on who is strong enough to scale the great mountain and find the damned flower for you? Since you have grown so *weak* to not recognise strength anymore, I will show you. I will defeat this demon and show you that I am the *rightful* heir to the throne.'

Unable to find rest, he couldn't head for Dharataj anymore, he kept wandering around in the hope of finding the monster somewhere. His head filled with one thought only, *Once I put down the demon, no one, not even my father would question my strength again.* The memories of his home, his siblings, and his mother, all seemed like a blur compared to the moves he kept practising to unleash against the monster once it showed up… if it showed up at all.

*

Another day went by in his frenzied search for the demon. Perhaps the heavens heard his war cry and aided him, or maybe it was sheer luck, he didn't care much when he finally came across the *Kabandha* while he wandered around. It was in deep sleep among the rocks, a massive figure lying on its back on the ground. It had long claws and there was no way of seeing its face from the ground level. Atikaya was filled with ecstasy, accompanied by a rage from the merry hunt he had to go through to find the monster. He challenged it with a proud and loud voice, 'Get up, you foul creature, get up and face me. Let justice be done upon you.'

The *Kabandha* groaned and turned; it took it a while to get back up from its back. The *Kabandha's* eyes were red when it woke from its slumber. In a furious voice, it spoke to the prince, 'Puny human, do not force me to incur my wrath upon you. Be gone, and I will forget I ever saw you.' Only if the creature had a head, for the first time in his life, Atikaya would have had to look up to match its eyes.

Offended by its words, he challenged again, 'I am not going anywhere until I have slain you. That is my duty as the prince of the kingdom that lies at your doorstep. Rise, demon of the underworld, let's test my sword against your claws.' The creature finally stood up, standing fairly taller than Atikaya as it looked down at him, wiping its eyes with one of its long hands.

Yes, the prince noticed that the accounts hadn't been fully correct, it had hands longer than its legs. Then again, no one must have survived it to tell the true tale. He could only imagine the looks on everyone's faces when they learned who had finally bested the legendary being. It said, still uninterested in the prince's challenge, 'I have no interest in fighting humans. I sleep when I like, and eat when I like. Since you disturbed me, I will just tear you open and go back to my sleep.' Atikaya's eyes were filled with rage and a lust for battle that he finally got to satisfy.

The demon leapt at him, faster than Atikaya had anticipated. As rare an event as it might be, he had to retreat a few steps, jumping back quickly. It truly enraged him to his bones to think that he had to retreat; the thought made him fume with anger. He had not expected to be bested by a creature with no legs or head. His swings of sword were barely able to deflect the *Kabandha's* claws; he hadn't been able to land an attack yet. The demon came charging fast, its jaws wide open as it tried to bite his head off. Atikaya had to drop his sword and use both his hands to stop the demon's mouth from closing. Its claws came at him from both sides; his only way was to slide under the demon. He tried to topple it by grabbing its leg, but the demon moved away before he could grip it hard enough.

The prince jumped away just in time to avoid getting sliced by its claws. He was panting, picking his sword he deflected the next few claw attacks. Worried that he might get his sword damaged too, and to turn the fight in his favour, he made some distance between himself and the monster. Then he brought forth his bow and arrows. His aim was precise, and his bow was strong, but the demon's hide was thick too. Though his arrows hit the creature, again and again, all of them bit the dust..

'What is this? Where did all your bravado go, human? Afraid to approach me that you fight from a distance?' the demon mocked, making his blood boil.

He roared back, 'You brainless dimwit, it is a battle and battles are won with strategy. Besides, don't look down on archery you fool, it is an art itself.' Desperate to win the fight, Atikaya kept searching for the *Kabandha's* weakness. Though it was fast at its leaps, it struggled at turning around or moving in small steps, thanks to its massive build and weird shape. Since the *Kabandha's* legs were short and distorted, they were a vulnerability. Atikaya kept running around the monster to tire it out. Though it kept him safe, the demon didn't show any sign of fatigue at all.

It was forbidden to attack anywhere below the waist in a fair battle, be it with a bow or mace and sword. Yet, Atikaya saw no other chance of winning, and he had taken the saying to his heart that *everything is fair in war.* He moved quickly behind the creature and shot at its hamstring tendon. The skin was thin there, the arrow getting buried into its flesh. The *Kabandha* screamed as it stumbled, and then it fell down as Atikaya shot at its other leg, right at the same spot. Then he aimed at its feet, making sure his arrows embedded themselves deep into its feet. With legs that were already distorted, the arrows rendered it impossible for it to move.

It cried out and cursed him, 'Foolish human, you boast of your skills and power, yet you resort to foul tricks in battle.'

'Foolish demon, a battle has no fixed rules, you fight with everything you have got. That is the sign of a warrior… the sign of who is stronger,' Atikaya laughed back at it, walking in a taunting manner around it, 'Look at you, rolling helplessly on the ground, because you were weak!'

The demon groaned back, filled with hatred, 'Know this, mortal, your own arrogance will drag you down one day.'

Atikaya came in front of it and said, 'Oh foolish creature, I still had some pity for you when I was merely angry at your cowardice, but now I have none.'

He raised his sword and buried it into the *Kabandha's* right eye; the monster screamed in pain again. Then he pushed the blade into its left eye, cutting open a line from one eye to the other. He couldn't stop himself there, he hacked and hacked at its limbs, till they were a dozen pieces. The monster tried to bite him and spat on him. Finally, when his temper was satisfied, he shoved his sword into its mouth. The monster screamed, and the land and sky echoed, as it took its last breath.

Even the villages near Pandhar's border heard its scream, some feared that it had been angered and would devour the villages whole. Some folks dared to venture into the rocky teeth. They brought back the dead body of the monster, but Atikaya had departed by then.

The prince mumbled to himself, 'If the flower matters so much more than true strength, I will bring the flower to show that I am no less than the heroes of old. I will be your saviour, Father.' After a few days of travel through the rocks, all that stood between him and the flower was a deep forest and Dharataj. That's what he thought at least.

It was the evening before he entered into the forest proper. He was rationing the last remains of his food and water. The sky was so beautiful, a voice in him said that the clouds had passed away to honour his might. He smirked, memories of the past coming back to him. *It was such a clear night, when his mother lay on her bed, so weak and fragile looking. Her five children are around her. The brothers stood around her bed, while Geetika was held by Ujjwal in his arms. Even the ever-chaotic Ujjwal had fallen silent that day.*

He looked at his wrist, where Ujjwal had grabbed him. 'How dare he?' he clenched his fist as he said to himself, 'Well, now that the demon has fallen by my hand, no one on this earth would dare question my might, challenge my actions.' He lay his head back against a rock, shaking off Ujjwal's thought as he was visited by his memory of a time when the fourth prince had jumped at him, clawing at his face before taking a punch to the face that had knocked him out. Atikaya touched his face, where the scratches would have lingered if Ujjwal's fingers had dug any deeper. He sighed, 'Always the troublemaker. Why do I even remember him right now? He isn't even in this game to begin with.'

The memories of his mother returned again – she was looking at her children as if saying something. Or maybe she was pleading with them, in her moment of weakness, begging them… begging him… maybe the same thing she had asked before Sarthak was born. He said to the stars, as if talking to his mother's soul, 'You were wrong Mother, I cannot protect people by just being strong. I have to become the strongest.' He closed his eyes to rest; he had a long hike ahead.

*

King Dharmendra lay on his bed as a messenger brought news of his sons. Bhimsen opened his eyes from the deep meditation he was in, Geetika was standing by the bed. The messenger gave him all the accounts he had heard of, the king absorbing it slowly. Once the messenger left, the king looked at the *pandit,* who replied, 'It seems to be true Your Majesty. I couldn't see anyone at the place where the flower blooms, it seems none of them have made it there yet.'

The king replied, 'It seems they have taken their own separate paths now. That is alright, as long as they overcome the test with their own skills.'

Bhimsen cleared his throat and said, 'Oh king, it is true that they have taken their own paths, but a time may come when their paths will intermingle. Do you not worry that the brothers will clash against each other to prove their worth?'

Dharmendra didn't get a chance to respond as Geetika spoke in anger, 'Yes, father, I always said it was a terrible idea. To send your sons to fight each other in forsaken wilderness! Only if you had consulted my opinion just once, they are my brothers too! But why would anyone bother to listen to the youngest child… the little *girl's* feelings? You are being a terrible father.'

The king took her criticism calmly and argued back, 'I am trying to be a good king here. Dear daughter, do you think I can just hand over the throne randomly to one of them? The Crown Prince must be decided based on merit, not through some outdated traditions!'

Geetika was still not convinced. The princess was visibly fuming, her breath heavy in the silent chamber. She gathered her composure to speak with her mind instead of emotions. She said again, 'Can you not see their merits yourself as their father? Don't act like you don't already have a choice or you don't already put your wager on one of them.'

Dharmendra was thoughtful for a moment, then he spoke, 'Yes, I think Chandreya is the most suited to be my successor. He has always been the polite, honest and honourable prince. But when it comes to capabilities, Atikaya and Sarthak are capable too. They are both strong and determined.'

Geetika pursued more, 'What about my other two brothers?'

He thought for a moment again, then said, 'I would not place my bet on them. Ujjwal is a hopeless case, he has done nothing useful as he just roamed around from place to place. I have even heard accounts of him singing and dancing like some stage entertainer, making trouble at houses of local lords and even as far as working in some farms and fields now and then. I don't think he is suited to be a prince at all, forget the Crown Prince.'

Geetika's face was fuming, but perhaps the king didn't notice as he continued, 'Ritikesh has skills, he has spent the most time in the court among my five sons, yet he lacks the confidence to take authority. He is too soft-hearted; that's a risk when one sits on a throne. Being brutal and decisive is an important trait for a leader.'

Geetika was visibly unhappy with such remarks about her most beloved brothers. She grunted, 'You underestimate them Father, and you underestimate elder brother Ujjwal by a lot.' The Pandit's lips curled to a smile at the princess's remark about her brothers, though he refrained from commenting as it was more of a family argument.

The king responded, 'Maybe I do, that is why I have put this test. Only the results will reveal the truth, so let's pray and wait for them, daughter.' Silence fell in the room.

*

In the wilderness that lay outside the kingdom, Viryanath and Sarthak made their way around the lake, unaware of the recent developments, of Atikaya and Ujjwal's journey. Finally, the princes came in contact with a tribe that had lived in those parts of the woods for centuries. The *Kuntha* tribe were happy to give them some accommodation, as part of their generous culture, after their false introduction as pilgrims. Behind them were Chandreya and Ujjwal, preparing to cross the lake and save time.

Ritikesh had already turned and followed Sarthak's path. He was keeping his profile low and tailing the second prince closely now. All his attention was set on him. He still had a little time to catch up to the duo. As he sat alone, memories of him came down like a mighty waterfall. Being the youngest prince meant he was well sheltered and protected by his elder brothers, save for Ujjwal. Every time he fell from a tree or got hurt on the field while playing, his three brothers would rush to him immediately. If his sword or bow did not work as he had hoped, they would show him the right technique in a heartbeat.

In a manner, he was the one who had truly a princely life, or so he thought as a child. Over time, the eldest seemed so far from him, while Sarthak and Chandreya still treated him like the youngest brother he was. They still cared, protected… and *sheltered* him. The word of the woman from Kundal reverberated in his ears, an echo that would not end.

He said to himself as he looked at the horizon, 'Now I see it, brother Ujjwal. You never rushed to me when I fell or gave your hand for me to grab, because you knew I too had the strength in me, to stand back on my own. I understand now, that look in your eyes, you trusted *my strength.* You never gave me your hand, but you were always there if I ever really needed it. When I was lost in the cornfield and bumped into you all exhausted, you offered me to walk with you. Only when you saw my exhaustion did you offer to carry me on your back? You always pointed out my flaws instead of teaching me the way, so I could learn and fix it myself.'

The youngest prince sighed, his hands lingering on his toxins a little longer. 'That is why I must act on my own, to find my *reputation* that suits me, as you had said. I must prove this time to all, for you, that I am capable too. No matter what path I have to walk.'

Three Questions

CHANDREYA woke up early to get ready for their journey ahead. Getting freshened up and after his morning prayers, he headed for the banyan tree. It was the biggest tree in the village, quite distinct in its location. His younger brother was not there yet. Chandreya wasn't surprised. He sat down to meditate and offer more prayers to the sun god. Soon his younger brother strolled in, a bag full of popped rice. Chandreya raised a brow, and the younger prince replied, 'Good morning, elder brother. This is for the way, popped rice seems to be readily available here in villages, and it is quite a great food for long journeys. Though it makes one thirsty too.' The third prince laughed softly.

Ignoring his long sentences he said, 'I am glad you managed to wake up at all brother. I was getting worried about how much did you end up drinking.'

Ujjwal laughed back playfully as he said, 'What can I say, dearest elder, there were some… unexpected events that I had to sort out. But let us not dwell on it.'

Chandreya's eyes narrowed as he spoke, 'I still feel uncomfortable about last night's events. It might be different in your eyes, but I will always find drinking and gossiping as a degrading act. It will be good for the name of our family if you adhere to some of the royal etiquette. Otherwise, no one, not a single soul will respect you, brother.'

Ujjwal gave a carefree yawn as he lifted his hands to stretch, 'I will try my best.'

'Let's head out then, we are already a little behind the time,' the elder prince suggested.

'Yes, we shall… But let's wait for a moment, someone is joining us. The sun hasn't risen yet after all,' said the younger prince.

Chandreya looked at him with a frown, 'Who is this new company of yours? Not some drunkard, I hope. And why are we taking a third person with us when we don't need to?'

Ujjwal smiled and pointed at Katyaki as she made her way to them, 'She.' Chandreya turned aside to see the beautiful woman walking towards them, though he couldn't recall her face from the previous night. He was quite surprised, perhaps Ujjwal had no limits of debauchery, he was about to ask something when Ujjwal said, 'Well, as per the rule of the quest, everyone can take one person to accompany them. You are taking me, but I still haven't chosen anyone to join me. So, it still follows the rule if I take her along.' Chandreya's glare didn't lower, so Ujjwal sighed and explained with a chuckle, 'Oh brother, stop giving such accusing looks. She is just well versed with the path we plan to take, no other reason for tagging her along.'

Katyaki gave a respectful bow and said, 'If I were to try and cause any harm to either of you, the other might feel free to slay me without question.' Ujjwal gasped, his heart skipping a beat as he stood between her and his brother.

'What she meant is, she is a safe company. You have my word brother,' he tried to convince Chandreya.

The third prince was still not buying it. 'But you were not competing in the quest if I remember your words. What is this sudden interest in the throne, for this woman?' He looked at the girl, who seemed quite decent in nature and attire, apart from her surprise appearance.

Ujjwal sighed and leaned his head back, 'I still don't care about the throne. I just want to help you reach there faster, for Father's sake and for your sake. So, if that is what will take, I, the Fourth Prince of Pandhar, officially join the quest then.' Chandreya looked at him for a long while, the younger prince groaned and said, 'Please, brother, I am trying to be helpful. She isn't some kind of *dayan* or something, just a lady with knowledge of the terrain we will travel to.' Katyaki grunted at that comment but kept it to herself. Chandreya finally gave in to his brother's persuasion, the girl was modestly dressed with no flaw in her manners. Perhaps she had better manners than the fourth prince.

*

They made their way to the lake. It stretched far and looked deep, reflecting the morning sun, with little ripples forming under the breeze. Ujjwal asked, 'So, how do we cross this? Do we hire a ferryman?'

Katyaki replied in a matter-of-fact voice, 'Unfortunately, no boatman would dare come near the lake. A spirit, a yakshya guards the water. One must answer his questions to be granted passage. A wrong answer would lead to petrification. It is not possible to cross the lake, nor would any ferryman be insane enough to give you a ride.'

Chandreya spoke before Ujjwal could say anything, worried that his younger brother might provoke the *yakshya.* He politely requested, 'Oh lord of the water, guardian of this lake, we are in great need of passing the lake and reaching its other shore. A lot depends on our passage; the very peace and stability of this region depends on our quest. Please, will you allow us passage so that we may do our duty to our father?' There was no response from the water.

'Brother, to be fair, I don't think an ancient spirit would be bothered with our politics,' Ujjwal said in a bored gesture.

'Besides, why can't we go around the lake?' Katyaki said, 'Like the other –' She didn't say more, her honour as assassin coming to stop her.

Ujjwal said, 'Our quest is time-sensitive. Going around will take time, something we are short on.'

She questioned further, 'Is this quest of yours so important that you are ready to risk your lives? There must be other ways to succeed without turning to stone.'

The prince politely said, 'Yes, there must be. But the life of our father depends on this quest. Is it not better to turn to stone if we can't save our own father?'

'I wouldn't know of such things, unfortunately,' replied the assassin with a distant gaze.

The prince explained, 'I mean, I would prefer turning to stone than watch another of my parents pass away when I could have done something. Besides, we are princes, handling a few trick questions is no big deal to us.'

Chandreya asked the lake again, 'Oh lord of the lake, please allow us to be tested by you and pass the lake if we are victorious.'

'But who will take the boat across? As I said, ferrymen stay clear from the lake,' Katyaki reiterated her point.

Chandreya was thoughtful, but Ujjwal casually said, 'Ugh, I can row the boat.'

'Do you even know how much strength is needed to row a boat? It looks easy, but don't be fooled by appearance,' Katyaki told him.

He smirked at her, 'My dear, rarely have I been fooled by *appearance.*' Making her flustered, he continued, 'But I have rowed boat before, down river Neri to the southern hills and many more places. I can handle it. But… are you sure that this yakshya is not just a folklore?' The prince was getting impatient as he picked a stone to skip across the lake. Chandreya grabbed his hand to stop him, the younger prince sighed and dropped the stone.

By grace, the *yakshya* appeared in front of them, water rising and the apparition coming out of it. It said, 'Children of humans, are you the ones who desire to step over my lake?'

'Yes, my lord, we are on a quest to save our father, the king, and time is of the essence. Passage through your lake will be a great aid to us,' Chandreya begged.

The spirit replied, 'I am more ancient than the kingdoms you speak of. I have no reason or interest to act on their device. However, if you are in such great need, you could try answering my questions.'

'And what are the rules, oh lord of water?' asked Ujjwal.

'You are three to pass, so three questions it will be. Answer them all correctly and you are free to pass, answer any wrong and you shall perish. Are you prepared for the challenge?'

Katyaki gasped and turned to the princes, 'I don't think I am ready for this, I will get us killed. His questions are not so straightforward or puzzles, they are twisted and complex.'

'O' ancient spirit, if I may ask, do we need to answer one question each, or the order is not of relevance?' Ujjwal asked.

'Yes, that is true, I do not care who answers which question. But all three questions must be answered correctly, and any wrong answer will lead to consequences for you all.'

'Wait,' the fourth prince questioned, 'shouldn't it be the one who fails to answer the question gets turned to stone?'

The yakshya looked at him and said, 'Why? Are you three not travelling together? Do you not have trust in each other? If you wish to travel together, you must face the challenge as a group. I have already been lenient enough to let whoever wants to answer give the answer.' Ujjwal grunted and looked at the ground, thinking of the best way to deal with the situation. They would need Katyaki, but risking her life didn't seem fair. How hard could these questions be, between him and Chandreya, they should manage to answer them.

He looked at the assassin, who seemed uncertain, as she said, 'I still don't think we are prepared for whatever strange question he has. I mean, there is a reason people avoid it.'

The fourth prince stood in front of her and said in a gentle voice, 'My dear…' That's when the horror hit him, embarrassment clearly visible on his face as he had not asked her name all this time.

The *vishakanya* saw his embarrassment and to save him from further of it, she said, 'Katyaki… Now I feel even less confident about you. It is like gambling our lives in the hands of your brother.'

He gritted his teeth, but responded with a playful look, 'Oh I would happily gamble my life for brother Chandreya. But, Katyaki dear, feel free to walk back if it scares you. After all, you are not bound by oath or obliged to help us, you are not shackled by our quest. You are *free* to leave whenever you wish. I can understand that death can be frightening even in your profession.'

She gasped and like a provoked cobra she hissed at him, 'Fine, let us see what you got in your mind. If we die here, we all go down anyway, my job will be complete at least,' making sure that the last part was only audible to the fourth prince.

She turned her face away from him, the prince chuckled and finally turned to his brother, 'Shall we then, Elder?' Chandreya nodded and they looked up at the spirit for his questions. A heavy silence fell around them, as if even the leaves had stopped shaking in the wind, and the lake had become free of any ripples. It was a silence of anticipation, only their mortal breaths audible. Even the princes, taught by great scholars, breathed in and out.

'What is truth?' asked the *yakshya*. They all fell silent, *was there even a possible correct answer to this question?*

While the other two thought, Ujjwal asked the spirit, 'Can you kindly explain your question or reveal which truth you mean here?' Chandreya and Katyaki gasped, but there was no answer from the spirit. Thus, the fourth prince sighed and said, 'In my knowledge, truth is of three types. First is the personal truth, then subjective truth, and finally the objective or absolute truth.' The *yakshya* was still silent, so he continued, 'A personal truth is something an individual believes in. If I were to say that I believe I had a delightful meal last night, there is no lie in that, since the truth depends on me. It doesn't speak of the meal in general but rather represents my opinion of it. However, it is a flawed truth, since it is mutable. It changes from individual to individual. A more solid truth is the subjective truth. It is a truth that is accepted by multiple individuals and thus has stood the test of time. If you ask any human whether it is true or false that the sun rises in the east, they will all agree it to be true. The nature of the subjective truth gives it more strength in arguments and policy making because it is accepted by many individuals and groups.'

The prince paused to catch his breath, then said, 'Yet, it is not immune to mutability. Depending on the views and beliefs of the group in consideration, even a subjective truth can change. That is why it is subjective to the group and their principles. Many human-made laws are based on subjective truths. Let us take the idea of revellers like dancers or singers. In many courts, they are looked down upon as entertainers and such. While in rare few courts, they are revered as *artists,* their skills getting great praises. Depending on which kingdom you are asking the question to, the truth can change.' Chandreya grunted, but before he could intervene, the younger prince continued after a quick breath.

'That brings us to the third, absolute truth. It is immutable and unaffected by human thought. Humans can try to interpret it differently, but it will not change. Changing the name of directions will not make the sun rise from the current north, it will only change the name of the sunrise direction to north. Wise leaders make their decisions based on objective truth, instead of following subjective truth to satisfy a select few. Though, it might feel painful and boorish to follow such decisions, in the long run, absolute truth prevails. Think of the mayhem it will cause in calculations if we start pretending two and two add to five. We can change the name of the number that comes from adding two and two, but its value remains unchanged as an immutable truth. Sooner or later, that pretend game will fall apart. However, that very nature of objective truth makes it bitter and unacceptable for many, because sometimes our beliefs may not align with that truth. That is the time when humans hide in the solace of subjective truth until the consequences come to find them.' Katyaki and Chandreya looked at him in surprise as he finished his talk, catching his breath after such a long answer. He fell silent, feeling satisfied with his answer, ignoring stares from his companions.

A great silence lay between them, Katyaki checking her hands if they had started turning to stone. The *yakshya* broke his silence, 'Very well, I will let you live for my second question. What is death?' Katyaki's mind raced for answers, she had delivered so many deaths after all. Yet, she had always been a good soldier following orders, an assassin never looking back at her victim. The moment she turned to look at them, the horror and nightmares would follow her forever. That's why, no matter how many lay dead in her wake, she had never given much thought about her victims. She should have perhaps… if she hadn't been an obedient soldier, maybe she could have answered this question. But she had none, at least no answer she could trust.

From her side, Ujjwal said, 'Death is an important part of life, one of the most important parts. It is the end of the journey, the final destination we all mortals travel to. Yet, it has a tranquillity and serenity about it. It sets humans free from all misery and pain there is. One could consider it as the ultimate bliss, there is nothing we can lose after we die, not even abstract things like memories. As humans age, they lose strength, and their senses and knowledge, even memories start to blur and fade. That's when life becomes painful and unbearable. Death gives us freedom; it breaks those shackles. It returns the body back to nature, from where it had come. Yet, even after the body has turned to ash or crumbled to dust, the soul lives on, to dance in another living body and embrace death again, or becomes part of the divine forever.'

The spirit looked at Chandreya and Katyaki, one after the other, the prince breathed and the assassin's legs twitched.

The ancient spirit spoke, 'It is always interesting how mortals give answers so different from each other, yet the wisest of them manage to tie their answers through invisible strings that make them the same at the core.' It asked and let the air settle, then said, 'Then my final question, what is the meaning of human life?' Chandreya's thought immediately went to the books he had learned from, so many scrolls debated the idea of life's meaning. He had firmly believed, as he was taught by great scholars of his court, *that human life is a divine gift, and humans must spend it in the service of gods and their creations.*

'But it can't be such a simple answer,' the prince thought to himself, 'Perhaps it has more to do with following the words of gods dutifully, to set ourselves free from all desires and bonds, to become one with the divine again. But could he be asking for something more… earthly meaning? Like our beliefs and honours as a human, our duties to the laws and ancestors…'

While the elder prince was busy in his thoughts, Ujjwal said out loud, 'It is meaningless.' The *yakshya* maintained its gaze on him as before, without any changes in its expression. Chandreya was baffled, looking at his brother with an open mouth. But before he could react, Ujjwal continued, 'Human life is meaningless, when considered individually. It is like a blank canvas; anyone will consider it blank. But then we become the painter of our own lives. We make connections and form bonds – become part of a society – part of something bigger than us. In doing so, we give meaning to our lives. Now, even when an artist fills a canvas with colours, people can still interpret it differently than what the artist had envisioned. I believe that is true in life too. We can only work our part, what meaning others will infer depends on them. That's why one life on its own might not seem meaningful, like a drop of water. But by adding together with others, human life gains a meaning like the same drops add up to create mighty rivers and beautiful lakes. To provide evidence, even though born into a royal family, I wouldn't have been a prince if I was not part of a kingdom, well, it wouldn't have been a royal family to begin with. I would have been a son, a brother, but being part of this kingdom gave my life another meaning, that of a prince. You can't define in one word or sentence what human life is. Or else, some philosopher or scholar would have gotten it already. Because it is an experience, that, one needs to feel through time by living it.'

Silence fell, and the *yakshya* waited patiently if the prince had anything more to add. Then the spirit of the lake asked the mortal prince, 'Then I must ask you, oh prince, do you think that what you said is an absolute truth?' The prince flinched a little, caught off guard with such a question, but he closed his eyes to think. This was a question for him and him only.

Moments passed till he opened his eyes, and then he said, 'I have searched through my kingdom and more, learned from books, scrolls, scholars and many others. But every one of them had a different answer to this question. If any of their answer had been an absolute truth, it wouldn't have varied so much. Yet, as much as my heart desires, I cannot claim my answer as the absolute truth. That would be arrogance since I have not seen everything, learned everything, and lived many lives to say exactly what the meaning of life is. At best, I could at least claim that my answer was a subjective truth, since different people experience life differently, according to their shared bonds.'

Katyaki grunted, 'You said you had three questions only; we have answered them all, can't you let us pass now?'

The spirit chuckled as if the ancient one could be amused after all. It said, 'How can I not let you pass after you pushed me to ask a fourth question? I have learned a lot from mortals, yet I have learned even more today. This truly pleases my ancient heart. Very well, mortals, you may travel through my waters unhindered, at will. May your wisdom guide others in the path of life.' The elemental being slowly descended into his lake, vanishing from sight. Katyaki left a long gasp of relief, so audible that Ujjwal chuckled, making her flustered in return.

*

The two princes dragged the boat to the lake shore, Katyaki following them. 'Is she coming further too?' Chandreya inquired.

'Oh, yes, she wants to help us see our quest done,' Ujjwal said as he helped her get into the boat. He started rowing.

'I can be of quite help in the wilderness, Your Highness,' she said. Chandreya gave her a blank stare, neither hateful nor filled with cheer. She continued, 'Although, I do not know what the quest is.'

Ujjwal chuckled and said, 'You just need to help put my brother on the throne, in the right way.'

She rolled her eyes, then replied, 'Well I would have thought you were the candidate for the throne, given how philosophical you are. I wonder how you knew all the answers.'

The prince blushed a little as he said, 'Please, my dear, no need to exaggerate it so much. They were questions which never had any definitive answers. Rather it was a test of confidence. An answer made after hours of personal reasoning and months of research feels more confident than an answer handed down to you.'

'I see, which indeed makes you quite the charming yet philosophical man that a throne deserves. Wouldn't you agree?' Katyaki said and looked at Chandreya.

For reasons unknown to her, the elder prince preferred to ignore her question, or perhaps ignore her completely. Although she wasn't sure if he was ignoring his brother. Ujjwal groaned out, 'Not in a hundred years. For one, I have avoided that thing for all my life. Second, all my knowledge comes from random trips I had taken years ago to some mathas and temples, where the priests and scholars would sing from their scrolls and bore me to death as they would tell their philosophies.'

'Oh yes, *bored* you with their *knowledge*, I get that, Your Highness,' she said playfully, teasing him. The prince looked away, knowing well by now that his illusions wouldn't work on her, she was the one person he would struggle to lie.

Still, he defended himself by raising his hands and said, 'Besides, my final point is that I don't even come close to Elder Brother when it is about politics and governing.'

Chandreya gave a smile to him and said, 'My younger brother, we all five are equally competent and qualified. Otherwise, Father wouldn't have assigned this task to all of us.' *Was there another layer to that smile?* Katyaki couldn't tell, but she decided to refrain from commenting since she barely knew the princes. They took turns rowing as they moved on the calm water silently, unaware of the happenings with their siblings.

Sinister Plot

VIRYANATH and Sarthak had found a shelter to rest for the night and food to regain their strength. The *Kuntha* tribe loved and revered their forest, not binding themselves to any king or kingdom. Rumours were that some of them were tree whisperers and shape-shifters. True or rumours, one thing was certain, they could be very hospitable to people who respected their boundaries. They would happily take guests when someone was in need, acting to the best of their skills to provide for the guests. They would not forgive anyone who tried harming their forest or its sacred trees though. Staying away from war and politics was their way of life, but it didn't prevent them from standing up for themselves.

Sarthak and Viryanath had a charm in their voice, they had a way of convincing people. Both were great minds undoubtedly, always plotting and calculating. It was not hard for them to pretend like pilgrims crossing from one kingdom to the next. They needed only a night's rest anyway. 'Our assassin has taken care of your younger brother by now for sure, which would also take Chandreya out of the equation,' said Viryanath as they washed their legs by the well.

Sarthak looked a bit distraught as he stared at the distance, not focused on anything particular. He didn't make any comment or protest this time. As they headed into the mud hut provided to them, Viryanath continued, 'We still don't know where Ritikesh is, and all that remains is your elder brother.'

'Though he has taken a risky path, I wouldn't underestimate him,' commented Sarthak after gaining back his composure, he seemed to have made peace with his decisions.

Their small talks were disturbed as a girl arrived at the door with drinks in bamboo-made glasses. She said politely, 'Dear guests from the realm of Pandhar, please accept this for your refreshment.' Sarthak looked away, but Viryanath's eyes lingered on her.

He walked to her for the drinks, Sarthak spoke from his place on the floor, 'Thank you for your hospitality, and the dinner was delicious too. But please, leave us to our own since we are tired.' The girl bowed and took her leave. This made Viryanath grunt a little, but he joined the prince with drinks. He said to Sarthak, 'Listen, my friend, in the savage wild, when bears or tigers meet their siblings, they fight with their own blood over the territory. At least you do not have to dirty your own hands.' He patted the prince on the back and handed him the drink.

They gulped down the sweet and sour drink from various fruits like mango or *bhel*. Sarthak said, 'I can understand that, after many thoughts. It would be a disaster if the arrogant Atikaya or the too-good Chandreya were to get the throne. The whole kingdom would get upturned.'

Viryanath gave him a reassuring smile, 'Exactly my friend, you are doing it for the greater good. There is nothing to be ashamed of, you are doing your duty to the kingdom and its citizens.'

'Yes, yet, is it truly righteous to hurt one's own blood to win the throne, wouldn't that make us animals like tigers and bears?' the prince questioned.

His company answered, 'Yes, it would be the same if you were to take it to a brawl of some sort. What we are doing is more humane, making plots and using others to do our work.' Sarthak didn't seem fully satisfied, yet he nodded in agreement. Viryanath offered him, 'Lie down and rest my friend, think it through. You will have better clarity, and you will see the nobility of what we did. You have the whole night for it. I will go get some fresh air before sleep.'

Sarthak agreed, only nodding instead of using words, and the minister walked out of the hut. Viryanath wandered around under the open sky, hoping to find some clarity for their next steps, or at least pleasure from some maiden of the tribe. He walked out of the premises of the tribe and stepped into the nearby woods.

'How is the quest going for you?' a familiar voice called to him from the darkness amidst trees. He suddenly turned, hand reaching to his waist, where he would have his sword sheathed if he had not left it behind in the hut. 'It is alright, I come in peace and alliance,' said the voice.

He looked at the shadowy figure as it approached closer, under a waxing moon, mingled with the shadow of the forest. 'Ritikesh? You can come out,' said the minister with a little surprise covered well by his composure.

The long breath didn't make Viryanath relax, yet he felt that Ritikesh was there to talk. 'Well, it seems you have come this far quite untroubled,' the youngest prince spoke as he stood out from the shadow into the moonlight, revealing his face.

Viryanath pressed on, not allowing the prince to get an edge over him, he said, 'And what might be the reason that you followed us here? Since it is definitely not possible that we both thought of this path independently.'

'I think we both are wise enough to visualise which path is the quickest to success,' the prince responded.

'Yet, it can't be the quickest way for you if someone else has got a head start over you. Unless…' Viryanath looked at Ritikesh with suspicion, letting the ominous silence settle in the air.

Ritikesh finished it, 'Unless I have a way to overtake you, is that what you are claiming? Think again, I might not need to overtake you. I only need to overtake my brother.'

The prince's words piqued interest on Viryanath's face, he said with a chuckle, 'And you think my alliance is so easy to win over?'

Ritikesh walked at a slow pace, still keeping his distance, he spoke, 'Tell me, why do you think only you are the non-royal in this quest? Why do you think no other prince chose someone else to take along?'

'What do you mean? Atikaya is too arrogant. Chandreya and Ujjwal are with each other, and I don't know much about you,' the minister said in the voice of someone who had done his calculations.

Ritikesh smiled, 'Do you not find that odd? Both elder brothers could have chosen someone else to come with them, yet they joined hands, each with another prince, none else. Brother Ujjwal isn't so interested in the throne to begin with. Eldest chose not to take even his brother along, so he didn't choose anyone else either. Now, you are the only non-royal in this quest, and let me ask you, how many sources did you have to get your information about the quest? Just one person, the person with whom you take this perilous journey?'

The prince's words made Viryanath agitated, he said, 'What is your point, Ritikesh?'

The prince said in a serious voice, 'You are a man of intellect, don't play the fool. Think ahead and think of your position. Are you really heading to the glory and prizes you deserve, or are you being downplayed, *underestimated?'*

Viryanath scoffed at the prince, 'You call me a man of intellect, yet you try to trick me with a puzzle of words. Why would you suddenly be interested in my role in this game instead of focusing on your own victory? Is it out of benevolence, I doubt not? Play of words won't be able to split me from my friend easily.'

Ritikesh smiled, 'Did he ever tell you, that the quest doesn't dictate that only a prince may bring back the flower? Anyone, whatever his status or profession might be, anyone who can bring back the flower will be crowned as the heir to the throne.'

Viryanath looked back with the same intense gaze, 'And why would you tell me that, even if it was true?'

'I do not think I need to think hard to know who is the brain behind your progress. Yes, it has been you, then will you settle for the position of a mere advisor or whatever was promised to you while holding all that intellect, when being a king is within your reach?'

The prince gave a minute to let the words sink into his mind. He continued, 'Will it not be better if you take the chain of commands yourself? I am sure you can rule better than him. For me, it will still be the same, never would I have been able to sit on the throne anyway. Yet, it will still be good news, if the kingdom and citizens are in the hands of a smart man.'

He paused to let Viryanath grow a lust for that idea. 'Tell me then, knowing that there is such a possibility, will my brother not take steps to prevent it from happening? He is not a fool; you would know that. We are not so benevolent after all, as you said. So, who will betray whom first? Think about it, you might have been already betrayed. Not everyone is what they appear to be, not even friends, are they? Thus, it is not about my victory, it is about his defeat.'

Ritikesh stepped back into the shadows and soon his footsteps receded. Viryanath returned to his chamber, the poison had already been administered, a poison of thoughts and words. Sarthak was lying on his bed, hearing him return he said, 'Did you come with any plans for our next move?'

Viryanath sat on his mat on the floor. He said while looking at the prince directly, 'Not yet. I was curious, what would happen if someone other than us, say from all of us who are competing, were to bring the flower back?'

Sarthak looked at him in confusion, 'How will anyone else know of this quest?'

'In a hypothetical situation my friend, the possibilities are endless.'

'You know my father is a man of word, so perhaps he would honour his promise and crown the man as a Crown Prince.'

Viryanath made a worried gasp, 'Even without royal blood? How could the king make such a claim? I thought you told me that the quest was for the princes only.'

Sarthak said in a reassuring voice, 'Do not worry friend, I don't think any of the princes will be fool enough to mention it to an outsider. There was no need to mention the unnecessary details of the quest, it was given to the five princes after all. Why do you bring such a question now?'

Viryanath couldn't read if there was any doubt in the prince's voice, but he cunningly replied, 'I am worried that your brothers might spill something if they are in the face of harm.'

The second prince chuckled, 'Do you think anyone would dare approach Atikaya with such an attempt? Chandreya can handle himself, no need of concern, his principles would stop him from betraying the throne.' He said in a dismissive voice, 'I had to hold Ritikesh to stay back, he would be wise to follow my words. But even then, I don't think he would spill such an important secret.'

Viryanath gave a faint smile, 'Let us rest then, we shall leave early morning.' They lay down to sleep.

*

Outside the hut a man moved, walking up to the well silently he dropped something carefully, something so light that there was no sound from the water. He silently walked out of the tribe's premises and turned around, approaching the night guards. He bowed respectfully as the guard asked, 'Who are you, a friend or foe? Speak.'

'I am neither a foe nor friend, just a well-wisher. If I am not wrong, some guests arrived here today, isn't it true?' the stranger chose his words carefully.

'That is not something for you to learn. We don't sell off our guests,' the guard grunted, the tribal marks on his paint clearly visible.

The man said to the guard, 'I respect that, but tell me, will you still treat them so generously even when you learn that they are the princes who have come here to steal your forest from you?' The guard groaned, but the man continued, 'You don't need to believe me, test it out yourself. But know this, if you don't act now, they will burn your forests, and poison your waters, and it will start from here. I just wish your safety, my friend, don't fall victim to their plots.' The youngest prince bowed to the guard and walked away, waiting in the dark for his plots to unfold.

*

An hour or more had passed since the prince and his friend had lay down to sleep. They heard a voice outside, asking for them. Sarthak groaned and woke up, the doors were made of bamboo, so there was no provision for knocking. He just walked up to the door and opened it, irritated at such disturbance, yet knew better not to insult their host. As he opened the door, the girl in front said, 'Oh Prince, Your Highness, I hope everything is alright with you and you are comfortable? If there are any mosquitos or insects, we can provide some flowers to burn and keep them off.'

Sarthak was sleepy and didn't bother with her words, 'Thank you, but we are fine. Please leave us to rest and don't bother us again.' He closed the door dismissively before she could bow and leave.

Viryanath had woken up, 'What was that?'

He said, 'Nothing of importance, asking if we needed insect repellent,' as he went back to sleep.

Another few hours passed as the night grew deeper, they could smell smoke and everything felt hot. Both of them woke up in horror as the hut was burning. 'What in the world happened?' roared

Viryanath. Sarthak was rushing to the door, and Viryanath stopped him by his arms. 'We should take the window, if they had any wish to save us, they would have attempted already,' his voice was firm and frightened. Sarthak nodded and they jumped out of the window. Viryanath's assumptions were correct. As soon as they emerged from the window with their mace and sword, the tribe was upon them with javelins, spears, axes, arrows, and scimitars. They ran in one breath, running for their lives as far as they could.

Brother of Mine

THEY crossed a ravine on their path as they ran mindlessly through the night, falling, tripping, getting bruised all over. The stars watched their plight silently. Luckily the ravine was a mark of the end of territory under the *Kuntha* tribe. The tribal folks stopped chasing them finally, being firm in their beliefs of territory. Gasping and panting for breath, the prince and his friend walked further ahead, finally resting to catch their breath. It was a great length of time before they could speak, their heartbeat returning close to normal. 'How did you know they wanted to kill us?' asked the prince.

'I didn't. But it was odd that the hut was on fire and no one attempted to put it out. What had you told to the girl that time? I don't see a reason they would turn against us.'

'I didn't say anything. She just –' the prince paused and gasped, 'Oh, no. She called me Your Majesty or something like that. I was sleepy, so I went along with it. But even then, I don't see –'

'Your youngest brother must have set them off against us. He must have informed them about you being a prince, mixed with some other lies.'

Sarthak was surprised, 'My youngest brother? How did Ritikesh come into the picture?' A heavy and gloomy silence fell between them, the air denying to move at all.

'He met me in the woods when I went out of our hut, but I don't know what he did after that,' the minister said to defend his point.

It was true that Viryanath had no knowledge of Ritikesh's doings. The poison he had put into the water started getting people sick, not enough to be lethal, yet discomforting. It was a potent poison brewed by him, quick to take effect and make people start vomiting or even lose consciousness. The inquiry made by the girl only strengthened Ritikesh's warnings.

The tribal folks waited till the night was deep and their guests were fast asleep. They realised that the only remaining option was to eliminate these guests before they could do any more harm. Blaming the prince and his friends for the sudden sickness in the tribe, they chose to burn them alive.

Surprised that Viryanath had conversed with Ritikesh in secret that night, Sarthak howled, 'And when were you planning to tell me about it? What did Ritikesh promise you in return? How long has this secret conspiracy been going on?'

His accusations brought fury into Viryanath's voice, 'I was hoping you would reveal your reasons to bring me along first.'

'To aid me of course. Did we not strike a bargain already?'

'Oh yes. Yet you knew that I could take the flower by myself and inherit the throne. Then why did you risk bringing me along?' Viryanath replied with a suspicious undertone. The moon was in the west, soon it would be dawn, a bright new day.

Sarthak gasped, 'What are you implying, Viryanath?'

His friend smirked when the prince used his name. He said in a feral voice, 'I wonder what sinister plan you had for me after you were done using me.'

Sarthak gripped his mace, 'I don't approve of your tone right now. It seems Ritikesh has managed to pour poison into your thoughts already.'

Seeing him grip his weapon, Viryanath pulled out his sword, 'I do not seek your approval. I am not your younger brother. I wish this didn't have to end this way.'

'It doesn't need to; you still have a chance to lower your weapon. We can still be friends, you can still be my Prime minister,' his friend tried to offer.

However, there was no surrender. Viryanath charged first, knowing that Sarthak would need time to swing his heavy weapon after the run. He was not war-trained like the prince, but even as a minister, he knew that a fraction of a second could be a difference between life and death. Sarthak used a quick manoeuvre to move aside as Viryanath thrust his sword towards him. Using his weight, Sarthak shoved Viryanath back, breaking his balance. His one swing of mace threw the sword out of the Viryanath's hand, but he couldn't land the second blow in time. Viryanath was nimble enough to jump away and pick up his sword, though his hand rang with pain from the previous blow. The cold wind of that night brushed against the sweat on his brows, sending a jolt of chill through his face.

He needed to get inside Sarthak's defence. On the other hand, Sarthak could feel the tiredness from their run catching up to him. He had barely any strength for two or three more swings with the heavy mace, he needed to end it quickly. Viryanath looked in his eyes and charged forward, thrusting his sword, and hoping that Sarthak would use his previous manoeuvre. He was smart and calculating, his guess was correct. Sarthak turned aside to dodge the point of his sword. Viryanath backed a step and quickly swung his sword parallel to the ground, hoping to sweep a wide area and slash some good parts from Sarthak's body.

Being a prince, Sarthak was more well-trained with weapons than a minister. He quickly brought his mace up, stopping the sword mid-swing. There was a ringing as the metals clashed, and a sound of chipping from the sword. Both knew they needed to finish it quickly before the sword broke or Sarthak's hand lost strength. Viryanath gritted his teeth as he knew it wouldn't take Sarthak much effort to raise his mace enough to block the sword. He lunged forward again for a thrust, and the prince jumped aside like before. This time Viryanath used his motion to take a swing just after the thrust, hoping to get into melee with Sarthak before he had a chance to bring up the mace between them.

It worked, almost. Sarthak couldn't block it. But he jumped back, his left hand raising in the air, his right hand swinging back with the mace to avoid getting slashed by the sword. If Viryanath had been just an inch forward or had a second swing, Sarthak would have bled to death. However, the ending was different that night. Sarthak used the momentum of his right hand to swing it in an arc till he had raised the mace high enough, his left hand joined it and he brought down the mace with all his might. He was hoping Viryanath would step back or doge and fall out of balance.

Unfortunately, the combination of thrust and swing had taken out any chance of stepping back for Viryanath, his momentum too focused on a forward attack. The mace fell on his head, crushing his skull immediately. It all happened instantaneously. The headless body dropped to its knees and fell flat on the floor. It had all happened already by the time Sarthak realised his horror. The smashed head was draining blood on the grass, the colours visible clearly as the sun rose in the east. He couldn't hold onto his weapon anymore, and falling to his knees by his friend's corpse, he cried out, 'Nooo! What have I done? What did you make me do?'

'That indeed is an interesting observation, the intelligent one bit the dust first,' Ritikesh said as he emerged from the treeline.

'Ritikesh!' shouted Sarthak with all his breath.

'Yes, brother?' his reply was cold like pale winter morning as he walked closer.

Sarthak stood up, 'Why? Why would you do it? Why, what is your goal?' His eyes were red with rage and sorrow. At that moment, Ritikesh didn't feel afraid of his elder brother's fury.

He stepped closer and said as if he was spitting venom like a snake, 'To make you lose, to show that you are as helpless as me when you are alone. No, I came all this way on my own, you, on the other hand, needed hand-holding. So, who is the pathetic one brother?'

Sarthak brandished his mace, 'I will make you regret that you ever dared cross my path.'

Ritikesh scoffed as if he knew what Sarthak would say, 'Sure, come and try it.'

He pulled out two daggers. Even though Sarthak was more skilled with weapons, he was exhausted. Ritikesh knew that, and he had another advantage, his poisons. Sarthak rushed at him like a mad bull. Ritikesh jumped out of the mace's reach, but he was still surprised at his elder brother's skills. Slashing at Sarthak's arm, he missed the first attack. He gritted his teeth, the light of dawn making him question his motives. But he swallowed, it had to be done, he needed to show his worth.

'Stop looking down on me,' he said, more like screamed.

Sarthak lifted his mace again and said, 'You think you can win this competition with your cowardly tricks?'

'No, but at least I can stop you from winning and show you your place,' the youngest prince said as he dodged the blow again. This time he attacked with his poison-dipped dagger at Sarthak's left hand when he was using it for balance to hoist the mace back in the air with his right hand. It was a minor cut to him, not enough to break the momentum of the mace. In his shock, Ritikesh brought up his left hand to block, the mace smashing his arm bones. Both tumbled back, falling flat on the ground. Sarthak was too tired already, as he tried to hold his mace in both hands, his left hand got a burning pain suddenly. He knew he couldn't fight with only his right hand.

Ritikesh saw the vulnerability and jumped on top of Sarthak, putting his dagger to his brother's throat. Their eyes met; their gazes collided. Ritikesh gave a mournful scream and threw his dagger away, falling onto the ground beside his brother. 'What am I doing?' he screamed at the sky. There was a moment of silence, only the heavy breathing of the two brothers. The sun was shining on the east; a new day had begun.

'I…' Sarthak said with a little struggle, 'I underestimated your skills by a lot.'

'I should have focused on the quest, on finding the flower, instead of proving myself to be a threat,' gasped Ritikesh.

'What did you do, brother?' asked Sarthak.

'I poisoned the water of that tribe, to make them fall sick and doubt you, I told them you wanted to take the forest for the kingdom,' said the young prince with a voice burdened with guilt.

'I and Viryanath sent an assassin after Ujjwal,' said the second prince with remorse in his quivering voice, unaware of what fate had befallen his brothers.

Ritikesh smiled at the sky and red sun, 'I wouldn't worry about that. If you underestimated me, imagine how much you might have underestimated him. If anyone among us could finish this quest, it might be him. Only if he was competing that is, but surely, he would make elder brother Chandreya the winner. Anyway, I should stop worrying about the quest, there is nothing I could do in this state.' He looked at his broken left hand.

Sarthak groaned and checked his left hand, lifting it with difficulty, 'Same goes for me it seems.' His muscles had started to look bad.

Ritikesh gasped in panic and immediately got to the other side of Sarthak. 'The blade was poisoned, I will need to draw it out,' he said as he took out a clean dagger. He cut a wound on that hand to make Sarthak's hand bleed the poison out. 'No, oh no, the damage has happened already,' he tied a cloth to stop the blood flow, 'This…

your hand... It might not...' his voice was trembling.

Sarthak said in a dismissive yet hopeful voice, 'It does not matter anymore, neither of us two can make it for the quest, even together. Let us put our faith in our brothers and hope that you are right, at least one of them would succeed. The only thing we can do now is return home.'

Birds were making their morning calls in the forest, and soon the shepherds would lead their cattle for grazing. The wives and girls would start cleaning the house while the men would get ready for the day. A sick king was still asleep on his bed as he waited for his sons to return. A princess had woken up from a sleepless night to attend to her father, as she too waited for her brothers to come home. The two brothers lay on soft grass, far from their home as they saw each other's truth for the first time. The sky had turned pink and slowly was changing to blue.

'I was blind in desperation,' said Ritikesh as he was satisfied with his medical intervention. He sat and wept there, at his own folly, while Sarthak's left hand slowly bled from the wound, removing as much poison as it could from his body.

Sarthak gathered some strength to sit up, as he softly said, 'No, I understand. Atikaya saw me as a fragile brother, always acting like I needed his protection as if I wouldn't survive without his grace. And I only had to suffer one brother. Your pain must have been compounded from all your brothers, from all of us. You did what you felt right to do, to prove yourself. It was I, who was blind.'

Ritikesh looked at the sun and then towards the north. With their hopes all placed on their three brothers, they stood up with each other's help. 'I pray to the heavens, at least they don't have to face the fate that has befallen us,' Ritikesh softly whispered, begging from his soul to the lords of heaven. Hands over shoulders, the two brothers slowly walked back towards Pandhar. The journey was going to be long, but with each small step, they would get close to the capital.

The Long Hike

ATIKAYA managed to reach the foot of the snowy mountain Dharataj, the pinnacle of the world. He took a deep breath as he looked up to see the height that he would need to scale. The mountain was touching the sky itself, as if like piercing through the sky into the heavens. There was still one final hurdle standing between him and his goal. A deep dark forest untouched and untravelled from ancient ages. No one in centuries had dared step into this part of the wilderness. Tales of monsters and demons were enough to keep people away. Even the heavy air and crooked shape of trees were doing a good job of deterring anyone daring to enter.

Atikaya sighed as he stepped into the shadows, his weapons ready to strike down any threat that dared oppose him. As he kept walking deeper into the woods, it became more eerie. Branches seemed more twisted in odd angles and birds' voices had become coarser. Any commoner would have turned back and run by that sight. Yet, the first prince of Pandhar had a mind of steel. Even as the roots twisted and turned on the ground to make the path difficult, he kept walking. It was hard to see the sun through the canopy of the forest, so he kept moving forward without much sense of direction, marking the trees to avoid running in circles.

Water was in plenty thanks to the brooks and tributaries of Neri. Food had become scarce though. He had gotten low on food rations he was carrying, so he was relying on fruits and hunts. He shot down some rabbits for dinner, but after seeing the texture of their meat he didn't dare eat it. He didn't want to eat the berries or fruits of this forest, even as hungry he kept pressing forward. Starving was not new to him, even as a prince. Many times, as part of rituals or missions, he had spent days only drinking water.

He had his trustworthy weapons with him, that was all he needed after all. He munched some rice cake he was gifted by the villagers near Neri. He looked at his hand, all calloused and scarred. He smiled, a hand of a warrior it was after all. But he hoped in the depths of his heart that he wouldn't have to fight any big battle along the way. Even if he managed to win the fights, time was running out. He needed the flower before his father succumbed to his illness, *how could you have become so weak oh father of mine,* he asked in his thoughts.

He regretted the time he wasted searching for the *Kabandha*, he could have saved a few days and a lot of food if he hadn't spent that time in such a manner. He smirked though – it was worth bringing down the monster. The roar was so loud that even villages miles away would have heard it. When he returned with the flower, they would be certain who it was that defeated such a foul and old creature. Yet, one more of such mad diversions could cost him days up to a week. He couldn't afford any such unwanted battles anymore, or any sort of diversions that would need him to walk around. While he entered a gorge, it was fate that he came across an *Ahisur (Ahi:* Snake, *Asur:* demon).

It had taken the form of a gigantic white python, silver glimmering from its scale. The demon slept in its serpentine coil, blocking the narrow path between the gorge. Atikaya hoped to preserve his strength for the final climb, and any other challenges it might give him. He resorted to negotiation, or rather what he *imagined* as negotiation. He said, 'Oh demon of ancient age, move from my path so I may proceed without having to kill you.' The python did not even budge, as if his voice was lost in the air. His patience was running low; he pulled out his sword and stabbed the sleeping demon.

The *Ahisur* finally woke from its sleep, looking at the prince. Its biforked tongue moving in and out of its mouth, it said, 'Human, what madness has possessed you that you come here to be my food? Though I am not hungry at this hour, come back later.'

Atikaya growled at it, 'Move away from my path and I won't have to slay you today.' The serpent's head lifted, its reptilian eyes staring at the first prince.

It said in a very slithering sound, 'Find another path, so I won't have to taste your blood.'

'Time is of the essence to me,' Atikaya replied, holding back his rage and annoyance, 'And I do not have time to search for a new path around this huge gorge, just for the convenience of a sleeping demon.'

Ahisur made an expression that might be equivalent to human laughter. It looked at him with both his eyes, one after the other, and the prince saw his reflection in its eyes. Saw the man he had become, a force to reckon with, yet he saw figments of weakness from his tiredness. He hated those eyes, wanting to claw them out of the serpent's face. It moved its head back enough to be able to see him with both eyes at once. It uncoiled itself slightly to look down at the prince, as it hissed to speak, 'I see, and what is the meaning of your insignificant life, lowly human, that you ask me to abandon my sleep for your convenience?'

This infuriated the prince, who answered with an arrogant voice, 'You ask the significance of my life, you fool?' He brandished his sword and said, 'I am a prince, no, I am the First Prince of Pandhar. A man chosen by the Devas and gods. I am the one who will one day wear the crown and rule Pandhar. My life gives meaning to so many lives that will follow me one day, as my subjects. I am like the sun that shines bright to give nourishment to those who seek it. I am Atikaya. They would sing my name from one border to the other, yet, you dare ask me what is the meaning of *my life?*'

His voice echoed through the gorge as if he was declaring it to the entire world, to the very foundations of the earth. The snake demon replied to him with its wisdom, 'Your answers have mostly been about the future, a future that neither you nor I can see for certainty. All your life's meaning is then a mere pipe dream. A dream that may become true, unless –' The serpent paused and its eyes stirred like that of a predator as it came at Atikaya to swallow him. This was no ordinary python, a gigantic creature with a mouth big enough to swallow a horse whole, its gargantuan body stretching far into the gorge.

Atikaya was about to counter its argument, but he jumped away as the demonic mouth lunged at him. His strength was diminishing each day, and he decided to be decisive. He pulled out his bow and shot at the demon's eye. The snake moved with tremendous speed, even with its large body. His arrows couldn't make their marks, especially when his weakness was getting into his head, making his aim less accurate. Even enchanted arrows couldn't entangle it enough to slow it. Fire and lightning arrows didn't make it flinch. He looked around, the gorge was scarce of trees, its tall figure not allowing much sunlight to enter.

He ran among the trees even as the demon teased him, 'Running like a mouse, are we? That suits, my prey.' For once, his weakness clouded his arrogance, letting him resorting strategy over brute force. The snake coiled from tree to tree, crushing many of them in its wake. It wasn't enough to entangle it, but the quick turns and large trees on its way slowed it down. That was enough for Atikaya to hit right in its eyes. As the arrows pierced into its eyes, the snake went into a frenzy of rage as it hissed wildly. Unable to see, it moved in random directions, unbothered by the trees it collided with and broke. It could only rely on its sense of smell to hunt down the prince. He managed to mingle his smell with the forest, moving all around the snake, yet, at one point the monstrous body collided with him. While trying to save himself from the impact, his bow broke in two.

He pulled out his sword from its scabbard and swung at the snake. It screamed in agony and rage, as it came straight at him. Its demonic scales looked beautiful, and they were tough to cut through. Even with such a fine-made sword, he didn't have the strength to cut open the whole width of its body. He risked it all and readied his sword as the snake came at him with its jaws open. He pierced right into its throat, the snake screamed and wreathed around with his sword imbued into its mouth. Atikaya knew it was either the demon's end or his. By good fate, the serpent fell dead to the ground.

Atikaya was exhausted, he could barely breathe. He was sure of one thing; he needed to finish the steep climb and get the flower soon before his body was broken. He looked at the great height of Dharataj, the mighty rock that would not move to even the powers of nature. Sitting under a tree he cleaned his sword, as he thought to himself about how little rest he could afford. He wasn't sure how much rest and food he could get once his climb began. His muscles cried out in tiredness, perhaps he could take the next few days lightly. He spat at the ground from such revolting thought, how could he take the throne if a little tiredness could slow him down.

He thought back on his journey, perhaps he could have asked the villagers for a little more food. But he was a prince, the eldest prince, how could he have begged some commoner, he was the provider after all. Maybe someone like Ujjwal or Ritikesh would have fallen to his knees and begged with both hands out, but he knew the value of a prince's position, unlike the younger princes. If a prince, especially as important as Atikaya, ever got on his knees in front of commoners, the entire image of the kingdom would be ruined forever. A stain that would take years of work and wars to erase, to show strength again. He, as the eldest prince couldn't afford to show such weakness, for the good of his kingdom and his subjects.

He had slain the demon alone, even at the cost of his bow, yet he couldn't shake off the eyes that had stared at him. He looked so broken in those eyes, so drained of strength. 'Ahhh,' he shouted, 'I need to finish this quest. I can't think of rest right now, not when I have come so close. If I feel so broken and… weak, I doubt any of my siblings would even make it to the top of Dharataj. So, for the sake of that faraway future, I will have to silence my pain, burn away my weakness, and keep moving forward, till I have won it all.'

Yet, he was no utter fool, he knew his body needed rest, it needed sleep to recover after the fight. It was such a short fight, yet he felt so tired from it. He sighed, 'Have I truly become weak? It can't be, it is just this long journey. Never had I ventured so far alone before, but, now that I am here, it will be over soon.' He leaned his head on a tree root while lying on the ground, as he slowly fell asleep.

Dreams took him, dreams of days long gone since his childhood. Dreams of him running around with his brothers through the royal garden. In those dreams, they were all laughing, except for the times when one or another brother fell down and started crying. *He was always there to pick them up, even if he knew they would fall again and again. But they were his brothers, and he had given his words to his mother. Oh yes, he had promised his mother that he would protect his siblings even before Sarthak was born. What happened to that promise? What happened to that mother?*

He trained hard with every weapon and fought with beasts in the arena. He got strong and kept getting stronger. Battlefields became his second home as he crushed his enemies. Yet, it all didn't feel enough, he remembered the face his mother had before she passed away during his childhood. She looked at him so tenderly, so delicately, so lovingly, as if he was a fragile flower. He was no flower, he was strong back then too, as strong as any child of his age could be. Then why did she look at him like that?

He had seen that look before too, much before that sad day. It was after he had that damned fight with Ujjwal, or rather when Ujjwal jumped at him to claw at his face. His mother came to take Ujjwal in her arms after he knocked the younger sibling out with one punch. She looked at Ujjwal with such tenderness, as she took care of the bleeding prince. But she had given that pathetic soft look to Atikaya too, as if he needed her care! He was the winner of that fight after all. Why had his brother even dared to jump at him anyway?

The first prince remembered it, in his frenzy he had pushed his mother down, making Ujjwal leap at him as if to defend her. He thought that it was the problem with his mother, always requiring someone to protect her. She was so weak to protect her own children, that she had asked him to protect them. He returned to the world living from his dreams as the sun rose in the east, night had passed. Yet, the looming figure of the gorge was not letting any sunlight reach the floor. Even at the hour of dawn, shadows lingered around him, and memories of the past lingered in his head.

'You were weak Mother, you couldn't protect your children and died so early, leaving them to be protected by me,' he said to himself as he freshened up. He asked the gorge, 'But what was the point? The weak always stay weak, they can't grow out of it. So, why must the strong waste their strength on protecting the weak? Is it not better to just build a world where only the strong stand? There won't be any conflict in that world, no pain, because everyone can fight and stand up for themselves… there won't be any weak.' Only silence was the answer the empty gorge gave him.

He started his journey towards the mountain, to claim the prize that waited for him. He looked up at the sky as if speaking to his mother he said, 'You were wrong. No, you were weak, so your words had no meaning. Being strongest is not enough for this world, even the strongest have weaknesses. If I have to eradicate every weakness, to build a kingdom of power that isn't affected by any disaster or challenged by any foe, I must become strength itself.'

Two Brothers

THE princes rowed the boat and Katyaki kept her gaze at the forest. The lake surface was quite calm under gentle breeze that day. 'What bothers you, my lady?' asked Chandreya.

Ujjwal cleared his throat and said, 'Bandits?'

She shook her head and said, 'Worse things. Things which I hope we don't have to run into.'

'Like what?' Chandreya asked her, ignoring Ujjwal's frowns.

'Vetal, evil undead spirits. They can't be harmed with our weapons, and they distort your thoughts to do their bidding. I know it is hard to believe,' her voice was so firm that neither of the princes challenged her claim.

'How do you know of all these things? Of this part of the woods,' questioned Chandreya. A fish jumped off the water, colliding with Ujjwal's face as the prince stumbled to keep his balance. Though he was flustered, they all laughed at the situation.

'Perhaps we should be more careful of things in the water,' she teased him. Before Ujjwal could tell a good lie to Chandreya, she turned to the elder prince and answered his query, 'I am a *vishakanya*, raised and trained outside the safety of kingdoms.' Chandreya's eyes widened at the mention of that word.

Ujjwal blew out air from his mouth and said, 'Uh, well, can you imagine it, brother? Even in this era, there are people so cruel to steal children and turn them into murder weapons. Stealing their childhood from them forever, under torture of worst kinds.'

Chandreya stared at him intensely, 'And you still brought her, an assassin, a murderer, even after knowing all this? Knowing what she was… a criminal?' Ujjwal closed his eyes as he composed himself, the air felt hotter between them. Katyaki felt she was boiling between the two brothers, regretting her honest answer. Perhaps honesty wasn't always the best policy, she should have known better as an assassin.

Ujjwal calmly replied, 'Yes, so that she might have one chance to breathe freely, instead of being commanded around by men who just see her as an object… a chance to live a life that was stolen from her. And so that, you, the future Crown Prince would learn of the evil that still goes on and maybe do something about it. Because all that happened to her and many others like her, happened because people like us – like you – did nothing to stop it. So, we owe it to her brother!' Chandreya sighed in an annoyed way, turning his face away.

Before he could reply, Katyaki bowed and said, 'Your Highness, I will accept the punishment for my crimes, if you will so. But let me help you finish this quest of yours, so that you may become the future king and no other child has to lose her childhood, drink poison, or face such torment in your reign.' Her voice had a pleading in it.

Chandreya looked her in the eyes as he asked, 'And what made you so convinced that I will be your salvation? That I will be the one who will end all this evil? You didn't even know me before this.'

She looked at Ujjwal first, then turned to Chandreya and said, 'I have met many men in my life, Your Highness. Men who were filled with so much self-confidence that arrogance danced in their eyes. Yet, none of their confidence in their own selves was as great as the confidence I see in your brother's eyes for *you*. That confidence makes me feel I can put my faith in you too.' Ujjwal hid his face with one hand as both stared at him.

The third prince's eyes darted from her to Ujjwal, 'And are you sure it is not an elaborate plan of the *assassin* to slit our throat in our sleep?'

Ujjwal smiled and playfully looked at Katyaki as he replied, 'A *vishakanya's* lips are more dangerous than knives, brother. Besides, she had all the chance to slit my throat last night as I slept so vulnerable on my bed.'

Katyaki blushed and shouted, 'Do not put it like that, I left as soon as you released me.'

Ujjwal laughed, but Chandreya grunted, still displeased, and losing hope in his younger brother slowly. 'I still do not approve of her,' said Chandreya as he stared at her accusingly.

Ujjwal rubbed his forehead and said, 'Unfortunately, she is the person I have chosen to bring along with me in this quest. You will not reject Father's word, will you brother?' His elder brother grunted, but Ujjwal grinned and kept rowing. Soon, they were at the other shore of the vast lake. They walked into the forest, leaving the boat behind.

Katyaki leaned to Ujjwal as they walked close to each other behind Chandreya. She whispered, only audible to him, 'Why did you not tell me he would get that serious? I didn't know he would be so aggressive about it. I wouldn't have said it like that if I knew.'

The prince whispered back, 'I am in no position to tell you anything my lady, I do not dictate your decisions. You do what you find to be right. I can only stand with you when you face the consequences. That is the price of freedom, that is the only way you can be free.'

'And will you always be there for me?'

'As long as you have shackled yourself to freedom, I will be there, physically or in your thoughts. The moment you abandon that shackle and become what *others* want you to become, I cannot help you.'

'Still, a warning would have been nice.'

'You didn't ask. If you ask me anything, I will happily offer my input. But I cannot command you, you are free.'

'And what if I use my freedom to harm someone because you didn't tell me anything?'

'If the said someone is innocent, I will protect the person, but I will not attempt to stop you from what you wish to do. However, if you ask me before acting, I could give some input, which might make you stop yourself, even if I can't stop you directly.'

She sighed and walked behind him, letting him catch up to his brother. The forest seemed dark, even in the daytime. The trees were high and wide. 'Brother, I think we might have to camp in the woods from now on,' said Ujjwal after around half an hour of walking. Then he turned to Katyaki and said, 'Will you be kind enough to lead us through the woods? Find a good spot to camp perhaps.'

'Yes,' she softly said with a bow and headed forward. She could feel Chandreya's gaze on her as if the prince was watching all her steps. They managed to find an open space to sleep, the first night wasn't very difficult for the fourth prince and Katyaki, Chandreya however found it quite a challenge to sleep on soil with twigs and leaves all around. He didn't make a show of it, but Ujjwal could tell that his brother was uncomfortable in his sleep.

*

The next day, they ventured deeper into the woods. Katyaki was walking behind the princes, not wanting to be stared at as a threat. Ujjwal was humming, his hand reached out into the bush randomly, but he squirmed and pulled away as he got stung by the fruits of a *Dhatura* plant. She laughed and said, 'What do you think you were doing, trying to grab a thorn-apple?'

'The fruit might be so spiky my lady, but the flower, oh so beautiful, like you.'

Her cheek blushed a little, but she replied with composure, though in a faint voice so Chandreya wouldn't overhear him from ahead, 'And poisonous too, just like me.'

Ujjwal grunted, 'Yet, they are often found in every healer's hut. What's more, they are offered at the feet of gods and goddesses.' He tilted his head to give her a soft smile.

She rolled her eyes and said, 'That is still not an excuse enough to get yourself stung.' He reached into the bushes and carefully brought out a thorn-apple, as he threw it back without looking at her. She easily moved out of its way and gasped, 'With aim as bad as that one, I could dodge it eyes closed.' The prince chuckled but didn't reply to her as he walked to catch up to his brother.

The flowers in the bushes brought back memories. The nightshades and their kin were often grown in the gardens of her training home. Children were lined up as they would be given small doses of the toxins extracted from the venom of scorpions, snakes, and spiders. They would often vomit, go into spasms or lose their sight. Those who survived, like her, would be then given more concentrated toxins extracted from flowers and fruits, and rarer insects. Just a mere look at the flower made her feel like vomiting, the taste and bitterness climbing up her throat. All she could do was look ahead, look at the princes walking in front of her. She focused on them, to get rid of the memories which were consuming her. The memories of her lying sick for weeks after a few doses of the toxins.

Ujjwal noticed her lagging, her stressful breathing. He gently stopped and looked at her. When their eyes met, she wanted to turn her face away, ashamed to be looking so weak and miserably. But the prince only stared at her, not with pity or curiosity. It was tender when he said, 'You are strong. You have consumed the poisons that would kill anyone and still walked off. Don't let it consume you, whatever you are fighting.' She breathed in, closing her eyes she relaxed herself and straightened up. She nodded at him and he turned around without further questions, just walking slowly enough so she could catch up.

She kept thinking, *is he just big talk or does he have other skills too,* as she looked at Ujjwal walking behind his elder brother. She was eager to test it out, without thinking much she pulled out daggers. Silently, with a false intention of killing him, she came at him from behind. Ujjwal turned so fast she couldn't realise when he had grabbed her hand, pressing her back to his chest. He held her hand such that her own dagger pointed at her throat. Chandreya had already put an arrow on his bow and was aiming at her, when Ujjwal playfully said, 'What was that, another attempt to charm me? Let me tell you, this time you almost succeeded.' He laughed playfully as he looked at her, then said, 'It is nothing to worry about brother, she is just fooling around.'

She gave a coy smile and said, 'I was just testing your reflexes, it seems like the forest hasn't gotten into your head yet.' He released her hand and Chandreya lowered the bow, though his eyes were still on her.

'Please, I have wandered in many forests before, a night or few on the ground won't affect me much,' Ujjwal replied playfully.

'That's good, because we will be in this forest for a while,' she said as she kept her daggers back. 'As your brother already mentioned my lord, daggers are not my weapons of choice,' she bowed to Chandreya as she walked to the front, seeking the best route for them.

'Umm, I suggest we head north from here on,' said Ujjwal, bringing out a makeshift map he had drawn.

She turned and replied, 'What? Why? That would take us too close to the bandits of this region.'

'Yes, the closer we are to our enemies, the safer we are.'

'That is stupid.'

'Yes, that doesn't have much logic in it brother, even though it sounds thoughtful. We should take the safer route,' Chandreya said.

Ujjwal breathed in to gasp and said, 'Fine. I talked to a man in the village, Sarat was his name. He gave me information about a secret path up to the mountains. It starts from some kind of temple ruin near the bandit camp.'

'And this man, was he another drunkard friend of yours? How do we even know that the bandits haven't moved their camp even if he was telling the truth? It still doesn't make me feel convinced to just walk up to their camp,' his elder brother said firmly.

'Well, because he was drunk, he couldn't be lying about what he said. Why did you think I was late in the morning yesterday? I was talking to the guy late in the night to find this path for you. Bandits might have moved, but they won't go far. They move around the same place even when they shift their camps.' Chandreya shook his head in disagreement, so Ujjwal sighed and said with a childish tantrum, 'Very well then, let us just camp here at someplace safe. We can decide tomorrow morning where to go.'

Crown of Flowers

THEY built a fire to cook some birds Chandreya had shot down. As the meat was getting cooked, Ujjwal sat to look after it. Chandreya was sitting under a tree and Katyaki was making something with flowers. 'So, do you travel to remote forests a lot? Seems like you are habituated to it by now,' asked Katyaki as she continued her handiwork.

'Yes, I like to learn, but there is only so much you can learn from books and scrolls of the library. So, I travel to meet people and learn from them,' the prince said while checking the tenderness of the meat. The assassin looked at him and caught him looking at her doing her craft of flowers, he darted his eyes aside and she chuckled. Chandreya couldn't hear what they talked about, but it had started to make him feel uncomfortable – his brother, a prince – was flirting with a criminal right in front of him.

The dinner passed in silence, and Ujjwal got busy with disposing of leftovers and cleaning around the place to prepare for their sleep, sending off Katyaki to continue whatever she was doing when she offered to help with the cleaning. She grunted, 'What happened to not commanding me?' He rolled his eyes but wouldn't let her leave the craftwork she was doing with the flowers.

When Ujjwal sat down finally, she walked up sneakily and placed a crown on his head, 'Your brother might get the golden crown, but here is a crown for you.' He laughed, delicately examining the crown on his head with his fingers. She said, 'It suits you, don't worry.'

He replied with a gentle smile, 'Of course it does. You have put so much care and thought into making it, after all, it is not like some hunk of metal.'

Chandreya growled from where he sat, 'So, you think a crown is a mere hunk of metal without any worth? A symbol of peace, power and law is meaningless to you, is it like that brother?'

Ujjwal kept his calm as he responded, 'A king gives a crown its worth, brother. A king becomes the symbol through work, not through some title or object. A crown can only be a symbol of power concentrated in one place, a symbol of tyranny and oppression if having a piece of metal on the head is what makes a king instead of people's trust and loyalty.'

Chandreya stood up, 'And what would you know of that, someone who has barely stayed in the court, always running off to gamble or whatever you do? Tell me, dearest brother, what kind of world do you think a world will become if people stop valuing the one with a metal crown?'

Ujjwal only smiled as he looked up at his brother, 'A world where people are not divided by power and do not live in fear of those who wield power. A world where people are free.'

'A chaotic world.'

'A beautiful chaos.'

'A lawless inhuman society.'

'What you speak of is called anarchy brother, the opposite of what I wish for. In anarchy, people misuse the freedom granted to them, they use it selfishly to create even bigger disparity in the society. The world I dream of is different; it is not bound by laws and traditions that benefit a select few. Rather, people and their laws are bound through love, compassion, and empathy. A world where people are free to choose their leader, and the leader is held responsible for his actions because no metal crown exists to save him,' Ujjwal stood up gently to meet his brother's gaze.

'And how do you think the people will be wise enough to choose someone worthy to rule them? What wisdom do peasants or merchants possess to challenge the laws made by our ancestors and rights given by gods?' the third prince challenged.

His brother met him with an equally firm voice, 'Then shall we not educate them, instead of keeping them in the dark? Only through knowledge can they get enlightenment, and become capable of choosing a worthy leader.'

'Education is a right my brother, a right one earns through their duty in previous lives. There is a reason the low borne must serve the nobles because their lack of dedication to the divine led them to a poor life in this birth,' Chandreya argued back.

Ujjwal's fist clenched, but he unclenched it with a soft breath, then said, 'Then is it not our duty even more so to educate them, so they may not get lost again?'

Katyaki so wished she had any words to calm down the brothers, their earlier argument over her feeling like a breeze compared to the storm brewing at that moment. Chandreya pressed on, 'They are hopelessly bound by their desires and mortal bonds. They cannot take education brother. Do you think they will want to serve and toil in the fields, once they find a little education to stand beside nobles and royals? Laws were made to remain firm for ages, a law that keeps changing is like a force of chaos that can never keep a kingdom stable.'

His brother replied, 'A firm law is like a well or pond brother. In the beginning, it is lifesaving, accessible and safe. But leave it like that for long and you will find worms growing in it, mosquitos breeding and murkiness everywhere. A river, as chaotic as it might be, remains clean because it keeps flowing.'

'And what happens when it floods? It destroys everything in its path, just like a chaotic society will ruin the entire kingdom.'

'And do we not stand back from that ruin again? To rebuild, we stand back even more resilient than before. It is true, that we cannot control the rain that will bring a flood, but we can prepare to reduce its effect. Time itself is a river, brother, the best we can do is prepare well to ride it, or else the stagnant pond's disease will destroy us for good. Unless, of course, we clean the pond every now and then.'

'You are talking of heresy brother. To clean the pond, you say? Do you mean to change the laws made by scholars ages ago? Do you think you are so wise to challenge the wisdom of the ancestors? What wisdom do you have, from your travel here and there?'

'Not much, but what wisdom do you have either? Or what wisdom does even the wisest have? Can you claim to be wiser about farming compared to a farmer? I guess not, just the way, a farmer is not much wiser about smithing than a blacksmith. Time changes brother, the ancestors' words need to change if that has become a problem to the general public, and we can collect all the wisdom from people who are *living* now, to make better laws that serve them. What good is a law that cannot serve those it binds, who are living to follow it? Is it truly law or has it become a power to be abused in that case?'

Chandreya roared, 'I will not be lectured and insulted by you. I am the elder brother here, far noble, and wiser than you. What are you even trying to gain here? Have you gone blind with your attachments to the peasants and lesser born? Don't forget, our bonds are the reason our souls never get free. The only way to heaven and being part of the divine is through transcending all those bonds, your selfishness will bind you to this mortal world forever, never letting you be truly free of death and rebirth.'

Ujjwal gasped as if he was failing to do what he wanted, to show his brother the truth. For once, Katyaki noticed him without a smile. He said, 'Dear Elder, I do not seek to insult you. But tell me, are we not equally blind if we abandon all human bonds? How do you think you would see the pain of your own people if you cannot connect with them? You speak of becoming part of the divine through selfless sacrifice of all human desires. Is that not selfish itself, the desire and greed to become one with the divine. I would rather be born a thousand times to suffer with the people I have forged my bonds with than abandon them while I enjoy heaven. I will use those bonds to make a heaven on earth instead.'

Chandreya looked at him, 'I have no reason or interest to argue with you brother, you may turn back now if you will, but I will not entertain your lawless ideologies after I have the crown. The rules and divisions were made for a reason; it is our duty as royals to uphold those laws and boundaries. I intend to do so as the Crown Prince and future King till the end.'

'My lord, if I may, your brother might have said words that don't come up as lawful, but he has a kind heart, and you will need that in your kingdom,' Katyaki dared speaking up even as Chandreya stared at her intensely. He scoffed and said, 'Oh, he has just grown soft to the peasants because no one ever gave him importance in the royal court, that is not kindness, just his escapism. Has he ever talked about the time he was drunk enough to run around half-clothed through the city, the kind of delinquent he is?'

Ujjwal groaned, acting embarrassed, 'Oh come on brother, you didn't have to talk about that.'

To lighten the mood, Katyaki grinned at him and said, 'Oh, too late Your Highness. Now, I want to know.'

Ujjwal gasped, meeting her grin with playfulness, and said, 'It is not like what people tell about me. I mean, they just have made things up, okay? It was nothing like the way it is described. I mean, yes, that's what happened, but there is more to it.'

She leaned in with a playful look in her eyes as she said, 'Tell me, oh princeling, you are not escaping easy.'

'Fine, I was with friends, I had declared that I would test my limits with alcohol. I drank and drank, till I couldn't stand straight,' Ujjwal said and walked around like a drunkard. Katyaki laughed, but her inner voice told her why she got tricked the first night she met him, he was an absolutely perfect actor when it came to acting drunk. He continued, 'Well, there was a pond nearby, my friends took me to help me wash my face and sober up a little. I couldn't even do that; I fell straight into the water.'

She laughed even more, making him bring out the storyteller in him. He said, 'When I came out, I had to take off half my clothes to dry up.' His tone changed, and Katyaki listened intently. 'Then I heard this woman, a mother, crying about her boy. I was worried that he was drowning or something. She told us that her boy, a child, was running around in the city street when some city guard bumped into him. They were dragging him away to punish him; they even threatened to spike him or just throw him off a wall or bridge. Especially since he was a lowborn.' Birds flew overhead, but Katyaki's eyes stayed on him.

The prince breathed and said, 'If I was sober, I would have thought something efficient. But I was drunk, so I ran, half-clothed, I ran through the crowd, the city street. I ran into the two guards, falling with them. They were about to punch or shout at me, but they then saw my face. I don't know how scared the kid looked when they were dragging him, but the two guards turned pale when they saw me. I even went as far as acting like I would get them hanged for running into their prince. Oh, their expression was worth the trouble. After a little threat, they escorted me to the palace, letting the kid go. You see, people paint a bad image of me. I admit, half the rumours about me were spread by myself, but I am not that bad.'

Katyaki laughed and said, 'Oh my, I would have expected you to hold your liquor better.'

The prince gasped and said, 'Is that what you got from this long story of mine?'

'I am just teasing, your princeling,' she said playfully.

'I am offended if you thought I couldn't get a joke,' he laughed to join her.

'I am quite impressed how you went through so much to save the boy,' she said with such admiration in her eyes that made Ujjwal turn his face aside in shyness.

He muttered, 'Oh I was just doing my duty, protecting a citizen.'

If Chandreya was uncomfortable with their flirting, he was clearly disgusted by the comment Ujjwal had just made. He said blankly from where he lay under the tree, 'And the boy was never reprimanded for his ramble. What kind of man will he grow up to be? One who doesn't respect authority.'

Ujjwal gasped loudly and replied, 'He was a child, brother. That's what children do, run around. Let him have his freedom while it lasted, he would have grown up one day.'

'You never did.'

'I am...' Ujjwal thought for a moment, then said in a comical voice, 'I was never a normal child, was I? Remember how much mother had to run around to feed me, and even when she caught me, I won't eat until I heard a story or song in her arms. That boy, he was just another normal kid.'

Chandreya was fuming when he replied, 'Yes, a peasant boy, who should have stayed on his farm or whatever, instead of running around in a city full of civilised people. See, this is what happens when people forget the value of social order and rules that uphold it, getting blinded by emotions.'

Ujjwal rolled his eyes, composed himself as much as he could and replied, 'Tell me, dear brother. Of all the virtues and honours we uphold, how much of them do we look back at when the time of our departure comes? Do you think a queen on her deathbed thinks of all the praise she had got as a royal, all the gods she had prayed, or does she seek the children she loves to be around her? Does she recall the number of times she had bowed to her husband and king, or does she think of the times she hugged and kissed her family?'

Chandreya grunted, his eyes flashing brightly at Ujjwal, but the memories of their mother's last moment ran through his head, the memory where all the six siblings were around her in her last moments. The third prince stayed silent.

Ujjwal sighed slowly and said, 'I think we should rest now; I would take the first watch.' His elder brother silently went to sleep, Katyaki gasped in relief as the quarrel came to an end. Ujjwal looked at her, 'You should rest too, you could take the next watch.' She felt tired, she was surprised how the prince was so energetic all the time. She yawned and lay down, soon falling deep asleep. Ujjwal looked at the stars, then at his brother. He sighed in relief as he realised his brother wasn't so uncomfortable outside anymore. However, his hyper-alertness throughout the whole day had consequences. Tiredness came to him like an inevitable season, even before the prince realised, he dozed off.

Dancing in the Shadows

HE woke up to points of arrows aimed at his face as bandits surrounded them. Katyaki woke in a flash, brandishing daggers in her hand, though Ujjwal brought his hands to stop her. 'Wake him up,' he said in a calm voice.

Chandreya woke up and said, 'How did this happen?'

Ujjwal smiled with regret, 'I sort of dozed off.' Katyaki and Chandreya stared at him in disbelief. One of the bandits pulled out a sword and rope, and Ujjwal immediately said, 'You won't be in need of entertainers, would you? You see, I am a singer and my wife here is a dancer. My brother is a mere hunter you see, we were banished to live in the woods and that's how we are trying to get going.' Katyaki was giving a venomous stare in his direction, but he only kept his eyes on the bandits.

One of the bandits stepped closer, and Ujjwal said again, 'Woah, we were banished, we don't have much gold.'

The bandit sneered as he spoke, 'That is fine. Gold can be obtained after selling you off to slavers.'

Chandreya was about to shout when Ujjwal stopped him and said, 'Are you sure your master or leader will be happy to let go of our performances? I mean, we have performed at royal courts. You might need some entertainment while staying so isolated. Are you sure you want to make a decision in your leader's stead?' There was uncertainty in the bandits' eyes as they looked at each other. Displeasing the leader could end in severe punishment, and trying to decide in his stead could become a death sentence.

Ujjwal smiled internally as he persuaded, 'As I thought, you don't appear to be his right hand either. I am certain your leader would much prefer to have a beauty like her dance in his halls over selling us off.' He looked at Katyaki and nudged her as the bandits looked unsure. She weaved her charm with her eyes and spiralling strands of hair around her finger. Some of the bandits smirked, and some were still uncertain.

One of them said, 'Fine, tie their hands and lead them. Take away their weapons, they look quite fancy.'

Ujjwal chatted with them, 'Yes, of course they do. They are for theatricals after all. These daggers are for juggling, and this sword is for blade dance. And that bow, that's for arts like blind archery.'

'Enough!' said one of the bandits as he hit Ujjwal on the head to shut him up. Their hands were tied and they were led through the woods. The walk was a bit painful, as the princes and the assassin were denied a chance to put on footwear. The rough ground with grit and twigs kept Chandreya groaning now and then. Though the ground didn't bother Ujjwal or Katyaki much, he hoped that his brother wouldn't make too much noise, after all, what kind of hunter he was if he couldn't walk in a forest properly.

Ujjwal had a clear expression of nervousness. This was not supposed to happen, yet Katyaki could see him forming some plan or other. After a long walk, as they emerged from the trees, they found themselves in the court of the bandit king. It looked like an old ruined fort. At the far end sat the bandit leader, eating fruits from a platter. He had turned a stone slab to his throne. On both sides were wooden braziers holding earthen pots where flames burned bright. 'Sire, we bring these travellers to you, since they claim they can entertain you,' one of the bandits told their leader.

He looked at them with examining eyes. 'And anything else of worth? Anything to sell off?' he grunted from his stone throne.

'My lord, not much in terms of gold, but we found some jewellery and these decorative weapons,' said the bandit and another one brought forth their properties. The bandit king looked at the bow and sword, his eyes narrowed. Toughed with experience in warfare, he was certain these weapons couldn't be for decoration.

Ujjwal stepped forward and said, 'My lord, we come from the –'

He was silenced as a bandit pointed a sword at his throat. 'And do you have an explanation as to why your decorative weapons are such fine crafts?' the leader replied.

Ujjwal took a deep breath and said, 'My good sir, we don't perform in village fairs. We perform in the presence of noble lords and royals; hence such precious things were their gifts. Yet, having a crown doesn't make someone a king.'

Before Ujjwal ended up saying something that could anger the leader, Katyaki said in a soft and seductive voice, 'Neither does one need a crown to be a king. So, will you allow us to offer a performance in this open court of yours?' Silence fell like a heavy wave crashing on a beach. Even before the bandits or their leader could respond, Katyaki started walking forward gracefully. Her steps turned to playful dances, as she turned and smiled at Ujjwal. Taking her hint, he started singing, as terrible as it might be, slowly walking around the court as Katyaki enchanted them with her graceful dance.

Chandreya scoffed in silence, so disgusted by his brother selling off himself with the criminal to a bandit. He was so ashamed to have travelled all this way with him. But Ujjwal's verses had some deeper meaning to them, upon listening, Chandreya found the cues and moved towards the pile where their weapons lay. The entire bandit camp was mesmerised by Katyaki's smooth steps, as she danced closer and closer to the throne. The ground was so uneven, so gritty and filled with rough pebbles. Thanks to her assassin training, she had many dance steps in her repository. She had been using steps that helped her move effortlessly even on such a forest floor. Ujjwal's eyes were stuck on her like he was gnawing at her body.

She gave him a furious look, he gasped and intensified his songs, trying to make the entire atmosphere feel drawn to him now. She had devised a plan of her own. Unaware of what she was doing, Ujjwal placed his faith in her and his brother. It all happened quite fast, Katyaki pulled out her hair stick, lethally pointed, and leapt at the bandit leader. Though, he was no ordinary man, years of experience had made his reflexes razor-sharp. Katyaki would have died if there had been a second delay by Ujjwal, who used all his might to throw a brazier towards them.

Katyaki and the bandit leader jumped away from each other, the fire spreading between them. Before the bandits could act, Chandreya sent an arrow into the chest of one bandit and another in the general direction of their leader. In the confusion and spreading fire, the trio grabbed their weapons and dropped a few more braziers on their run into the forest. 'What was that? What were you doing?' Ujjwal groaned at Katyaki as they left the light behind.

'I was trying to save your skins,' replied Katyaki with equal intensity, 'You could have burned me.'

'Hey, I was saving you, that guy almost got you there.'

'That is enough! Stop bickering like some married couple,' ordered his older brother. Both fell silent and turned their faces away from each other. There was noise of movement from the bandit camp, the trio kept running deeper into the forest, only using the moon's light as their guide.

After a while, they stopped, gasping, and panting to catch their breath. 'Thank you,' said Katyaki, though not looking at Ujjwal directly.

'Don't get reckless, you have no reason to risk your life for us,' he replied.

'Reason or not, we three are on the same boat at this moment,' said Chandreya. Before they could proceed much further, they saw flames in the distance, the bandits were pursuing them.

Ujjwal said to Katyaki, 'Dear lady, we are in the dark, but we should move forward a little till we find some elevation.'

She replied, 'What good will that do? Not like they can't climb.'

Ujjwal grinned, 'I have an idea. Can you lead us through the darkness?' She nodded and they followed her for a while. After a little chase from the bandits, they saw a scarp rising from the ground, not more than a hundred yards away.

She stopped and said, 'There, some elevation and from what I can make out in the moonlight, it becomes a rising slope beyond it.' Ujjwal sighed, the flames still following them.

He said, 'From what Sarat told me, these bandits use hit-and-run tactics against our military, which is why we have always failed to bring them down. We are just three, heavily outnumbered, so let's use their tactic on them. Katyaki and I can hide in the woods, attack, and split their team as we run after each attack. Brother, you can hide on top of the scarp, gain a vantage point and shoot at them from the shadows, they have torches to show where they are exactly.' Katyaki's eyes brightened at the plan, but Chandreya's eyes darkened.

The elder prince said, 'How can you suggest me to be hiding in shadows like a coward? I am a prince, a warrior, facing our enemies up front is the true way.'

'Dear brother, look around you, we are in a forest, not a battlefield. This is not a battle for valour and glory, it is for survival. They use this trick on our soldiers, and our army fails because they don't know how to fight anywhere outside battlefields,' Ujjwal grunted, a bit impatient in that tense situation.

But Chandreya was adamant, 'What good of a Crown Prince would I make if I fight like them, hiding and sneaking?'

'Better than a dead one, brother. This is not the time to argue. Trust on my strategy, will you?' Ujjwal pressed on desperately.

Chandreya turned his face aside, 'I would rather die here than live with this shame.'

'And abandon all those citizens to whom you have to serve as a Crown Prince? Is that honourable? Fine, if your honour is so damn important, then stay here and do what you like, or escape to the mountain when Katyaki and I keep them busy!' Ujjwal groaned this time.

Chandreya looked at him, the younger prince added, 'I am going to fight them – in whatever manner I like. Even if I die, at least I would take down a few to thin their number, that is the least I could do for the villagers who gave me such hospitality, lessen their sorrows from the bandits. Lessen the number of children who are stolen and enslaved!' Katyaki didn't dare say a word, but she told him with her eyes that she would follow him to this bitter end. Ujjwal said, 'A coward is not the one who hides and attacks, a coward is who makes excuses like tradition and valour to abandon a real battle, a battle for the people and their own brothers,' and headed into the woods. Katyaki followed him, leaving Chandreya standing with his bow.

The bandits were armed with swords and bows, though only a few carried torches to keep their numbers less visible. Ujjwal and Katyaki hid behind trees, far from each other, ready to pounce whenever a bandit came near them. Ujjwal leapt with his sword when a bandit came by, slashing at his throat precisely. Katyaki gave the same response, jumping at another bandit to stab at his throat twice with her daggers. As the bodies dropped, both of them ran around, hiding to attack again. The strategy worked a little at first when the bandits were spread over.

Soon, they were surrounding the two. Ujjwal couldn't imagine Katyaki falling into their hands, he rushed at a group and unleashed a flurry of blade work. He slashed around, dodging their attacks, as if… dancing. Katyaki felt something familiar with his moves, of course, they were her moves, the steps she had used at the bandit camp. But it was not just hers, there were so many other dance forms merged together, or rather, moulded to be used as sword fight techniques. He wasn't gnawing at her that time, he was studying. She sighed and thanked the heavens that he bore no ill to her the day she came for his life. Things could have ended lethally for her or else.

Yet, even his best steps had limit, as waves of bandits poured in. He just hoped that his elder brother had made the run for it and headed to the mountains by now. An arrow struck into his calf, making him groan as he got imbalanced. He got shoved and fell to the floor; a bandit raised his sword to end the prince. An arrow struck the bandit on his head, making him topple back. Arrows after arrows, precise even in that dark, hit bandits one by one. The bandits hid in confusion, Katyaki took the chance to run and pull out the arrow from his leg. Crawling forward, they hid behind a tree and slowly stood up. Katyaki felt pressed between Ujjwal and the tree, so close that she could feel his warmth. Her heart pounded, but she kept a straight face.

'Is that the *Sound seeker* arrow?' she asked as Chandreya was shooting into the dark, yet any bandit that was not hiding well, fell to the ground. 'No, my dear, it's my brother's ear,' the prince said playfully, looking quite proud at his rhyme. Katyaki grunted, but she saw something in his eyes when he looked towards the bandits. Eyes she had seen countless times. They were eyes like hers, eyes filled with rage, but unlike her, his rage seemed to be coming from pain instead of hatred. She gently put a hand on his chest, and a shiver ran down her body. This was not the body of a prince or a warrior, it was the body of a man who knew hard work. He said, 'We need to incapacitate them a little more.' She nodded, it wasn't the voice of a prince either, it was the voice of a leader.

Ujjwal picked a pebble and threw it away, Katyaki did the same. The bandits shot in that direction, some following it. Ujjwal sneaked up to a torch bearer and slashed at him from behind. He extinguished the torch, but two other bandits were rushing at him, one of them with a torch in hand. Katyaki threw a stone hard at the torch-bearing bandit, knocking him out. Ujjwal grabbed the torch and smacked it at the other one's head, knocking him out and extinguishing the torch. He limped and joined Katyaki, 'Okay, that is the best we can do at this moment, it is time to retreat and run.' She nodded, without questions, she followed him towards the scarp.

Chandreya provided them with cover with arrows as he saw the duo walk closer to the scarp. It seemed a bit tall for Katyaki to climb. Ujjwal placed his hands to hoist her up first, 'Climb on, then you two will have to pull me up.'

Katyaki gasped, 'My lord, how can I step on you? I mean, you are a prince… and a man I respect now.'

Ujjwal looked at her with an open mouth, completely baffled. He said, 'What makes you think I care anything about any of such tradition? We are running for our lives, get on with it already.' She smiled and stepped on his hand. Chandreya was not happy pulling her up, but he did it anyway. The two then helped the limping Ujjwal climb up.

Before the prince could make it up, an arrow passed by Chandreya, almost missing him. But it had wounded his left arm, enough to make him grunt and release Ujjwal. The fourth prince was holding onto Katyaki and the other hand gripping the ground at her feet. Chandreya immediately picked his bow and shot into the darkness, the sound of a body falling onto the ground followed. His brother managed to climb up after all, getting them a chance to retreat away from the shooting range of bandits. Ujjwal was catching his breath, his elder brother staying alert for any more bandit archers.

Katyaki immediately tore a piece of her cloth to tie up the wound on Ujjwal's leg. Then she turned to the elder prince, her voice firm but careful, 'Your Highness, that wound... I am afraid the arrow might have been poisoned. If you allow me, I could draw it out.'

Her voice was almost pleading, but Chandreya was adamant when he said, 'What? What are you bickering about? I crossed a line to save my brother already; I am not stooping so low to take aid from you. If I am to die by poison, then let it be my end.'

'Brother!' Ujjwal hissed and continued, 'We do not have time for this. Your life is important, more important than the rules you uphold so firmly. Let her help.'

'What help can she give? All she has given is death to the innocent.'

'I don't know who was innocent and who wasn't, but I know you are a man with honour and nobility, that is why I want to help you,' Katyaki gasped, her voice filled with urgency.

'What good was it to put myself in danger if I am to lose you at the end?' Ujjwal said with equal urgency. Chandreya felt cornered as he felt the slow decay of his flesh where the arrow had hurt him.

He turned his face away and lifted Ujjwal's sword, 'If you want me alive, you shall have me alive. But I will not remain attached to a hand that will not serve me any good.'

Katyaki almost squirmed, 'I can draw out the poison without all these theatrical.' Ujjwal stopped Chandreya's hand from slicing his wounded hand with a firm grip.

'Don't you dare touch me, younger brother!' Chandreya hissed. But Katyaki, to both the prince's surprise, took the chance to slice at the wound with her dagger, placing her mouth on the wound as she drew the poison out. She spat the blood on the ground when she was finished, her tongue looked blue but she was unaffected otherwise. Silence fell as she offered a piece of cloth to tie the wound up. Chandreya couldn't speak anything while Ujjwal tied the cloth tightly around his hand.

'We should move, gain more distance, please lead us,' Ujjwal told Katyaki. Chandreya helped Ujjwal walk as Katyaki tried to find a way in that dim light of the moon. The third prince grunted at Ujjwal while walking, 'This is the last time I will entertain your madness. There will never be another time, be certain of that.'

Ujjwal teased, 'Come on brother, admit it, you could not resist to protect your adorable little brother.' The elder prince turned his face aside.

They managed to get some distance when they sat down. 'No torches in the forest or footsteps audible. I think they went back,' Ujjwal said.

'We can't be sure that they won't come after us later,' Katyaki replied.

Chandreya sighed, 'That is why I will take the watch this time.' Ujjwal tried to speak, but Katyaki stopped him, her eyes reminding him that they got into trouble because he dozed off. He sighed and admitted defeat, as he needed rest more than the two. From the scarp, the ground had been a smooth slope. They were almost at another edge of the elevation, a steep fall in front of them. It felt like a secure place to rest, high to reach from either side. Thus began Chandreya's watch as the other two slept.

A World without Ujjwal

SARTHAK and Ritikesh reached the village Kundal, tired and weak from their long journey. The youngest prince had taken great care to tend to his brother's left arm. Even if all the poison was drained out, it had done severe damage to the muscles, rendering the hand useless. 'We should head to the lord's house in this village, we need to rest,' Sarthak said as he sat under a fig tree with his brother. It was early morning; bullock carts were carrying grain and sugar-cane. The wives were busy wiping the courtyards and *verandas* with brooms. The poorer ones were also applying layers of cow dung to the mud huts, while others were placing dung cakes to dry so that they could be used as fuel later.

Ritikesh was thoughtful for a moment, then said, 'I don't think that would be a great idea, brother. Would anyone even recognise us as princes, in this state?'

His elder brother sighed and replied, 'We still have our royal rings. It is not so easy to steal one, that they would doubt our claims.'

'Then what? Even if we prove ourselves to be princes, do you think it will paint a good image if they see their princes in this horrible condition?' the younger prince added.

'Do we really have time to think about image and reputation?' the elder prince said as he caught a leaf drifting in the wind. Ritikesh looked at him, trying to encourage him, he said,

'Not ours, but the image of the kingdom still matters. Its king is sick, and if anyone hears that two of the princes were roaming in remote villages while injured, actors from inside and outside the borders will try to stir trouble.'

Sarthak laughed to himself, almost in melancholy. He let the leaf fall off his fingers as he said, 'Perhaps you are right. I have forgotten what I want, or what shall I do. Nothing really matters to me anymore; all these complex thoughts and politics are the least of my worries now.'

Ritikesh took a deep breath and pressed again, 'Even if you... we are out of this competition, we are still princes of this kingdom, part of its royal court, part of its future.'

Sarthak raised his left hand, bandaged to prevent the decayed flesh from rotting and allowing it a chance to heal to whatever extent it could. He placed it on Ritikesh's shoulder and said, 'I am glad you still have so much spirit left in you. When Father announced the quest, I had placed all my heart and mind to ensure I would win. But here I sit, not even being able to continue the quest anymore.'

'I never had interest in winning this race. I just wanted to be of value to Father, to feel valued by the family I held dear,' Ritikesh said with a soft voice.

'Then you have already won your personal quest, little brother,' Sarthak rubbed his shoulder.

The festival was long over, and the upcoming festive days were months away. People had gotten busy with their everyday lives, from farming to crafting, whatever their professions were. Ritikesh said, 'There was this man I had tried to help, I do not know how he is doing right now, but we could ask him for a little food or shelter. There was another man, whose barn I had slept in, for a little silver or copper, he won't mind letting us stay with the goats.'

Sarthak looked at him, surprise all over his face. He said, 'You sound like Ujjwal right now, but I do see the point in your words.

Perhaps talking to the commoners is not that bad, but sleeping in a barn might be new to me still.'

Ritikesh chuckled, 'Yes, the sound and smell of beasts can be repulsive, but when you are trying to keep a low profile or have not much of an option, it can still be a secure bet.'

Sarthak slowly stood up, 'Very well, let's ask this man you had helped, and see if the wise words are true that when you help someone, help finds its way to you.' Ritikesh helped him walk as they made their way to the mud huts. The shepherds were taking goats, cows, and bulls for grazing, sometimes there were buffalos in the herd too. The sky had a few clouds, though no signs of rain were visible. Travellers were not rare in those villages, yet rarely any traveller was as ragged as the two princes. A few eyes were staring at them, though they kept their heads bowed to avoid any unwanted attention or trouble.

'How far have we fallen!' sighed Sarthak in a voice barely audible.

'As much as we deserved,' replied Ritikesh in the same voice.

The youngest prince recognised the mud hut he had visited last time when the couple were having a fight. He straightened himself and tried to appear presentable. 'Excuse me, sir and madam,' he said as he stood outside the bamboo door. The door opened slightly and the familiar face of a woman peeked out.

'Who are you?' she asked, and once she recognised his face, 'Oh, it is you, the good man from that day.' Ritikesh gave a gentle bow, and she gasped, 'My lord, you saved my family, you do not need to bow.' She stepped out, put on her *saree* over her head and joined her hands, bowing to the prince.

'I am glad I could be of help,' Ritikesh said politely, 'How is your husband doing?'

'I must admit, he hasn't gambled from that day. But he still has a long way to go when it comes to managing money. But he is working at least, which is good,' there was a strained smile on her face.

The prince returned her a faint smile and said, 'I am glad he has you with him then, he won't be losing all his money.' The lady wanted to laugh perhaps, but she nodded in agreement to not appear inappropriate in front of a stranger man. She looked at his left arm, bruised and bandaged with a cloth, then she looked at the even more bruised Sarthak. The youngest prince spoke, 'I never had the chance to give you my name, my lady. I am Ritikesh. I, and my brother here, got into a kind of accident, beyond the Sondar village. We only seek a place to rest and recover for a night, before we can head back to the capital. Could you recommend any?'

The lady looked at both of them and said, 'We have nothing much to offer, oh Lords, but we will never say no to a guest.'

'A roof overhead and something to eat are all we can ask, my lady,' Sarthak walked closer. The lady gestured for them to come into the house.

The lady called out to her husband who was still asleep. He grunted and sat up on his cot, rubbing his face with his cotton towel. 'My lord, you have returned,' he said as he stood up, giving a respectful bow. His wife told him of the prince's request and he immediately offered them the room to rest as he went to wash his face and freshen up.

The lady sighed, 'He still hasn't gotten over his drinking habits, though it has got lesser nowadays.'

Ritikesh chuckled, 'My lady, sometimes addictions take years to get over. Give him the time, and credit for his attempts. Pardon me, I never asked your names as I never expected to cross your paths again. But it seems I was wrong about it, like many other things in my life.'

'I am Lataa, my lord,' she said and waited for her husband to return, as it was not so civil to take one's husband's name.

The man returned and offered his name, 'My lords, I am Hari. My wife told me you go by Ritikesh, I haven't learned your brother's name though,' as he talked with Ritikesh.

'I am Sarthak, my good sir,' the second Prince said. The couple's eyes widened, and the lady shivered as she spoke, 'Are you… the princes?'

Ritikesh rubbed his head and said reassuringly, 'Please, it matters not at this moment. In fact, we would be grateful if you could ignore our titles and keep them out of your mouth. We do not want to draw unwanted attention.'

Hari nodded, his body still stiff from fear, 'I… we will do our best to make it comfortable for you my lords… Your Highness.'

Sarthak said with a soft smile, 'My dear Hari, we have been sleeping on bare ground under an open sky for many nights. You do not need to worry about comfort at this moment.' Their hosts sighed; a bit relaxed around the princes now.

Lataa reminded Hari, 'Do you not have to leave for your work soon? The merchant will kick you out if you are late again.'

'Yes, yes, I will be on my way. Take care of our guests,' he grunted and prepared to depart for his day job. The princes chuckled as they sat on the cot.

Once Hari had left, Lataa said, 'My lords, I will go fetch water for you to freshen yourselves.'

Ritikesh stood up to offer, 'My lady, it is alright. I mean, you do not need to put in so much effort. We can fetch water ourselves.' He looked at his brother, who nodded in indifference.

Lataa bowed and said, 'Your Highness, I mean no insult, but I don't think you could do that in your current condition,' as she looked at his hand.

Ritikesh looked a bit embarrassed, he smiled, 'Yes, you seem to be right. We will be grateful for your help.' She left as she took their leave.

Ritikesh sat on the cot, 'Ah, I was trying to act generous, but it backfired.'

Sarthak said, 'She had logic, I don't think you can win against logic.'

'I wonder what other brothers would have done if they were here. Maybe brother Ujjwal would have said something along the lines like depending on others is not a sign of weakness, Ritikesh,' the youngest prince said with a voice mimicking his elder brother.

'Atikaya would have let himself drown before he would ever ask for help,' Sarthak said firmly. They both fell silent, the air filled with a strange feeling they couldn't describe.

Lataa had fetched enough water for the bothers to get fresh. They didn't care about breakfast that day, both rested on the floor on a mat till lunchtime. They woke up when Hari returned for lunch, Lataa had placed two earthen jugs of water for them to wash their faces and hands. 'Did you rest well, my lords?' Hari asked them as they sat down for lunch.

'Yes, we feel much better than how we felt this morning. We are rested and have got a little of our strength back. We will not make you suffer our presence for long, dear sir. We plan to depart early tomorrow,' Sarthak said.

Hari replied, 'Please, it is no burden to us to give you a space to rest.'

Ritikesh added, 'We need to head back to the capital my lord, we do not doubt your hospitality at all.'

Hari lowered his head as Lataa was serving food on banana leaves, saying, 'Then I am grateful to the Fate maker, that I had the chance to pay you back for the aid you had given me. I would have happily let you stay as many nights as you need.'

Lataa gasped at him, 'Can you stop talking and let them eat now, please?' They all chuckled and got started with the lunch.

Sarthak felt a feeling of belonging he had never felt before. Even if they were lowborn, living in a mud hut with just one jute-woven cot, he felt a strange familiarity with them. He didn't feel like a prince at that moment, not as an intelligent schemer, not as a contestant for the throne... he just felt like a human, a fragile and weak human who needed others like him to survive. Perhaps Ritikesh shared the same feeling beside him, after all, he looked like he would have cried out if they were not sharing the space with the couple.

They ate *khichdi* for lunch, Lataa looking anxious as she kept staring now and then to verify that they weren't too uncomfortable with her cooking. Ritikesh licked the banana leaf clean as he finished eating, 'I haven't had anything delicious in so many days, my lady. I cannot describe my gratitude.'

Hari spoke with a mouthful of *khichdi*, 'Your Highness, you have already done this house a great favour. This is merely us paying you back.' The princes smiled, a new kind of delight it was, being treated with goodwill born as a reciprocation of their own action, not some respect given to them on a silver platter thanks to their royal lineage. It felt warm like a campfire, not a scorching summer sun.

Hari left again for his job, Lataa got busy with household chores as the princes rested through the afternoon. Sarthak looked at the straw ceiling and said, 'When was the last time we ate like this, brother? Not as a group of siblings in the same dinner hall, but more as a family sharing a meal. I know, you have had a couple of meals with Ujjwal and Geetika often, sometimes Chandreya with you too. Maybe it was just me who had been missing out on the best part of having so many siblings.' There was a sorrow in his voice, and he made no effort to hide it.

'Oh, we... they were not much different than our usual meals when all six siblings were eating together. Brother Ujjwal talking of his tales of travel, Geetika ranting about the dramatic lives of her friends... nothing out of the ordinary,' Ritikesh said with a consoling voice.

Sarthak sighed, 'Is that not the point? To have an ordinary meal as a family, sharing banters and laughter, instead of princes and princesses eating silently to maintain the decorum.'

'I mean, it's not like Eldest Brother would have joined us for such silly gossip, but you were always welcome,' Ritikesh said as he looked at his brother.

Sarthak kept looking at the simple straw-made slanted ceiling, as he said, 'Yes, but I was a fool back then. Chasing the shadows of an elder brother, wanting to prove myself, always looking at my own ambition. But I was scared all the time. Scared of a world where Atikaya rules and I become a mere shadow itself.'

Ritikesh sat up, the evening was slowly creeping in outside. Lataa must have started cooking dinner, a faint light of the earthen stove was visible outside the door, towards the kitchen. Some delicious aroma followed the light, filling the chamber.

'Please brother, I don't think we should be talking ill of our brothers when they are facing challenges that we will never,' Ritikesh sighed.

'Will that change the reality? Will it change what kind of person Atikaya is? If anything, we should prepare to act accordingly, so that people like Hari and such don't suffer in a kingdom that is ruled by Atikaya if he gets the throne by fate,' Sarthak said in a firm voice this time.

Ritikesh grunted, 'Brother Chandreya is still competing, it won't be easy for Eldest Brother to get the throne. Especially, as long as brother Ujjwal is with him.'

His elder brother looked him in the face and said, 'I always kept thinking, what kind of scary world it will become if Atikaya takes the throne, but I didn't want Chandreya to get the throne either. He is easy to manipulate, a few words of laws and order, and he will let the vilest of acts go unpunished. He lacks the courage and ruthlessness needed by a leader to stand against chaos. But I was a fool all along while trying to stop them, I never even took a moment to think what would happen if I was out of the quest myself.'

Ritikesh lowered his gaze as he said, 'Did you try to stop Brother Atikaya? Brother Chandreya might be a bit too strict with his codes, but he is still the best option we have I feel.'

'Is he though?' Sarthak challenged, 'What do you think would happen if their paths crossed? If Atikaya asked him to hand over the flower, do you think Chandreya would resist? He would give it up to his *eldest brother* as the nice prince he is. Oh, he would not speak back to Atikaya, he didn't do it when Atikaya was punishing the fishmongers when their yield was reduced from polluted ponds.' He was quiet for a moment, letting the heaviness of his words settle, giving Ritikesh a chance to respond if he wanted.

He continued with a voice like fire of forges, coming deep from his soul, 'He didn't even dare stand up to Atikaya when our eldest sibling raised hand on Mother. It won't make a difference, whether Chandreya gets the flower or not. Because if Atikaya meets him anywhere, it will become Atikaya's victory by default.'

Ritikesh gasped, 'Brother, neither of us two were around to witness what happened when Brother Atikaya was furious at Mother. But from the accounts we have heard, Brother Ujjwal had fought back against him, and he is with Brother Chandreya this time.'

'To what end? Everyone knows how that fight had ended, Ujjwal getting beaten up by Atikaya. Besides, we cannot be sure that Ujjwal is still with Chandreya. In my fear of seeing a world ruled by Atikaya, I didn't give much thought to a world without Ujjwal,' Sarthak said with a broken man's voice. He continued before Ritikesh could speak, 'I always thought, a world without Ujjwal wouldn't be much different, because he seemed so insignificant in the grand schemes. But I was so wrong, if our assassin has succeeded, if she got Ujjwal, then Chandreya will lose even if he wins.'

Ritikesh gave a soft laugh, 'Did you just say *she*? Did you send a woman after brother Ujjwal? No way she will ever be able to harm him, dear brother.' His eyes had a brightness of hope.

'What makes you say so?' Sarthak said, a bit hopeful now, 'She was immune to any princely charms and such.'

'It is not just the charm that our brother wields, his true skills lie in seeing at people's heart. She might be an assassin, but she might slip on his words before she realises,' Ritikesh said with a soft smile.

Sarthak's smile was faint, mingled with sorrow and fear when he said, 'I don't know Youngest, she was not so ordinary maiden. Her lethal tricks could have many layers, challenging to see through, even for Ujjwal. But I dread more of a situation where Chandreya just hands over the flower to Atikaya, to maintain that image of a young brother who lives by law and words, fully loyal and respectful to his eldest brother. I cannot believe I am saying it, but I fear to live in a world without Ujjwal. I hope he keeps Chandreya in the right mind, or else all is lost.'

*

The evening passed lightly, even though the air between the brothers felt heavy. Hari tried to tell some of his tales and stories from around the village. His hands still trembled from staying away from his alcohol, but Ritikesh tried to help him with the name of herbs that might help him improve the situation. The couple didn't bother the princes much during dinner, clearly seeing the tension around them. The brothers rested through the night and headed out before crows and hens had greeted the dawn. Soon, they would be home. Sarthak asked on their way out of the village, 'What do we tell them, brother? About how we ended up like this.'

Ritikesh sighed, 'Nothing other than the truth, dear brother. They deserve to know. And it will only bear us ill if we try to run away from our truths, so we have to face it.' Sarthak sighed, smiling at the wisdom of his little brother, as they helped each other walk back to their home.

Whispers in the Dark

THERE was no sign of bandits anymore as the three rested on the mound. Dawn was still a few hours away and they needed proper rest for the night. Chandreya sat against a tree and rested his head. The air was soothing for a late summer night, the sky looked so peaceful without any clouds to shroud the stars. He was still tired, even though he had gotten some sleep. The run and fight had worn him down. He did his best not to follow his brother, yet, soon his visions started getting… misty.

Katyaki's eyes opened to a foggy ground, it felt eerily silent. The night was still dark and there was no sign of dawn yet. An unsettling feeling surrounded her; a memory that haunted her forever had returned. *The loneliness, the sense of being weak and vulnerable. The nights she had spent on cold stone floors, lying on her own blood the poisons had made her vomit. She struggled to get up, but her visions blurred again.* When she could see again, she was back in the forest, lying on the soil. She stood up, it was strangely silent, not even the rustling of leaves could be heard. Her every sense was on high alert, ready to kill or defend. She took a few steps forward. Ujjwal was lying on the ground. He was sleeping so carefree, so peacefully, like the rest of the world didn't exist. She felt jealous of him for that, to feel so safe and free.

It reminded her of the days she could only half sleep, her dreams and nightmares waking her up every few hours. A vast majority of her training was supervised by women, yet sometimes her clients wanted to test her skills. She was left among stranger men to fend for herself, her only way of salvation being eliminating her targets. Be it through blade or venom, all she could do was kill. Her trainers used to tell her that *taking a life is an art, and vishakanya like her were professional artists.* Every time she found herself alone and vulnerable with men, she could only think of killing them before they harmed her. Peaceful sleep was a luxury she could never afford.

She gasped, returning to the present, forgetting all her sorrows of that long-gone moment. She felt oddly safe with Ujjwal around. Kneeling by the young prince, her hand reached out towards the prince. Before her hand could brush his skin, Chandreya was standing with his bow aimed at her. 'So, this is what you were planning?' he said in an accusing voice.

Before she could reply, he said, 'Brother, wake up and look at the scheme of your slave.' Ujjwal turned and looked at her. She stepped back a little, but Chandreya kept the arrow pointed at her, faint moonlight glistening from the tip.

Ujjwal sat up, 'Woah, it seems you were really good at acting. But then again, your uses for us are over now anyway.'

She gasped, 'No, I wasn't trying to hurt –'

'Oh, lady, you are a venomous snake, I don't hold it against you. It's your nature to bite the very hand that feeds you,' Ujjwal accused her.

'Then why would you not hand me over to the authority or slay me the first time we met?' she hissed at him.

'Because you had a good use, helping us through the lake and more. Alas,' Chandreya prepared his shot, 'Your uses end here.'

'No, wait brother,' Ujjwal smirked with a wicked smirk, 'She is a comely woman after all. I can see one last use of her, at least for me.'

Chandreya grunted, 'You and your never-ending desires. Very well, I will keep my weapon at ready. She will draw her last breath as soon as you are done.'

In a flash Ujjwal had pinned her down, 'So where shall we start from, shall I cut off your garb first?' She could see the moonlight reflecting from the dagger pommel on his waist.

She shouted, 'Ujjwal, get back to your senses!'

The prince chuckled and lashed back at her, 'Silence, wench. Long have you used your body to please men, come and serve your prince.' There was a strange desire and malice in his eyes, not something she had ever seen before. He reached for his blade, but she was faster, with lightning speed, she drew out his dagger and shoved it into his chest.

*

Ujjwal was lost in his dream world. *Many friends were at the ceremony, with loads of cuisines and lots of drinks. Women, of beauty hard to describe in words, walked around the hall. There was soothing music as he sat on a relaxing chair, laughing as he chattered with his friends from all over the kingdom. Some had travelled from their hilly homes; some had come through the river while others made their way from the eastern villages… all of them to attend his coronation. Coronation? He touched his head, a jewel-decorated metal sat atop it. He immediately pulled his crown away and smashed it on the floor in disgust.* The dream broke. When he turned around after opening his eyes, Katyaki was sitting beside him, under the night sky in the woods.

She had a strange look in her eyes. She smiled and placed her hand on his chest, it was gentle, playful, and *arousing*. She smiled again as she pushed him back, making him lean slightly. He gasped and said, 'Katyaki, what are you doing?'

'Shh… The night is still young, Your Highness. Your brother is too busy with the watch or perhaps asleep.'

She straddled his legs, a shine shimmered in her eyes, filled with desires. He put a hand on her cheek, the other one holding her wrist, he joked, 'Why do I feel like a prey caught in a serpent's coil?'

'Oh, because you are, I will devour you. And let you devour me.

Don't hold back my lord,' she said in a sensual voice as she pushed him back further.

'Katyaki, we shouldn't be doing this. I am not really –'

'Oh, stop making excuses. I know what lies in your heart, the way you look at my curves, my lips. So, enjoy it when I offer myself to you, oh princeling. Once you have the crown, we will rule together, me as your queen. You can do whatever you please, wherever and whenever you please.' She pushed him back further, her hand running down from his chest.

He gasped, 'Queen? But I have told you, I have no desire for the throne.'

'Please, my lord, don't be so foolish. You have every skill a king needs, you are so much more fitting than your older brother,' she said in voice filled with mockery. She reached to his waist to undo his garment. He gently put her hands to the side. 'I can give you what no woman can, and once you become the king, we will have everything,' her voice filled with seduction. He pretended to reach for his garment to undo it, but he grabbed his sword lying beside him in a flash and slashed through her throat. Her eyes went wide and black as she shrieked, dissipating into a black mist.

*

Chandreya was having a dream, a dream where he was sitting in the woods, watching over his younger brother and a woman. But he was awake now, on his bed back in the palace. He stepped out and cleared his throat, servants and maids came in to attend to him. Soon, he was fresh and ready for the day. He walked to the throne room. To his shock and dismay, it was not the throne room he remembered. A fountain flowing with mead was installed at the centre. At the end of the room sat the king on his throne, too old and weak. He seemed to be sitting there for ceremonial purposes.

Some ministers and court members looked disgusted by the situation, while others laughed and drank as women sat on their laps. A few village drunkards were rolling on the floor or teasing women standing near the ministers. Some of them were saying something, their face towards the throne, or rather the seat by the throne. The seat of the Crown Prince. The Crown Prince sat there, with a gem decorated golden crown decorated on his head. The woman from his dreams, Katyaki, was pouring wine into the Crown Prince's mouth, it ran down his chin as he looked at Chandreya. 'Ah, brother, you are finally here. Come, join us for the celebration.'

'What celebration?' shouted Chandreya, 'What is going on here? Should you not be looking at the royal matters, discussing border security? Keeping up with our finances?'

Ujjwal stopped Katyaki's hand and scoffed, 'Please, brother, why do you think I let you live? Those are the things you are supposed to be taking care of. I am a Crown Prince, let me enjoy my life. If you don't want to celebrate, then please, get back to work so that I can enjoy in peace.'

Chandreya was furious as he lashed at his younger brother, 'Ujjwal, you might be the Crown Prince, but I am not your servant! You have responsibilities to take.'

Katyaki rolled her eyes and adjusted herself on Ujjwal's lap, 'My lord, hadn't I told you he is better off dead than alive to us, utter nuisance,' as she played with Ujjwal's face. Her eyes darted to Chandreya as she said, 'Don't forget, oh princeling, even if you are older, just like everyone else, except for the king, you are a servant to the Crown Prince.'

'How dare you speak to me like that? You are a lowlife criminal, a murderer!' shouted the third prince.

Ujjwal's eyes flashed as he said, 'Oh, please, don't make me regret bringing you back alive.' Chandreya's visions blurred, the next time he opened his eyes, he found himself locked in a cell.

It was damp and cold, a voice from the cell in front of him said, 'So, even you couldn't last long.' He couldn't place if it was one of his brother's voices, nor could he see the face in that dark cell.

'What is going on? Why are you here, brother?' Chandreya questioned. He couldn't move far to see as he found his hands chained.

The voice replied, 'Because I talked against the policies of our Crown Prince. The kingdom is hollowed from the inside, our military scattered to villages and such, and morale is in the sewers. With me on the crown, I could have raised an army to destroy all our foes beyond our borders. If you were on the throne, you could have ensured laws were uniform for everyone, justice was done for crimes and rewards were delivered for good deeds. We could have shared our greatness, and wisdom, throughout the world. YOU could have become a symbol of honour and peace to the entire world! But Father chose him, just because he brought the flower! And, you… you were with him, he brought it right under your nose and you did nothing. Even when you knew very well where his mind lay, saw him scheming right behind your back. How foolish.'

'What are you saying brother? He was helping me, I don't know how it came to this,' Chandreya said in a pleading voice as if asking for forgiveness.

'Oh, don't play the fool. Did he not offer you his help, to the best options among us all? He knew that everyone would vouch for you… that is why he chose you. Recall his words, to keep enemies close.' The figure in the other cell didn't move, but the voice seemed to be coming from all around Chandreya, up close.

The prince gasped, 'He was my brother, and he hated the crown to his guts.'

The voice echoed in his head, 'And were you not there when he cooked up lies in mere seconds? He hid his true skills, just like he hid his true intentions. Why do you think he brought an assassin out of the blue, especially one that favours him so much?'

'He is my brother!' said Chandreya, trying to drown the voice. But the voice echoed back harder, 'Then test it yourself, who does he choose, the woman he desires so badly, or you? Or have you gone blind in love for him, even when all he sees you as a tool to his goal?'

'I will never close my eyes to any wrongdoing even if it is my brother, I would have seen through his lies, if there were any!' Chandreya argued.

The voice was firm, 'Oh, could you? But what if he had corrupted you from the inside already, blinding you with his brotherly love? Did he not make you sit with drunkards like one of them, whatever his excuses might be?' There was a moment of silence, Chandreya's brows twitched in thought. The voice continued, 'Did he not turn you to a coward, hiding in the shadows to shoot at your enemies so dishonourably? You have no honour left in you, the ministers who once praised you would laugh at you, spit at you. Your own father, family and citizens will look down upon you, the way they look at him. No one will ever respect you, value you, or praise your qualities again. You are a failure now, like him, a far cry from the great prince of everyone's dream you were.'

The prince screamed, he felt the headache so bad he woke up, finding himself back in the woods. His bow was on the ground beside him. Then he heard voices as he got his senses back. He could hear rustling and whispers from behind, where his brother and the criminal slept. They should have been asleep! His heart pounded, and a voice called to him, 'Do you realise now, what will happen if you fail? You must get the flower yourself. You are not safe anymore, they will act, unless, you act first.' He could hear them stand up, and without delay he picked his bow and quiver, standing up himself. The *vetal* vanished into mist from the tree above, with a smile filled with evil.

*

As Ujjwal turned and saw Katyaki, he pulled out his sword from its scabbard on the ground. Luckily, she was fast enough to jump back when he pointed it at her. 'It is me, Katyaki, the real one,' she said with hands in the air. Katyaki pinched her hand, asking him to follow. He used the point of his sword to poke at his finger; he gasped but was certain that he was awake now.

He gasped and sat up, relaxing. 'Did you get dreams too? What was it?' he asked.

She said, 'It must have been the works of some *vetal*, phantoms. When I killed it in my dream, it turned into a black mist. I would not dare tell the kind of dreams it induced, but know that I placed my trust in you.'

'Same here,' Ujjwal said as he gently placed a hand on her cheek. She purred a little, but let him touch her. She turned her direction where Chandreya was keeping watch.

She gasped, 'Do you think they might have…?' Ujjwal nodded and slowly stood up with her. Before they could step forward to check on his brother, Chandreya emerged from the tree line, his arrow aimed at Katyaki.

For Love

THEY both had verified it was not a dream, still, she poked her nail into her finger as her fist clenched. Ujjwal took a defensive stance, sword at ready as he kept himself between her and his brother. He asked Chandreya, 'What are you doing, brother?'

'What are *you* doing by keeping her on your side always? What is your goal, with a killer like her? What did she promise you, her body?'

'Brother that is enough! Even as a criminal, she is a woman, you shouldn't be demeaning her like that. It doesn't suit you.'

'Oh, I know what suits me and what doesn't. Following your order like a dog is definitely in the later part.'

'I am the one following you brother. And she joined us because she knew the road and could guide us. And because she seeks redemption.'

'Ah yes, every crime will be redeemed when one has the wealth of an entire kingdom at their disposal, won't it?'

Ujjwal moved Katyaki aside as she felt an arrow fly past her. He was fast and ready. 'What are you talking about? Stop this brother. The phantoms have filled your head with lies through dreams. You know I hate that metal crown. We need to work together to help Father get well,' the fourth prince shouted at his brother, then he said to Katyaki, 'Take cover.'

'Oh yes, one more lie, just like so many lies you have told in your life. The ungraceful prince, who can dodge my arrows, what kind of irony is that?' Chandreya challenged.

Ujjwal tried to maintain a respectful voice as he replied, 'I have watched your archery brother, for years. It's precise, but a little predictable.'

The prince kept his brother busy, as Katyaki made use of the dim sky before dawn. Her steps, practised to be silent as an assassin, managed to escape the trained ears of Chandreya. She hid behind a tree, Ujjwal keeping himself between the two in a defensive stance. There was a clang of metal as an arrow bounced off Ujjwal's sword. 'You are taking it too far brother, there is no reason to hurt her. If you have so much issue with her, I will ask her to leave and we can continue just like before, just two of us, seeking the flower for Father,' Ujjwal gasped as he tried to walk towards Chandreya slowly.

His brother grunted, 'Do you mean, help you take what you desire? Your assassin lover and all other women you crave for?'

Ujjwal wasn't sure where Katyaki was hiding, so his best option was to disarm Chandreya. He dropped his sword as he said, 'I do not wish any such things. I don't need a crown to get what I want. Because I want simple things brother, a garden with flowers, a peaceful house with a soft bed. And she… she was a victim of the inaction of people like us; our ignorance turned her like that. She deserves a chance to live free.'

'So, she has seduced you after all, blinding you to all honour and duty as a prince, as a royal?' Chandreya pressed on.

Ujjwal screamed out loud, 'Yes, she did. She seduced me with her zeal to be free, her heart that wants to make the right decision, and her resilience to stand up even after the world has wronged her so much. What can I say, I am a sucker for such traits!'

Katyaki gasped at such words, unfortunately revealing her position. Chandreya said a few words of enchantment and the tip of his arrow started glowing red as he aimed it towards her. Ujjwal shouted, 'Katyaki, RUN!' as he leapt at his brother, praying that he could stop him. Perhaps his jump made Chandreya move enough to make him miss. As Katyaki ran in desperation, a tree near her exploded in a ball of flame as the arrow struck it. There was only a cinder left of the tree. She would have turned to ash and bone if it had hit her. Ujjwal was immediately in front of Chandreya, grabbing his bow. They wrestled for the bow as Ujjwal shouted, 'Drop it, brother, I will not let you harm her.'

His brother responded, 'So, have you chosen desire over your virtues, a stranger woman over your family, your own blood?'

'Blood makes us relatives, brother; trust and love are what makes us family. And I trust that you still have kindness in your heart. She already accepted punishment when this is over, you don't need to aim your weapon at her,' Ujjwal pleaded, his eyes filled with tears.

Chandreya hissed, 'My heart is filled with my duty and justice to the society. If kindness becomes a weakness, I will cast it off. Just as I will cast you and any bonds with you if you don't move now. I wanted to see where your loyalty lies, and it is clear to me now, how far your desires have corrupted you.'

Ujjwal lowered his gaze, tears falling onto the grass below, 'I cannot move brother, I cannot let you harm her. I will always be loyal to you, and to those whom I love. Just like you love me brother, or loved me at least when you protected me from the bandits when you fought the made-up honours to uphold your love for me.'

Chandreya sighed, 'If I have become so weak and blind with my love, I must forfeit it then. I will start with releasing your soul from this miserable existence.' He kicked Ujjwal in the guts, sending the younger prince tumbling back. Ujjwal used a stone as leverage to propel himself as Chandreya sang another enchantment, his arrow crackling with lightning. Ujjwal was just in time to push the bow upward, sending the lightning-enchanted arrow to the sky. He managed to bump his head on Chandreya's making the prince release his grip on the bow as he tumbled back. His brother had more options than a bow though, he sang an enchantment as pure radiance took the shape of a spear in his hand. Ujjwal grappled him with both hands and wrestled, the brothers turned against each other.

Chandreya kicked him again and again, smashing his head on him too. But Ujjwal held on as he screamed in pain, 'If love is such a weakness and dishonourable, what will you call Mother for loving us so unconditionally?'

Chandreya's eyes widened as he resisted, 'I will not be swayed by your words brother, I have made up my mind. This kingdom doesn't need people like you, lying and tricking, dishonouring the value of a crown and its role.'

Ujjwal felt a pang of pain as Chandreya pressed fingers into his abdomen from both sides. He was not ready to let go of his brother, the light of dawn slowly visible now. They had walked quite a bit in their wrestling for Katyaki to follow, but she managed to catch up. She screamed, seeing where they were standing, as she saw them, 'Prince Chandreya, my lord, please stop already, please come back. I give you my word, I will take your punishment, please don't fight your brother.'

'Stay out of it, please. Don't make it more difficult for me, I cannot let any harm fall on you in my watch, that is the least I need to do, for love,' Ujjwal groaned.

'Mother spoiled you with love, younger brother. She should have let you learn your position as a prince instead of always holding you in her arms,' Chandreya said.

'It was me who kept asking her to carry me in her arms, brother, because I wanted her affection, not the other way around,' Ujjwal said as he started to bleed where Chandreya was gripping, but not letting go of his brother. The fourth prince tried to hold his brother's wrist, to move his hands away and to restrain him at his place as they wrestled a little more.

'If your love for the murderer is so important, you can die with her then. This is where I will bury my affection for you here, alongside your bodies. So that I can make a kingdom on values and virtues, an honourable kingdom that symbolises peace for the entire world,' his brother replied as he summoned a magical serpent arrow. The arrow turned into a snake and bit Ujjwal, wrapping itself around the prince to restrain him. He grunted as his hands loosened while the snake tightened around him.

Free from his brother's grip, Chandreya stepped back. However, he hadn't realised that Ujjwal's hands were the only thing holding him back from the deep cliff at whose edge they were standing. The only path left for him to go was downwards. In that moment he saw horror in Ujjwal's eyes, a view so familiar. The horror he had seen in his mother's eyes when he fell from a horse once, almost getting trampled. She rushed to him, covering him with her body, taking the horse's hoofs to her before it could be taken away. She was in pain, she was wounded so bad she never recovered, yet she held him so tenderly, with horror in her eyes. A fear borne from love, a very primal love that transcends any desires and laws, a love so pure that binds humans and living beings together, a love that builds family and society.

He fell far and hard on a rock, his body breaking from the impact. Before he hit the rock, a thought returned that had haunted him for all his life – *could a king be so devoted to his own citizens that he neglected his duty to the world?* Perhaps trying to be a dutiful king to the world, he had turned blind to his citizens. While Ujjwal had tried so hard to show him the truth, he couldn't see it. As the light of dawn poured upon him, shadows that had veiled his eyes vanished like fog vanishes under a waking sun. Only tears filled his eyes, from sorrow instead of pain of the fall. 'How could I do that? How could I hurt my own kin?' he cried.

Ujjwal quickly freed himself from the serpent with the help of Katyaki, the serpent vanishing into thin air as Chandreya's enchantment faded. He made his way around the cliff with Katyaki as fast as they could. Chandreya's body was too broken to be repaired by mortal means, and none of them were sages so great to undo such damage. 'No, no, it was the phantoms, the vetals. It wasn't you brother,' Ujjwal cried beside him as he tried to console him.

Chandreya tried to put a hand on his younger brother's palm, too weak to lift it in his last moments. 'My dear brother, I failed to see your heart. However, imagine, if I, the one considered the best option for the throne by many wise ones and even you, could fall so low in the blindness of honour and legacy, how far can brother Atikaya or Sarthak would go in arrogance or ambition.'

'It doesn't matter anymore brother, the kingdom won't be the same, the home won't be the same without you,' Ujjwal was weeping.

Chandreya continued, 'Not if you stop it. You have become wise my little brother, but even you couldn't see one truth. No one can do your will to the perfection as you can, because only you will be able to pour your soul into it. You and Katyaki have my blessings at least, to whatever future you choose. You must promise me, you must find the flower to heal Father and take the throne, to build that world you envisioned.'

The prince was struggling to speak, but he continued before Ujjwal could beg him to stop, 'I would like to be born in that world, where I can run free through the city, without fearing what my birth circumstances are. Give me your word, brother, that is my last wish.' It was certain that the prince didn't have more than a minute left.

Ujjwal wiped his tears and said, 'I cannot bind myself with a promise, but be assured that because of the same personal principle, I will ensure that the one who sits on the throne, whoever it is, rules with fairness and justice.'

Chandreya gave a fading smile, 'And kindness, brother, most importantly, kindness,' as he touched his brother's cheek before closing his eyes forever.

Ujjwal kept weeping by his body as he placed him on his lap. Katyaki stood there, for a long time. She had given death to many, without question, without ever looking back at her victims. She never dared to look at their eyes, their pain. Always fearing that it might break her, losing her sharpness as a weapon. But that is why she didn't know how people processed death, how to console someone in such pain. She walked up to him and gently placed a hand on his shoulder. He looked up at her and said, 'We can't build a pyre in the forest, but we must give him an honourable burial at least.'

They dug the soil, Ujjwal with his bare hand and Katyaki with a dagger. It took a long long while to make it deep enough. Finally, Ujjwal placed his brother's body in it and put the soil on top. He touched his brother's feet one last time, as he covered the last part of the grave with soil. He looked up at the starless sky of the afternoon with weeping eyes and said, 'Oh Mother, wherever you are in the sky, please take brother in your arms and keep him safe. Forgive me, I couldn't protect Brother Chandreya, I was not strong like Brother Atikaya.'

After his tears were all dry, he picked some flowers and made a makeshift crown like Katyaki had. 'Where did you learn that?' she asked softly as he placed the crown at the head of the grave.

'From you, when you were making it,' his gaze was distant.

Unable to find the right words for the sorrowful situation, she said, 'I see, you learn very fast.'

He replied, 'I like to learn, from any source I can. I used to annoy my mother to tell me stories of all kinds. I would go talk to random boys and old men around the city to hear their stories, as bizarre as they might seem at times. Then I finished all the stories and poetries in the library, they were not enough. When I grew up, I decided to travel and learn things personally.'

She kept listening patiently as he continued, 'I learned the hard way that no matter how far I travel and how much of the world I see, I can only learn passively. It was just like reading those books or hearing those songs, just observing. To learn actively, I needed to become one with the people. That's why I starved alongside the poor, toiled in agriculture fields with the farmers, and pulled carts with the merchants. In doing so, I understood them deeply and shared their pain, saw their true selves. That's when I realised just how much sorrow is in this world, so much sorrow that I can't do anything about. So, the best I could do as a prince, born into privilege, was to take all their pain and put it on myself. The pain of everyone I have ever met, just so that one day, even though through my brother's power, I could lessen that pain a little. But now that brother is gone, and I will have to find a way to fight that pain before it crushes me.'

The assassin took a moment to think, to find words befitting such an hour of mourning. 'Have you ever shared this pain with anyone? Or is that a sign of weakness to you, oh prince?' she asked softly.

Ujjwal looked at the sky, his lips recovering a little strength as he said, 'Of course, it is a sign of weakness. But I am weak myself like every other human ever born. What is there to hide in that? After all, through sharing and forming bonds do we overpower that weakness, through mutual compassion we defeat the greatest pain in our lives.' Ujjwal rubbed his sides gently, in a gesture to comfort himself from the pain he was suffering.

She momentarily closed her eyes and breathed in, gathering the courage in her pounding heart to ask what she desired the most at that moment. She said in a voice too tender even by her reckoning, 'And will you allow me to share the load, to give you a shoulder to lean on, if the pain becomes too heavy?' His smile was his only answer, and that was enough for her. Soon, they headed for the mountain.

A Sister's Sorrow

PRINCESS Geetika was getting ready for the morning, her maids decorating her braid with flowers as they talked about their previous evening. She tried to join them in their giggles, but her smile was faint under the sorrow and uncertainty of her brothers' fates. Once she was ready for the day, she emerged from her chamber. A messenger who was waiting outside offered his respect with a bow. He said without looking up, 'Your Highness, your brothers, the second and fifth prince have returned home.'

'Where are they?' she spoke with excitement, but soon, she enquired with a tone of grief, 'Did they… not bring the flower?'

The messenger kept his head down as he shook his head, and softly replied, 'They are being treated by the herbalist.'

She headed straight to the healer's chamber, entering silently as the healer was busy with his ingredients and mortal pestle. When he turned to her, she gestured to maintain silence, not wanting to trouble her resting brothers. They were lying on the bed, their hands bandaged, and herbal paste covering many wounds. She turned to the herbalist and said, 'Kindly send word to me as soon as they wake up.' The herbalist nodded and the princess walked out as silently as she had come. There was an entire day ahead, she gathered her strength as she held back her tears, making her way towards her father's chamber. *Pandit* Bhimsen was not in the room, only her father lying on his bed, a goblet filled with tonic mixed water on the side table. She sighed and quietly organised the room, watering the flowers in an earthen vase that decorated the space near the window.

King Dharmendra's breathing was faint and weak, yet he was breathing, he was still alive. She was only a child when she lost her mother. She could barely remember her mother lying on her deathbed. She was perhaps sitting on the bed beside her mother, or perhaps one of her brothers was holding her in his arms, she couldn't remember it properly. There was nothing she could have done to change that fate, but it was different now. She couldn't have gone searching for the flower that could cure her father, but she was not a child anymore. She placed all her focus and strength on keeping him alive and well, till her brothers would come back with the cure, just like she had given her word to one of her brothers before he left. She was not ready to let her father fade without giving a fight for his life.

'Your Highness, I have brought more medicine. And the two princes have woken up, but I would feel they need to rest a few more hours,' the healer spoke from the doorway.

Geetika bowed to him and said, 'Thank you, I will leave my father in your care for now.' She walked back to meet her brothers and talk if they could. Had it been a different day, or had they returned in better condition, she would have laughed with them, hugged them, or touched their feet, depending on which brother it was. But all she could feel at that moment was a sister's sorrow.

The two princes were looking at the ceiling when Geetika entered, bringing their attention to her. The light around the chamber was calm and comforting. She joined hands silently to show respect to her elder brothers. 'Geetika,' said Ritikesh softly, followed by Sarthak, 'How are you, dear sister?'

'Better than you it seems,' she replied, trying to make them laugh. A soft chuckle was all they could manage, yet it felt more heart-lifting than the last few days of their travel.

'That indeed is good news, to know that you are well,' Ritikesh said with a genuine smile.

Geetika dropped her hands and asked in a cold but calm voice, 'What happened with you two?' as her eyes lingered on their wounded hands.

Her brothers fell silently, looking at each other as they fumbled for words. She waited patiently as they silently eyed each other. Her patience ran out, as she said, 'I asked you a question,' a voice filled with such authority that even Atikaya would have staggered.

'I did it,' gasped Ritikesh, keeping his gaze down.

'What do you mean?' enquired his sister with a shocked voice.

'I created… I schemed and created a situation to bring down Elder Brother, but I saw the truth before it was too late thankfully,' the youngest prince confessed, not daring to meet her eyes. She gave him a moment to continue, but he was silent.

'And what is the truth brother? What did you come to realise?' her voice was unyielding, less as a younger sister, instead as someone more regal than they could have been as princes.

Ritikesh searched for the words, but couldn't speak it out, only think. Geetika offered him more patience this time, her fist clenched and eyes set on him. 'That I was wrong. I just wanted to prove my worth and stop being looked down on. But I did wrong, I should not have tried to harm my brother just to show that we are equal,' he said with a tender and broken voice, as he looked at Sarthak apologetically. The second prince's eyes were forgiving, but Geetika's were not.

She lashed at him, saying, 'Is that so? You thought bringing down your brother was the same as proving your worth because you were talked down by a few brothers? Have you ever thought about me?' He looked at her, gathering all his courage to look into her eyes to see what she felt, and he saw her rage.

'Do you think when this quest was decided and declared, anyone bothered to ask me, the youngest sibling, the only sister and princess, what I felt? No. Does that give me any right to resent anyone? Does that give me any right to think of you as any less than as my brothers?' she said with a voice like a mighty river bringing its flood.

'No,' replied the youngest brother with a faint voice, his eyes filled with sorrow.

'No. Exactly. Did you ever take a moment to think before you went ahead with your plans to prove your worth, that he is your brother? Did you at least think of him as my brother, about how would I feel to hear of it? Did you ever care about your value in my eyes?' she rained questions on him before he could answer.

Only the sound of her breathing could be heard in the chamber. Sarthak came to the youngest prince's rescue and said, 'My dear sister, we all make mistakes while blinded by emotions. I wish we were wiser then, but now that we are through this, never will such a mistake be repeated in our lives.'

There was a momentary silence, as she considered his words. She calmed down for their sake and asked politely, 'You left with your friend, elder brother. What happened to him?' That was enough to make Sarthak gasp for breath, and hold onto his very soul.

He gulped and said with guilt-ridden voice, 'He fell, by my hand.'

'It was my device, my plot. I didn't know how it was going to end, but I just was trying to break them apart,' said Ritikesh to protect him. Geetika closed her eyes, tilting her face to the ceiling, tears rolling down her face.

'How could you take someone's life so easily, brother? Did you not think of his friends and family, and what they would go through when they learn of this? How can anyone take a friend's life so easily, even if they are in disagreement and standing on opposite sides?' she said as she looked at Sarthak with tear-filled eyes.

The prince looked down in shame and sorrow as he said, 'It was an accident. Forgive me, sister.'

Geetika wiped her tears as she said softly, 'Why do you ask my forgiveness? What good will it do? I am your sister and will stay your sister. It's the ones who have lost a friend, a brother, a son or whatever Lord Viryanath was to them, they are the ones you should be asking forgiveness from.'

'We will. We will personally ask their forgiveness, and accept their resentment,' said Ritikesh, seeing her with a new clarity.

Sarthak nodded too, the thought of slaying his friend still haunting him, but perhaps now he could move on, having received the resentment he felt he deserved. The thought of his attempts on Ujjwal's life also passed through his mind, making his lips twitch. Geetika said, 'What is it, brother?' When Sarthak looked up, she was staring at… into him. 'Speak,' the youngest sibling ordered him.

'Is that why they refer to you as Ujjwal's sister? Always looking through the details,' Sarthak said with a soft playful voice.

She would have laughed at such a funny comment at a different time, but this time she coldly replied, 'Perhaps yes. But that is not the answer to my question I believe, brother.' There was no running away from her anymore, Sarthak clenched his fist when he looked at Ritikesh, hoping he would rescue him again.

This time Ritikesh said, 'Brother, that is a burden for you to bear. A question for you to answer, I cannot answer for you this time.'

Sarthak looked at their sister, his heart beating fast. 'We… Viryanath sent an assassin after Ujjwal.' If Geetika's fury had been a storm before, it turned into a cyclone, an all-consuming wildfire.

'How dare you? How could you accept it?' she screamed at him, forgetting all bonds and traditions.

Ritikesh tried to come to his rescue finally, 'Dearest sister, think of it again. Do you think an assassin can easily harm brother Ujjwal? Of us all, you would know him better.' She looked at him with the same furious eyes, eyes laden with tears as she leaned against the wall, almost collapsing on it.

Even as her lips trembled, she spoke, 'I know. At least I hope he is unharmed. Yet, it cannot be forgiven, what you have done brother. I will never forgive you.' The words settled like a mighty blow of a hammer. Their broken hands couldn't even be compared to the pain they felt as they watched their sister weep. 'Pray to the gods that he comes back alright, they all come back alright,' she cried out, as the two princes silently prayed at her command.

'I did not want to do it, but at least I ensured to tell her that she should only try to slow him down, instead of going after his life,' Sarthak said as he gathered his breath.

Geetika wiped her tears as she said, 'Is that supposed to make me feel any better?' A silence followed as the answer.

The princess stood straight, gathering herself together as she declared, 'I wanted to see my brothers and ask how they are, but I don't know any more if my brothers returned at all. Think what you have done to your own family, brothers. I have to attend to father meanwhile.' They could only nod and silently watch her as she walked out of the chamber.

*

She placed her hand on the door to her father's chamber as she said, 'Father, I am coming in.' *Pandit* Bhimsen was sitting on a wooden stool by the window as he conversed with the king.

He stood up and gently gave the princess a bow, 'Your Highness.'

She stopped him and said, 'Please, oh Enlightened One, your wisdom surpasses my titles,' as she joined her hands and bowed to him. She turned to her father, the king, and said with a sorrowful yet soft voice, 'Father, do you know that two of your sons have returned?'

'Yes, I heard. From what I heard, they couldn't bring the flower with them,' the king's weak voice came from the bed.

Her eyes widened and her voice thundered, 'The flower? That's what you think about when two of your sons came home with arms broken? Father, if the flower was so important, why not send them all together?'

The king sighed and replied in a composed voice, 'My dearest daughter, I understand your pain and anger. But you need to calm yourself and see them as more than just your brothers. One of them would have to sit on the throne, and he must be chosen carefully.'

The princess breathed in, like a silence before the storm, then spoke her heart out in a clear and sharp voice, 'I will not be quietened. I will not be calm until you admit that you were wrong. That this whole quest to send my brothers to a doomed fate was absurd and would only cause pain to everyone involved. Do you even know the kind of things they have done to each other?'

The king tried to calm her down, 'My heart cries too, to think of the kind of challenges they must have endured and will be facing. But do you think they would have silently accepted whoever sat on the throne if they had not tested themselves out?'

Geetika argued back as her fists clenched, 'Is that so Father? Do the ancient texts we hold in such high regard not give a list of tests to find a true heir when needed? Empathy can be tested through how a man treats the beggars and injured, might and strategy can be examined in mock battles and arenas. You could have held debates to test their wit and wisdom and challenged them to solve problems people face in everyday life to see their intellect. Yet, you chose this madness!'

The king was about to speak when her eyes flashed in anger and she raised her finger, stopping him from interrupting. 'What was the real reason to send them on this quest, Father? Was it to test their quality or to demonstrate that you have freed yourself from the bonds you shared with your sons? To show that you have become a true king of his citizens who wouldn't mind making his sons clash against each other to find the best suitor to his throne?'

'That throne holds far more lives in its cradle than just my sons, dear daughter. So much of the kingdom and lives of its citizens depend on who sits on the throne,' her father made his point.

The princess of Pandhar was not ready to back down as she argued, 'Why? Why must we suffer so much for a damned overly decorated chair? Why must there be so much struggle to seize it? Always a challenge or battle by those in power, to pick someone who would rule over those who had no say in that selection process.'

'Because that is how the world is meant to be, my daughter,' he replied.

'Is it? Or is that the way our ancestors made it, and now we are making it?' her voice rang firm.

Pandit Bhimsen had to step in before the air burst into flame from the intensity of their gaze. 'Your Highness, if I may speak a word or two,' he offered politely.

She wiped her tears and turned to him, 'Pardon me, oh *Pandit*. I shouldn't have spoken out loud.'

'No, it is important to be heard, otherwise greatest of ideas will get buried beneath hubris. It is too late to undo what is done, even if it was a mistake. Your brothers are already in this quest, some have returned even,' he reassured her.

As she panted, calming down her breath, she said, 'Brothers they were to me, but I don't know what they are now. Turning against each other, are they still the brothers I knew?'

Bhimsen stepped closer to her and replied in a tender yet wise voice, 'Certainly not, princess. They are no more the men who had started the journey, but that is not bad. They have returned, and changed into individuals wiser than before, not because they achieved some enlightenment, but because they lost so much. That lesson learned through pain is like writing set on metal or stone.'

'But I can't just close my eyes to what they have done,' she wept, not like a princess, as a sister.

'Then don't. But you cannot close your heart to them either. This is a moment when they need you more than ever. Tell me oh daughter of Pandhar, what would you do if something precious to you broke?' said Bhimsen and looked around the room, continued, 'Like that vase let's say. Consider a vase your mother had gifted you. What would you do if it fell down by mistake or by someone's malice and shattered into pieces?'

She looked at him and said, 'If it was from my mother, it would be precious to me. I will gather the pieces and put them together, glue them to make the vase whole again.'

The wise man continued, 'Yes, and you are the glue to them, to hold their broken pieces together. The moment the five princes walked into this room together, I noticed something. Even though they were all so different from each other, they had one thing in common. Their tenderness for their sister.'

The princess's face brightened. The *Pandit* felt the burden weighing her down, as he kindly said, 'Forgiving another one's mistake takes great courage and strength, you don't have to do it immediately, you don't have to do it at all if you wish. It is important to understand their pain though. Don't abandon their already broken soul, or else when it is too late, you will not be able to forgive yourself. That is your duty to them, not as a princess, but as their sister.'

The princess stood in silence as she watched the vase on the table, holding the flowers she had placed in them. She looked at him as she erased her sorrow, 'I will do my best.'

The day was spent tending to her father, taking care of his medicine and treatments. Afternoon rolled by and evening came when she sat with her maids and servants to hear their daily lives. Their simple lives seemed so luxurious compared to hers at that moment. It was her only source of delight recently, their laughter-filled banter, carefree gossip that wasn't burdened by any throne, destiny, or duty. When dinner was over and royal chefs had retired, she prepared some pudding herself, carrying it to the chamber where her brothers were resting. They were delighted to see her again, their joy outweighing the fear of getting another verbal lashing.

She placed the bowls of pudding – *kheer* – near their beds. 'I have not forgiven you, I don't know if I will. But you are still my brothers, I will still care for you.'

'That is more than any kingdom's worth of treasure to us,' said Ritikesh as he took his bowl in hand.

Sarthak carefully placed his bowl on his lap as he said, 'I won't demand your forgiveness sister, though I hope for it dearly. Yet, I would like to keep the title of being your brother if you would let us keep it. That is more valuable to us than being a prince or such.'

They looked at the pudding curiously as they took the bowls in their hand. Their sister looked at them and said in a kind voice, 'It is like how Mother used to make when you were sick. I don't really remember it as I was too young. But I tried to make it as brother Ujjwal had described it to me when he told tales of Mother.' Tears rolled down the eyes of Ritikesh and Sarthak as they closed their eyes and savoured the pudding without wasting a single thought.

Atikaya's Mercy

ATIKAYA sat on a rock, the cold wind smashing all around the small cave-like space he was in. He leaned back against the rock wall and looked at the sky, counting the days and weeks it would take him to reach the flower. Sun was setting in the west; it was a beautiful view to behold. He had seen many such sunrises and sunsets from the mountaintop, and he would see a few more before he could start his return journey with his prize. There was nothing much growing in those cold heights, but by fate, he had managed to pull out some edible roots from the snow. He roasted it with the fire he had started with great effort. Melting snow to provide enough water was not a challenge there, yet his body was feeling the toll it had taken from the journey.

'Brace yourself, Atikaya, you are stronger than this. You have to become stronger than the mountain, if you wish to rule Pandhar,' he said to himself, the fire momentarily feeling bright as if it was encouraged by his words. He looked at his sword, his only companion left on that journey, many foes he had slain with it. A sword blessed by a priest and bathed in the blood of his enemies. The intricately designed hilt gem decorated pommel brought back memories of wartimes. He tried to push the thoughts aside, it was not a good idea to be thinking of bloodshed when he was on a journey to seal the fate of his kingdom, and perhaps the fate of the entire land. The thoughts were unyielding though. Soon, in his tiredness, the mountain turned into a battlefield, where he was riding on his chariot.

*

It was a battle from a long time ago. The kingdom of Dangri, a long-time ally of Pandhar was facing against invasive forces of the southeast, led by the kingdom Vastali. In their desperate hour, they sought military aid from Pandhar. The eldest two princes were sent to lead their armies and save Dangri from foreign control. Sarthak was aiding Dangri with defensive formations like the *Padhmavyuha* (Lotus formation) or more transport and supply-oriented *Sakatvyuha* (Cart formation). It had helped them reduce a lot of fatalities, though few still questioned the interference of a foreign prince, even if it was to their aid. Perhaps the questions and doubts were based on the eldest prince of Pandhar but misdirected towards his younger brother.

Atikaya had brought his army, experts in offensive formations like *Vajravyuha* (Thunderbolt formation) or *Makarvyuha* (Crocodile formation) to destroy through enemy lines with mighty strikes. Though it was inspiring to watch the eldest prince of Pandhar lead his armies, some even from Dangri seemed worried. The prince was clearly demonstrating the military superiority of Pandhar, and perhaps his own glory. They worried, and aptly so, that the army of Dangri itself might find itself awed by the prince's acts and perhaps in his command one day. What difference was it from the invasion then? Instead of an enemy state, they would get taken over by an ally, or former ally.

They did not question the first prince though; they were scared after all. So, the majority of questions and doubts were directed towards Sarthak, a shadow of the first prince as many considered him. Sarthak felt bitter at times, yet, he stayed true to his duty, proving his quality in times of war. He had strategies and spies at his disposal, which helped them prepare counterstrike even before enemy attacks arrived. He could sway the ministers and commanders to use unconventional strategies to gain an advantage.

Yet, his own brother would not hear a word of him. It was coming towards the end of the war, and many of the enemy generals had fallen by then. Morale was high for Dangri and its allies, the enemy forces were discussing whether to disband or make a final effort. Atikaya remembered when his younger brother met him in front of his tent to say, 'Dear Eldest, I do not see a reason for us to go full offensive at this moment. The enemy forces have thinned and we could just wait, till they lose morale to fight anymore. We are here to aid Dangri, not to destroy Vastali and its allies.'

'Do we not share the same blood, my younger brother? How could your blood go so cold then? Do you think ending this battle will be the end of it?' questioned Atikaya harshly.

Sarthak looked down and sighed, 'It is not our battle. It is their battle; we are just here to help them when needed.'

The first prince replied like he was teaching a young child, 'And what do we gain from it? Gold, their songs of glory, or perhaps their support? Do we need any of it? Have we not already shown them how ahead of them we are in the matters of war and wealth?' Sarthak was about to reply, but Atikaya shut him up with a stare and continued, 'If we don't end this war once and for all, Vastali and any of its allies will return in the future. They will come after Dangri, and we will be called for aid again. Our soldiers will bleed and die for another land once more. I do not want to see a day like that. I would end this war, and free Pandhar from future pain that is not ours to bear.'

Sarthak wanted to stop Atikaya from making any rash decision, the global geopolitics was in question, but the eldest had headed for his chariot already. Sarthak could only shout from a distance, 'They are humans too, just like us.' He wasn't sure if Atikaya had heard him. The only thing he could have done was to stay in the backline and provide his support, even amidst all the questions and mistrust. It didn't matter to Atikaya, it was a problem for his brother, not for him.

The conch of the generals of both sides rang through the frontlines. The battle had begun. Atikaya was shooting arrow after arrow, enchanting some of them with blessings and wisdom of Devas to rain lightning from the sky or mould the earth to sand. The enemy general had taken a lotus formation approach to keep their king, Kushanu, safe in the centre. Atikaya tried hammering from different sides, using both crocodile formation and thunderbolt formation now and then. It was to his folly, as the defensive nature of lotus formation was resilient against any direct attack. Atikaya thought hard to use an Eagle formation, to attack from three directions through the beak and wings. But the ever-shifting nature of lotus formation made it difficult even for an Eagle formation to break through.

Sweat dripped from his forehead, even as he stood under the shade of that chariot. He tried exploding his way through the first ring of the lotus, but they easily reformed it right after his arrow created the explosion. He looked at the captains around him and shouted, 'This is not something I would like to do, but it seems our disciplined attacks have turned to our disadvantage now. It is time to fight it with chaos itself. We will use the *Asurvyuha.*' The captains understood they were on their own, every captain acting independently to use the chaotic formation that *Asurvyuha* (Demon formation) was. The beauty of Lotus formation was not to be underestimated, it was no easy job to tear it layer by layer, petal by petal as they made their way to the central rings. Even the captains knew though, that the final blow had to be from Atikaya.

The circles of the lotus formation were scattered at the end, and the small troops of Atikaya's forces were spread all around. Then the final battle began. Atikaya took King Kushanu's challenge as they showed their archery skills. Enchanted arrows had created walls of fire and lakes of mud. One of his exploded near Kushanu's chariot, throwing him off his vehicle to the ground. Watching him get to his knees, Atikaya said to his own charioteer, 'Please stop the chariot. I would like to face him on equal ground.' Atikaya descended and walked closer to the king as he announced, 'Get up oh king of Vastali. This is not how you shall find your end. Stand and pick your sword, fight me like a warrior.'

The king didn't disappoint him, with a sword in hand and shield in other, he charged at Atikaya. As a prince, only Atikaya could have challenged King Kushanu, as no other royals were near them at that moment. So, he battled with joy. The swords clanged and clashed, though Atikaya didn't feel pushed back yet. His opponent was a formidable warrior; he had to dodge and take defensive steps now and then. But all that time, he only had a smile on his face. A smile born from his joy in battle. 'You are quite a dangerous foe, Your Majesty, I must admit,' he claimed as Kushanu pushed him back a couple of steps.

'Pandhar has been blessed with a mighty warrior, I would agree,' said the king. He spoke, 'No doubt your military influence in these parts is strong, or else Dangri would have been flying our banners by now,' and charged at Atikaya. The prince used his weight to create momentum, as he met the king head-on.

A few slashes and thrusts of their blades were exchanged before the king toppled back, his sword and shield lying on his sides. 'Get up oh king, you still have the strength to fight,' roared Atikaya as he challenged him again, letting him catch his breath. However, the king did not pick his weapon again. He only stared at Atikaya, blood dripping from his broken lips. The air around was filled with the scent of blood and shouts of dying men.

'What is the point, oh prince? When I will end up on the ground again,' the king muttered. The prince did not attack, he would not attack a man who had no weapon in his hand, and who was lying flat on the ground.

'What was the point of your conquest? What was the point in all the death and suffering you brought along with your war?' he questioned the lying king.

The generals of Vastali and its allies only stood and watched. Even the kings and princes of the other kingdoms didn't have the right to interfere as it had turned into a duel. Pandhar's prince hissed, 'Your men are watching as you wallow on the ground. Stand up like a king and face me as the warrior you are. There is glory in defeat too.'

'All the glory I sought has been in vain,' king Kushanu replied. Atikaya scoffed and said, 'If not glory, then for whatever little respect you and your crown are left with, fight for it. Do you think they will wash your feet when they see their defeated king return? They will laugh and spit at you.'

'Perhaps they will. But their laughter and mockery are far better than the tears of my loved ones I think,' the broken king said as his eyes were not looking at Atikaya anymore, they were set at the sky. The evening was nigh, once the sun was set, the war would be over and Atikaya would not be able to slay his opponent.

Even then, the prince's sword did not rise to make the final blow. It was not just his honour that stopped his hand, his eyes had turned tender for a moment. 'Will your loved one still accept you, when you return as a defeated and broken man?' he asked the king.

Kushanu replied, 'Perhaps not, perhaps they will. It is not their validation that I seek as a warrior, I only wish to return to their affection. I am sure even in my defeat, they would find something in me to love me still. That is all I need. Would you not have wanted to be returned to your brothers and your family, if you were standing in front of death, not that I would wish that fate upon you?'

The prince stood tall and proud, yet with a firm and gentle voice he said, 'I see your honour is intact in defeat, and you still yearn for those whom you love. I don't know if I share such a feeling. I think I would much rather meet a warrior's end on the battlefield than return home in shame. But if that is the fate you have chosen, I would not be cruel to steal it from you. Know this, Your Majesty, if you ever return to bring ruin upon Dangri or any of our allies, you will not be graced with this mercy again.'

Atikaya sheathed his sword and returned to his chariot, letting the king take his banners back and return home. The war was over and Dangri was saved, at least from that invasion. The rest of their fate was not of his interest and he didn't even bother staying long after the war was over. The king of Dangri offered his daughter's hand to Atikaya, but the prince refused to be wed to someone as a token of reward. He was only following his father's order when he came to fight for Dangri, and doing his duty had been enough reward for him. He returned home and Sarthak followed soon after.

*

The sky had gone completely dark by the time Atikaya regained his thoughts, his eyes turning to the waxing moon. 'Only if I wasn't so foolish at that time. So many lives could have been saved. Only if I hadn't become so weak to offer him my mercy,' he said to the sky, not seeking any answer from it. He wrapped the *shawl* around him tightly as the evening had started getting colder.

He held a fistful of snow in hand and watched it melt between his fingers. 'That coward of a king wouldn't have met his end at the hand of assassins if I had finished him off in an honourable way. I had warned him, they would look down on him, but he was not ready to listen,' he kept talking to the empty winds.

Everyone was aware of what happened next. Dangri and the kingdoms affected from the invasion made Vastali pay for its crimes. The economic load of the war and then reparation became a heavy burden for Vastali, causing instability within its realm. Once the nobles of Vastali decided that Kushanu was unsuitable for its throne, he was silently removed from its court through poison. Then a new coalition was formed, to strike back Dangri. Their attack came swift and powerful, without any honourable challenge of war.

Pandhar had its own economic troubles to deal with after the previous aid. Their support for Dangri came too late, almost half the kingdom had been ransacked. Though the three eldest princes of Pandhar worked together to drive off the invaders, the damage was done already. That time Atikaya was not ready to listen to Sarthak or Chandreya if they tried speaking of any negotiations, though his younger brothers didn't make any such attempts, be it out of duty, fear, or mutual hatred for their enemies.

Atikaya ensured to slay the enemy generals himself, while Chandreya and Sarthak also defeated some of the royalties. It was a message for the world, to stay away from allies and border of Pandhar, a clear display of power and their wrath. Even in their economically fragile state, King Dharmendra sent aid to rebuild Dangri. None of that was important to Atikaya though, his thoughts had only one conclusion.

Never again, shall I show such weakness. If this world needs to be a better place, someone needs to fortify his heart and make tough decisions. If no one else is there to take that burden, I will be that man, Atikaya thought to himself while warming his hands at the dying fire. He lay down to sleep, though memories of those moments of his weakness, of his merciful acts, returned to haunt him. His night was spent in a sleep mingled with dreams. The next morning, he felt tired still, but he had a quest to complete. He freshened up and grabbed his sword, as he continued his slow ascension.

Far in the distance, his brother too was making his way towards the flower.

Battle of Songs

IT took Ujjwal and Katyaki a few days of wandering around to finally reach the steps Sarat had mentioned. There was a ruined temple and vines all over its walls. Its entrance arch was half broken, and a statue of a goddess on a tiger was at its prayer hall. The walls had fallen around, exposing the statue of black granite to the forces of nature. Few of the many hands of that goddess were broken, yet the shine of the granite hadn't faded, as if some truly divine power was in it. They both joined their hands and bowed, offering a silent prayer.

Finally, Ujjwal turned to Katyaki as he said, 'I cannot thank you enough for guiding me… us, through these woods. And, be there for me when I lost my closest brother.' Katyaki waited for him to continue. He said, 'My dear, I will not ask you to walk any further than you have. This is where I need to start walking alone, to understand myself.'

'Why? Do you think I can't –'

'No, I have seen your skills, and I would rather drown in Neri than doubt you. But even the greatest have bad days. I don't know what awaits in the path ahead, so I can't let you put yourself at risk for me.'

She scoffed, 'Is that not exactly why you should have someone with you, you idiot! Pardon me, Your Highness, but what if some ill befalls you and no one is there to help? We have already been through bandits, what more can be there that could scare me?' her voice getting tender at the end.

'True, but I cannot have you risk yourself for me. Besides, more importantly, I need to know that someone is waiting for me to get back, apart from my family of course. I know my sister must be worried sick, I don't know where my brothers are, so my father must be waiting for his sons to return, though one will not,' Ujjwal replied with a grief-filled voice.

Katyaki placed a hand on his cheek and said, 'Stop making excuses.'

'I am not. I just need to know you are safe. Also, I want to contemplate if I can really take the throne, and I need to take this part of the journey myself to learn that answer. You don't need to follow me, you are free.'

'And I am using my freedom to choose for myself, to follow the one I love,' she said, her voice not ready to yield, 'What are you afraid of? That the cold will get me? That I am too weak to climb up the mountain? That you will have to spend your strength protecting me?'

Ujjwal held her cheeks in both hands, delicately like a flower. He said, 'What even made you think like that? I will not doubt the physical resilience of someone who has conquered all poisons. And no, I don't think I need to protect you because you are weak, I want to protect you because you are important to me. Even if you don't need me.'

'But I need you.'

'I need you too. More than ever, yet, if I cannot find my inner strength by myself, I cannot bear the load of the crown. Please, my dear, allow me to go alone,' Ujjwal pleaded.

Katyaki grunted, then softly said, 'What will you do, if the flower is already taken?'

'I don't know, but I will not stand against Father's decision, even though that would be so typical and in character for me. I will find a way to have my influence. I hope I can convince other brothers to see through my eyes for once,' Ujjwal said as he looked up at the snowy peaks in the distance. Katyaki took a long breath.

Though assassins worked in the shadows, using methods often considered dishonourable, they had few strict codes of conduct. Their existence relied on their adherence to their words. One of the most forbidden acts for any assassin was revealing the clients. No amount of torture could justify the crime of giving away a client's name. Katyaki said, 'I don't know which of your brothers was it, but one of the two had a sapphire ring.'

Ujjwal's brows raised, 'Viryanath, which means brother Sarthak was involved. My dear, there is no need for you to tell me any of it.'

She shook her head, 'I needed to tell you this. It was my last assignment, after all, assigned by *you* to kill fate itself, a fate that was bestowed on me. After giving away my client's name, I can never be an assassin again.' She smiled at him, a free smile, a bright smile that had burned away her dark past.

Ujjwal sighed, amused at her. He walked around a little and picked a wildflower growing on the snow-touched soil. He offered it to her, 'For you my lady, a flower that suits you. A wildflower whose name I do not know, a flower that doesn't bend to the harsh cold of snow. It doesn't care for the quality of the soil. It blooms wherever it likes, whenever it prefers. Please, take the safest road home. Once this is all over, I will come and find you, wherever you are.'

She raised her head as she took the flower, 'And you must make sure to return home safely, to the family you still have.'

He nodded and said, 'Don't follow me, you know already we can't really lie to each other, given how easily we see through one another's illusions. At least I can sleep in peace if I know you are safe somewhere.'

Katyaki was bowing to him, but he held her firm on each side, staring into her eyes. She sighed with a happy smile and turned around, walking back home. Once he felt that she was safe, out of the dangers of the mountain ahead, he started climbing up the stairs. He had to admire Sarat for his speed, even if he was descending in his time, it was a long way. Ujjwal spent many cold nights sleeping outside by the stairs, covered with just a *shawl* beside a dying fire, but he was getting closer to the cave each day.

One night, memories of his mother came flooding into his mind, memories where she was holding him in her arms like he wished she would hold Chandreya in heaven. *He was getting chased by some maids for a bath, but he was faster, running all around the palace. He was still a small boy, though he already had a brother and sister after him, he could easily pass-through small gaps. He bumped into his mother. He raised his hands in the air and said, 'Mother, pick me up.'*

She stared at him, 'Really? You were giving the maids and servant a merry chase all around the palace, and the moment you saw me, your legs stopped working?' She picked him up in her arms nonetheless, carrying him for his bath. The memory itself was enough to give him warmth, letting him sleep peacefully through the night in that harsh cold.

*

His journey continued the next day, leading him to a cave indeed. There was no tiger at the cave entrance. Instead, there was something far worse, a *Brahmarakshas.* It was one of the immortal demons, who were once mortal men, mostly priests or scholars. When such an enlightened individual strayed away from their path, gods cursed them to become *Brahmarakshas,* who couldn't die, nor be killed by mortals. They roamed the world with all their wisdom and knowledge, yet were driven by demonic instinct to kill and eat humans. That was their curse, their suffering, to be conscious of it, yet unable to stop themselves from eating those who were once their kin. This *Brahmarakshas* had a hideous face, asymmetric eyes, and no nose on it. His hands were twisted oddly. The demon was meditating when

Ujjwal appeared from the stepping stones. He opened his eyes to see the approaching prince but didn't say anything or act hostile, yet.

Ujjwal sighed, knowing that he was once a human, the prince approached the demon, with hopes of reasoning with it. 'Oh, lord of the cave, I seek a flower from the mountaintop in haste, to heal my father. Will you be kind enough to let me through?'

The demon laughed menacing laughter as it said, 'Then give me a reason, why shall I not devour you outright.'

The prince replied, 'Have you forgotten who you were? As a scholar or priest, you should have been giving knowledge to others. Didn't you fall from grace to this hideous form because you strayed away from the path of wisdom and teaching? Tell me, do you find any peace in eating other humans?'

The demon grunted, and with a sigh, he said, 'I do not. Yes, I was arrogant of my knowledge, and that led to my fall. I still remember my wisdom, my humanity. I couldn't bring myself to eat the villagers I met, there was no peace. That is why I abandoned society, coming here to live in the mountains, to penance. I have submitted myself to the gods, spending every moment of my life offering my prayers to them as I meditate here. Hopefully, one day they will hear my pleading and relieve me of this fate.' A sorrow lay in the immortal's voice, a burden of long life he was bearing.

Ujjwal said carefully, 'Yet, it does not seem like it has worked. Maybe an act of generosity of letting me pass could help?'

The demon laughed, 'Good try, young man. But still, I cannot let you pass freely, unless you defeat me.' Ujjwal knew the curse of *Brahmarakshas*, damned to suffer for eternity.

The prince said, 'Very well, I will battle you.'

The demon laughed, 'So tell me, mortal man, how do you think you would defeat me? Do you have the knowledge of the celestial weapon crafted by the Creator himself? Because no other weapon that a mortal can wield, nor any spells save for one used by gods themselves could harm me.'

Ujjwal said with a grin after his sigh, 'Oh, I am not a great warrior to know the arts of such powerful weapons. Perhaps my eldest brother could have pulled such a feat, but not me. But I don't recall you saying anything about slaying you. I only have to defeat you.'

The demon looked at his grin and said, 'Such arrogance. Even if you were to wrestle me, I would win. I do not tire; I don't need food to keep my strength. What chance does a mortal like you have to stand against me?' It was true, a *Brahmarakshas* couldn't die even if it tried. Unless a god slayed it or the curse was lifted, it was fated to suffer for eternity.

Ujjwal sighed, 'You were a scholar once – an expert of *mantras* and hymns, armed with songs praising the gods. I challenge you, oh immortal demon, to a battle of songs.'

The demon's laugh echoed through the mountains, 'Such arrogance, just like I was in my old days. Do you want to challenge me to a contest I already have the upper hand in? Very well, accepted.' He looked at the prince, wondering why a man would damn himself to such a decision. He had learned from so many scriptures and scrolls, that a mere man would stand no chance against an immortal ancient being like him. He asked, 'Fool, are you not afraid of defeat and the doom that waits you thereupon?'

Ujjwal replied, 'Why shall I be afraid of defeat?' The demon raised an eyebrow at one of its asymmetric eyes. He thought to himself, *this man must have noble blood, perhaps royal blood itself, such arrogance is rare to see.* The prince continued, 'It is such a beautiful thing after all. When you are defeated, it means that you have given your best effort, without holding back anything that the Divine had gifted you. A victory might be gained with luck, but defeat is earned when you have emptied all your skills. That is why there is peace and beauty even in defeat, in a true defeat.'

The demon kept looking at him, awestruck for a second. He asked, 'Who are you? I must know before we start this battle.'

The prince sighed and said, 'A son seeking a cure for his father. A brother trying to uphold his dead brother's wish. A lover wishing to keep his promise. A prince trying to find the best future for his kingdom. Most importantly, a human finding his place in the world.'

The *Brahmarakshas* straightened himself and said in a respectful voice, 'Let us begin then.'

The duel began, and to the surprise of the demon, Ujjwal battled all his challenges. But the fallen scholar was persistent too. He was a little surprised to see a prince singing such poetry, filled with music and emotions. The royal had learned many a song from priests all over the kingdom. He sang the praises of gods and sang of the cycle of birth and death. The demon sang back with lore of creations and battles of long past. They sang the tales of warrior princes fighting demons of the ancient world, songs of gods in mortal flesh guiding humans in the ways of duty. The prince kept singing back whatever the demon challenged him with. Yet, victory was not near.

They were both on equal grounds. Ujjwal switched to peasant songs and tribal poems. The demon smirked but replied with the lyrics of such songs with equal intensity. He had travelled around too, for a time much longer than Ujjwal could comprehend. The prince gritted his teeth; he needed something to catch his opponent off-guard. He decided to sing the most vulgar of songs he had learned from low-born folks. Perhaps the demon was corrupted so much that a little vulgarity didn't make it flinch. It returned his challenge with lyrics of the songs Ujjwal had started.

The prince was thinking, he needed some song that the priest won't know, or can't sing. He looked at the demon's face, the hideous face. The prince grinned. He started singing with his nose, and the demon tried to meet his challenge. Without its nose, it couldn't create the rhythms, finally falling back. The *Brahmarakshas* sighed,

'Very well, you won after all. A defeat is a defeat. You may pass, prince.' Ujjwal bowed with respect and made his way into the cave. 'Wait, victory was yours, even if through trickery. Let me sing one last song to you, oh prince,' the demon called out. The prince turned to face him as the demon said, 'You said you seek a rare flower to cure your father. If you have come all this way, it must be the Royal Blue poppy.' Ujjwal's brows rose for a moment, and then the ancient being sang songs which had no rhyme or rhythm. Yet, through the puzzles of words, he revealed the secrets of the passages through the cave to the prince.

Ujjwal took everything in, or whatever he could. He said, 'Before I part my ways, if I may tell this, I feel your meditations might not be the best way to repent, oh Wise One. It is not so selfless, you see. You are seeking redemption for *yourself.*'

The demon looked at him and said, 'What would you recommend then, prince?'

'You should abandon this mountain and go back to the duty you have long forsaken. You abandoned your duty of teaching, and that is what brought this fate upon you. You abandoned the people your duty was meant for. Go back to them, go teach them, teach everyone you can, share your wisdom.'

The prince paused and thought of something as if some memory that troubled him, the memory of a brother. 'I have started to learn, that we cannot accept someone else to act on our behalf, when we have a duty to do, we must act ourselves. No gods will save you oh Wise One, you must save yourself through your actions.'

'Who would want to learn from a demon like me?'

'The wise, the fool, the curious. If you let your demon form define you, that is all they would see. Let your wisdom define you, oh great teacher. Let them see the truth of your heart. They will hate you, resent you, fear you… But they cannot harm you. You were cursed to be immortal and invulnerable to everything, wield that curse as a gift. Take all the harm they throw at you, take their resentment and pain, because that will be your cure, your salvation. Even when your desire to consume them is overwhelming, or when you drown in their insults, act for their sake, because that is true selflessness.'

The demon looked at him, humbled at the royal's wisdom. He said, 'Your Highness, you already know the path to the flower. You could have walked away, why must you try to help me?'

Ujjwal leaned against the stone of the entrance and looked at the sky, it was getting dark then. He said, 'Because I hope that you can be redeemed. There are people in my life, people I hold dear, who have gone or might go through dark paths in their lives. I need to know that they have a chance to redeem themselves. If a demon like you can be redeemed, certainly they can be. That is why, do your duty oh Wise One, and it will be a thousandfold more impactful than the empty prayers you give here. You just taught me the ways through the cave, does that make you feel any different?'

The fallen scholar's eyes brightened as he looked at Ujjwal and he said, 'Yes, I do feel a little more humane. I cannot place how, but I do. Thank you, oh prince, you are a wise one yourself. May you find the flower and I hope to see your kingdom one day.'

Ujjwal smiled, 'I will gladly take you as an advisor to the court if you ever decide to visit.' They bowed to each other and headed on their way. The demon descended from the mountain, to find true redemption. The prince headed into the cave, guided by torchlight and the walls. Soon, he should be reaching the peaks to collect the Royal Blue poppy, the cure for his father's illness.

The Last Duel

IT took him a few days to navigate through the caves. The cold was getting him slower; the snow had gotten into the cave. But that meant there was an opening somewhere, which was a hopeful thought. When Ujjwal emerged from the cave path, the mountain in front of him was pure white. The snow shined under the bright light of a waxing moon. Another day or two of following the path suggested by the demon and he would see the peaks, and flowers all around.

The prince was gasping for breath throughout his walk. He looked towards the south and said, 'Thank you, my friends, I cannot thank you enough for teaching me your ways, ways of controlling one's breath at high heights. Without your lessons, I would have needed a few more days to reach here.' The flowers were poking out of the thick layers of snow as if their presence itself embodied warmth.

He sighed, if the flowers were still around, his brothers hadn't made it there yet. He walked closer to examine the flowers, ensuring he was looking at the Royal Blue poppies themselves. Three white lines coming from the centre decorated each petal. It looked so beautiful under the full moonlight. He was about to climb up to pick them up gently when a voice came from the other side, 'I am surprised you made it here.' The fog moved aside to make way as Atikaya emerged from the fog, like a mighty force of nature tearing through the thin fog. His eyes were set on the flower as if Ujjwal wasn't even there.

He said to Ujjwal, 'Now that I am here, you need not worry about it anymore. I will take them.' The younger prince stood silently, unmoving, unyielding. 'Ujjwal, move aside,' Atikaya's voice fell like a mighty wave.

His brother took a deep breath to sigh, 'I cannot, Eldest. I made a promise to brother Chandreya, my last promise to him.' He turned around to face Atikaya, his eyes filled with sorrow.

Atikaya shifted a little, 'What happened to him?'

Ujjwal lowered his head and said softly, 'He fell, I couldn't save him. But I will not fail him or the words I gave him.' Upon hearing Chandreya's demise, Atikaya's demeanour changed a bit, there was grief in his eyes. A hint of humanity.

The eldest prince straightened his face and said, 'I care not, there are more important things to attend to. So, unless you want to battle your eldest brother for the crown, I recommend you step aside.'

Ujjwal found himself in a dilemma, *was it really worth fighting one's sibling for a crown, something he had considered a hunk of metal all his life?* 'I do not wish to fight you, but I cannot just walk aside either,' he said to Atikaya.

His brother's brows rose as he said, 'And what will you do then? How do you think you can stop me? You, the weakling who couldn't stay away from Mother, needing to be in her arms in his entire childhood… how do you even think you would challenge me?'

A pain surrounded Ujjwal's visions. He softly said, 'Dear Eldest Brother, there is a set amount of time in someone's life that they can spend in their mother's arms. With time, we grow too big to fit there. That is why, I made the most of my childhood to be with her. Perhaps you would have turned out to be a different person if you had spent more time with her.'

Atikaya groaned, 'Turned into a pathetic excuse of human existence like you, that's what I would have been.' His hands reached to his sword pommel, and Ujjwal immediately threw his own sword to the ground, taking a sit on a nearby rock.

Atikaya stopped, and Ujjwal said, 'Thank you, for upholding some honours still. I wouldn't have expected a great warrior like you to strike at an unarmed man, and you showed your quality.'

'I don't have time for your idle chatter.'

'Then tell me brother, what does it mean to you to be a Crown Prince? What does *ruling* mean to you? I will make my decision according to your answer,' Ujjwal said as he looked straight into his brother's eyes.

Atikaya laughed and said, 'Even if you were to fight me, we both know that the results will be in my favour. Why shall I bother wasting my time chattering? Is it not delaying father's recovery?'

There was truth in that question, Ujjwal took a moment to think. He answered, 'Brother, Father must have known that this kind of confrontation might happen when he gave us the quest. Yet, he sent us in this manner, instead of simply asking us to bring the flower. I am sure he knew of the possible delays, and he knew how long he could hold his health. He wouldn't have risked his life in a folly. To honour his decision and the last wish of Brother Chandreya, I will not move an inch. The question is, are you ready to cooperate and answer my simple questions, for father's sake?'

Atikaya drew out his blade, his patience was running thin. He said, 'Maybe it will be faster to cut you down. Do you not remember what happened when you fought me last time? I knocked you out with one punch.'

Ujjwal taunted, 'I was defending Mother back then, not fighting you. You were the one who couldn't handle his rage when he lost a silly game with friends and lashed at Mother when she tried to console you. Perhaps you are unsure of your own feelings and obligations, brother, which leaves you at a disadvantage against my questions.'

Even though fuming with anger, the eldest prince said, 'Being a Crown Prince is the first step to becoming a king. A fate gifted by the gods to the chosen few. The power to command the fate of an entire kingdom, bearing its weight on your shoulders. To decide how your subjects live their lives, devote their work for your kingdom, that is what ruling is.'

Ujjwal looked around the snow-covered peak, the air too thin for them to breathe and so dry. He replied, 'Brother, if your desire to become a Crown Prince is rooted in the betterment of the citizens, not in personal satisfaction, would you not be able to give this duty to someone else, to your own younger brother, as long as the end goal is met?'

'To someone incompetent like you? Who do you think will keep the kingdom safe with his might? Keep the laws and order maintained with his command? You or me?' Atikaya mocked him. His eyes narrowed as he pointed his sword at Ujjwal and said, 'I had enough of your chatter, draw your blade or walk away. I won't warn again.'

The younger prince gasped at the realisation that negotiations were off the table. He drew his sword and slowly stood up as he said, 'Please think again brother. I have watched you for years since *that day*. I have heard songs of your battles, and seen you wrestle bears and bulls in the arena. As a warrior, you should know, that information is power. I have watched your every battle skill, on the contrary, you know nothing, absolutely nothing about my skills.'

Atikaya laughed, his voice echoing through the mountains. 'Is that so? Let us test it out then,' he said and leapt at Ujjwal with his sword.

The duel between the brothers began. Their last duel. They battled at the peak of the world, atop Dharataj mountain, under a sky filled with stars and moon, with heaven as their witness. Atikaya's mighty swings came fast at his brother, pushing Ujjwal to a defensive manoeuvre. Every strike rang with metallic vibrations as his sword clashed with Ujjwal's. Yet, none of his attacks managed to cut through the younger prince's defence. His brother's defensive moves were quite precise, stopping each of his attacks as if they were designed specifically for his attacks.

He groaned at Ujjwal, 'Why shall I hand it over, instead of bearing the weight myself? And if you are so noble, oh younger brother, why do you stand in my way instead of giving up your desire?'

Ujjwal shouted back, 'It was never my desire. All my life I ran away from it. But I don't agree with your definition of ruling. Since there is no one else to take the mantle and serve the citizens, I must do it myself.'

'Is that not arrogance? To think that only your way is correct?' Atikaya questioned him, pushing him back.

Ujjwal tried to keep to the higher elevation, a small advantage he could manage against Atikaya. The question had caught him off-guard. He shouted from his heart, hoping to reach his brother's heart, 'Had I been one of those who chased after such power and crown, it would indeed be arrogance to say that my way is the only right way. But you know me, how much I detest the rank and how much have I avoided the court. Yet, in my travel, I have seen the kingdom, and its people, and now I see you. I cannot allow the fate of the kingdom to fall into the hands of someone so ruthless.'

Ujjwal saw something that the eldest prince had been blind to, the exhaustion in Atikaya's body. His attacks were getting slower and more predictable every time. The eldest prince said, 'You have seen how hollow this kingdom has become, weakness festering everywhere. Do you think you could rid this world of its pain, its sorrow that stems from this weakness? I think not. It needs a strong ruler who will not fear to transcend the limits of human beings, to become one with the divine and to create a heaven on this earth. A world free of pain and suffering.'

Ujjwal scoffed, 'A fictional world. A world cannot exist without pain and sorrow, the way light cannot exist without shadow, day without night. It is poetic, but not practical. All we can do is build a world where pain and sorrow exist, yet it is balanced with compassion and empathy. That is the kind of world I had promised to Brother Chandreya. Since brother Chandreya is no more, it is a weight I will carry. I know my way won't be the best. But I will keep learning and growing, taking the help of the wise ones.'

Atikaya's eyes burned with fury, he said, 'And you think you will become a good ruler with such half-hearted obligation? Needing the fools and ministers to direct you, instead of commanding them with authority bestowed on you. You think you can be fair and just when you take the role just to please a dead brother?'

He knew Ujjwal was cunning enough to handle his attack patterns. He abandoned techniques and embraced chaos; his attacks became completely random. Ujjwal struggled to keep up, retreating as he tried to reorient himself to the incoming volley of slashes.

Atikaya howled, 'Are you trying to taunt me, Ujjwal? Come, show me your true skill. Attack me, brother, I will be sad to kill you without giving you a chance to fight.'

The fourth prince ignored the challenge and focused on the earlier point Atikaya had made. 'It is not half-hearted; I am not doing it just to keep my promise. There are lots of wrongs that I want to correct. I will work hard for it. I was never interested in it because it felt boring and like a heavy burden. But now I see, if I don't take that burden, no one could fix the things I want to see changed.'

'And you think you can change anything?' roared Atikaya while slashing at his chest, a cut opening. The cold of the heights stopped Ujjwal from bleeding too much, but he needed to act soon. His brother continued, 'You were weak, you travelled with Chandreya.

And look what happened? A fragile man he was at the end, falling to his death, leaving you alone. You still think you can rely on others?'

Ujjwal gritted his teeth, balancing himself on the slippery rocks, moving from side to side to not give Atikaya a clean opening. He said, 'And you started with three weapons I had heard. Here you are, with just a sword on your side. Seems like we are on the same ground, brother.'

The heights were testing Atikaya, and he was surprised to see Ujjwal maintaining so much control while moving. Even with superior skills in weapons, the eldest prince found himself evenly matched by his younger brother then. Ujjwal kept his breath steady with all his skills. He roared, 'Are you calling me weak?' His attacks turned ruthless, unleashing many lethal techniques he had rarely used, or rather rarely needed before.

Ujjwal shouted, almost crying out with tears, 'No, you have NEVER been weak. That is exactly the problem. You can never know weakness; that's why you can never help those who are weak. You can never understand their struggles; the battles they fight that won't be sung in songs or read in stories. Because those battles are fought in silence. I can't let you have the throne if power in your hands will only make the weak more miserable.'

'When a forest burns, it's the weak and old trees who perish first. There is no place for them in this world,' Atikaya gasped as he thrust his sword, almost making Ujjwal lose his balance. But the younger prince gracefully rebalanced himself, as if like a well-rehearsed step of dance.

'Yet, the young and new plants keep standing, as weak as they might be. Just like humans show resilience when faced with great calamities beyond the strength of any single man. They hold hands together with love and share the pain, reducing its impact so they can rebuild,' he answered.

Atikaya said, 'Fool, many perish by the time help reaches them. The weak mostly. In a world free of the weak, the strong won't have to fear anyone, not even calamities. That's why, I must become a king who can touch heaven, the one who will unite the world under one banner. And even calamities will bow to me, so give up already! Give up already, because you are standing in the way of Fate itself, a Fate that had chosen me as the first prince of Pandhar, the heir to its throne.'

Ujjwal said with eyes filled with tears, 'Then I will cut down that Fate if I need to.'

Atikaya had practiced that one attack so many times, and used it with pride in the arena many times. An attack that couldn't be stopped, at least no one had managed to stop it yet. He went straight for Ujjwal's head. The young prince gasped, deflecting the attack as he arched back, a move he had practised so many times, just to stand against that attack from Atikaya. He needed some way to attack fast and break Atikaya's defences. But the slippery stones were making it hard to even stand straight. A memory flashed through his mind, the time he was chasing children in their game, atop the hills in the south of Pandhar.

Using the muscle memories of those tricky terrain, he attacked back at Atikaya. To the eldest prince's surprise, Ujjwal used a mimicry of his own unstoppable attack. Not only had his younger brother stopped his previous attack, but he also dared to replicate it to suit his physique. He must have practised it so many times, to be able to even mimic it. Atikaya saw the attack coming, but couldn't do anything. He had taken so much pride in calling it the unstoppable attack, why would he ever need to find a way to defend against it, how could anyone else have managed to use it against him. Yet, he found himself in exactly that situation. Ujjwal disarmed him in a quick flourish of blade work, his feet moving on the stones like dance steps. He pointed the sword at his elder brother's chest and said, 'I am not so weak either, brother. So, please, accept defeat already. It is alright, we are brothers, and we can go home like that… at least I wish to.'

Atikaya's sword, one he had gotten blessed in the temple of the god of destruction, clanged a few times as it fell from the top of Dharataj mountain. He could only look at Ujjwal, wondering how could he lose to a man like him. He looked for the flirt, drunkard, or spoiled kid. Instead, he found a man, who didn't stand alone, one who had lived thousands of lives through the lives he touched. A man moulded and shaped by such people. Such a weak man who relied on so many others had surpassed him in blade work.

Other than rage, Atikaya could not feel anything. His anger boiled over as he found himself insulted by his scoundrel brother. Since Ujjwal was looking at him with pity, or whatever those looks his mother used to give him, Atikaya managed to push aside the sword in a quick motion of his hand. He leapt at Ujjwal, trying to grab him by the throat. But the elder prince's foot slipped and tumbled back, rolling a few times before he slid off a cliff edge.

He grabbed hold of a rock and watched as Ujjwal had abandoned his sword and was running down to him. His younger brother offered him a hand, saying 'Please brother, take my hand. I cannot lose another of my kin, please. If the throne is so important to you, we can take the flower together and talk this through with Father. Please, just come back up, take my hand.'

Such *insults,* he was the first prince, the eldest of the siblings, how dare his younger brother offer him help! Atikaya was filled with fury. His inner voice called out, 'If you can't have it, he shall not have it either. It will be the greatest insult to your legacy, your strength… if a loser like him takes the throne.'

Be it jealousy, shame, or anger, Atikaya reached out to grab Ujjwal by his hand and drag him down. Before his hands could connect, the sudden change in load from his leap caused the rock he was holding to give away. Atikaya, through intention or nature, had brought the *Kabandha's* words to fruition. And so, from the pinnacle of the world, fell Atikaya, the first prince of Pandhar, for one last time.

Ujjwal cried out in horror, only able to watch his elder brother disappear into the darkness. He won't even find the body to give a respectful burial. He kneeled and cried, cried out loud as he looked at the sky. His voice echoed through the mountain as he wept, 'Oh Father, was it the only way you had to test us? Was there no way to choose an heir without pitting your sons against each other in a deadly journey?'

His heart was heavy and breathing laboured. His tears were getting frozen from the cold. Though grieving and distraught, he knew that he had to finish the quest. Wiping his tears away, he made his way to the flower. The beautiful royal blue coloured petals with white stripes from the centre shined under the full moon. He slowly picked them one by one, placing them in a pouch.

He looked around himself, at the vast darkness that he could see from the top of *Dharataj*. The road ahead was going to be equally challenging, but he had to walk it nonetheless. Walk alone at that, much different from the happy journey he had dreamed of. He hoped as he looked at the sky that his other two brothers had not met a fate so cruel. He could only speak with a quiet voice coming from his soul, 'I hope you can forgive me, Mother, I wish I could have saved my brothers.' He rested a little to regain his strength, and then he descended to continue his journey home.

A Promise Kept

IT took Ritikesh and Sarthak a few weeks to recover, though, the damage to their hands was permanent. The deeper wound was to their soul, which would linger for a long time. Yet, as siblings, they helped each other heal. Geetika, though still angry at them both, showered them with all the kindness a younger sister could muster, only wishing them to get well soon. It had been a week or so since they had fully healed, and they visited their father after a long time since they had headed out for the quest. They took seats by the wall; King Dharmendra was lying on the bed. His eyes had gone weak; he was struggling to even look at them. Geetika was tending to him at that moment, she looked at her brothers as they sat. They could only hope that she would forgive them soon one day.

The king struggled to utter words, only in fragments could he talk now. 'The flower… did someone bring?' His voice was so faint and distant, that the brothers had to lean closer.

Geetika pressed her father's digits and said, 'No father, we don't have the flower yet. Though Pandit had said that one of the other three had gotten it, he could see it he said.' She adjusted the pillow under his head. A messenger came and stood by the door, bowing, breathless.

'Yes?' Sarthak said as the eldest sibling there.

'My lord,' the man said to him and turned to the king, 'My king, Prince Ujjwal has returned with the cure.'

Geetika ran to meet her brother when he arrived at the palace's threshold. Yet, Ujjwal's face was filled with grief. She didn't have to ask where their elder brother Chandreya was. With a heavy heart, she realised that at least one of her brothers won't be returning. She fell to her knees as tears rolled down her eyes. Ujjwal kneeled by her and hugged her. Bhimsen came to see them, giving the siblings a moment to mourn. When Ujjwal noticed him, he pulled out the pouch filled with Royal Blue poppy and handed it to Bhimsen. The Pandit nodded and took his leave. Ujjwal had no interest in discussing medicine, politics or even philosophy, he only focused on calming his grieving sister.

The scholars and medics of the kingdom worked day and night, extracting the essence of Royal Blue poppies meticulously. They had to be careful with the limited raw material they had at hand, concentrating it to a suitable amount. Ritikesh tried to help them when he could spare. Even the ultimate cure was not something divine blessing that could have cured the king in a day. It took him weeks to fully heal, through daily doses of the viscous medicine brewed by his herbalists and Geetika's devoted care. He was delighted to see her face again when his visions improved. He was still struggling to walk without support from a staff or a stick. Yet, important things needed to be discussed.

*

The king summoned a court, with only important ministers present. There was no music or dances that day in the throne room. The air felt heavy as everyone sat in anticipation, watching the king take his throne after such a long time. The king slowly lowered himself on his seat, one hand holding tight on his staff. The three princes, Geetika and *Pandit* Bhimsen were also there. There was no question what the meeting was for, an heir was to be decided. Sarthak took a deep breath and questioned, 'Father, can you really hand over the inheritance to him just because he returned with the flower? He left with Chandreya, yet returned alone. Do we know for sure if he did not betray his own brother? What fate befell Atikaya, do we know?'

Before the king could respond, Ujjwal spoke, 'Yes, Father, how will you ensure that my victory was an honest one? Or had you not considered the possibility that brothers might turn against each other?' his eyes turned to Sarthak, accusingly. Sarthak and Ritikesh both lowered their heads, falling silent.

Tears rolled down Dharmendra's eyes, he said with a tender voice broken from pain, 'Yes, you are right my son. To be a just king, I failed as a father. All this time, I failed to see the hearts of my sons. I failed to see the insecurities my youngest son festered because I stayed silent every time someone talked down to him. I thought I was being fair by not being partial to my youngest, yet I was the most unjust by depriving him of a father's love.' He looked at Ritikesh with eyes begging for forgiveness, the youngest prince looked back with eyes filled with tears and forgiveness.

The king turned to Sarthak and said, 'I could not feel the pain of my second son as he always had to stand in the shadows of his elder brother. Never having an elder brother myself, I couldn't comprehend the weight. Always, in my own stupidity, I saw him as someone to replace Atikaya if ill befell the eldest son. I wish I had seen them equally, loved them equally as a father should.' Sarthak nodded, his eyes heavy, yet he was ready to accept the past and build a better future.

Geetika offered the king some water as his lips looked dry. He sipped and continued, 'Only if I could have looked clearly at how arrogance had taken over my eldest son. I abandoned him to his own device, thinking foolishly that I was granting him independence. All I gave him were ambitions and the rage that comes from failing to fulfil those ambitions. No amount of grieving would bring him back.' The court sighed, at the thought that mighty Atikaya had fallen at the end.

He looked at Geetika, seeking her forgiveness instead, as he said,

'The son I had loved the most perhaps, the son I thought was filled with kindness, had been blinded by the laws and honours he tried to uphold. I couldn't have ever imagined that he would be consumed by them, but the truth is always inevitable. Only if I had given him the right lessons of empathy and the freedom to show compassion, he would still be here.'

He looked at Ujjwal, the prince's face completely unreadable. He said, 'In the end, the son I always thought was a spoiled child, returned with the prize and my cure. Only if I had seen the true depth of your heart, I could have been a better father to you.'

'That does not answer my query, Your Majesty,' Ujjwal said in a firm unyielding voice, making the entire court gasp and fall silent. He elaborated, 'Was there no other ways to test your sons? I understand that the flower was essential to be obtained, but was it essential to turn it into a competition filled with bloodshed?'

'My son,' Dharmendra said after a long breath, 'A quest that hadn't been done in centuries could only be completed by the best of the best. I had hoped that the challenge would help you all grow as a person. I wished you all would see people as they live and fight battles of your own inner minds. I had wished that this quest would make you all more cooperative, bringing my five sons closer than ever before.'

'And what if you were wrong? What if elder brother Sarthak was right? Will you let me wear this blood-soaked crown? No, I am just trying to find someone to blame for the deaths of my brothers,' Ujjwal's voice turned to distraught, 'Only if I had challenged this quest the time you announced, only if I had called out its hubris instead of accepting it, maybe two of my brothers would still be here.'

Bhimsen stood up and said, 'Your Highness, even though your siblings and other members of the courts are unaware of it, I have been gifted with Divine Eyes. I can see and hear far even while sitting here in the palace. I saw your battle with Atikaya, as I have already described it to your father while he was healing. What's more, I have listened to the philosophical exchange you made with your eldest brother, I have seen your suffering too, at his demise.'

'Then, oh wise one, how can you expect me to put on a crown that has been bathed in the blood of my blood?' the prince questioned him.

'Yet, you must wear it. A king needs kindness first of all, with honour, strength, and skills too. But above all, he must see the truth and be just. This journey has tested all your inner selves, the persons who have returned are completely different than the ones who had set off. Tell me oh prince, do you still think the role of a Crown Prince is fooling around with power? Others saw power in the crown, some saw a label of honour, while you ran away from it all your life. Because you were the only one who saw its truth, the burden, the responsibility. Because you saw its truth, you were the only one ever worthy of it, whether you like it or not.'

Ujjwal was about to speak, but the *pandit* continued, 'It is soaked in the blood of your kin now, yet would you resort to cowardice and still keep away from it, or brave it and put that burden, that pain, on your head to serve the subjects who need you. Long have you travelled around, it is time to put that knowledge and wisdom you have gained into use. Imagine the darkness that would have fallen if Atikaya had taken the role as he had become. Or think of the insecurities and divisions that would have been birthed from the Chandreya's rigidity. Will you still abandon this kingdom and its people to a dying fate?'

Once allowed to speak, Ujjwal grunted, but asked politely, 'But how can you be sure that I won't change in future, that I won't bring upon another kind of darkness?'

'Because you are questioning. The only one who ever questioned if he was the right choice to be a ruler. Only when one questions and criticises himself, can he see through his flaws and improve upon them. Your doubts won't become darkness, they are not your insecurities, but rather a proof of your rational thinking and humility. They will be the origin of that divine light that will guide you. I see it in your eyes, your desire to keep yourself away from this great burden. Yet, you fought your eldest brother, because you knew the responsibility,' Bhimsen enlightened him. He turned to the court and told of the battle at the peak of the world, the last duel of two brothers. Some took it to their hearts, others to their mind.

In the end, the *pandit* turned to Ujjwal and said, 'Oh prince, this kingdom needs a future king, and we have our best candidate in you. So, please take up the mantle of your father. If you ever go astray, your brothers and so many ministers are here to help.' He looked at the other two princes and the court. They all nodded in agreement. Dharmendra felt a great peace when Ujjwal finally accepted to become his successor.

Though, the prince announced, 'There are certain conditions to my Crowing Ceremony. If they cannot be met, I would rather take up farming than the throne. Two brothers we have lost, two princes. For the next twenty days, we will all mourn for them. In these days of mourning, there shall be feasts every day, asking the gods to give peace to their souls.'

He turned from his father to face the rest of the court and said, 'In these feasts, every person from the capital must be invited, irre spective of their profession, birth, age or gender. To the very last child. Send words to the farthest corners of the kingdom, that every lord and chief must organise such feast in their lands, ensuring every man, woman and child is fed in these days. On the last day, ensure that guests, representatives of villages and towns of this kingdom, scholars and spiritual leaders, artists, and performers, are here to witness the Crowning ceremony the next day. I would like to meet each of these guests personally.'

Some ministers grunted, not fully accepting Ujjwal's ascension or his idea of mourning. One said, 'My lord, will that not affect the royal treasury? To arrange a feast of such a scale is a nightmare, we will have to employ so many people for security, transportation, hospitality, cooking and other services.' They immediately fell silent as they were met with Ujjwal's gaze, a silent declaration that things were going to be different from then on, whether they liked it or not.

Silence fell in the throne room, the king sighed and said, 'If that is the will of a Crown Prince, then it will be done.' Geetika smiled in relief, all the pain was not for naught after all.

*

The feast happened as Ujjwal had demanded, to the point that some of the local lords of villages had to empty their treasure hoards. Every guest of the final day, irrespective of where they hailed from, was requested to stay for the next day. Ujjwal knew he would not remember all of them, but ensured to meet and greet every last one of them, even if that was the only thing he got to do through the entire day. The next day was a day worthy of remembrance.

Horses and elephants were displayed; a display of the kingdom's military might. Music and dances were arranged to celebrate cultures and art forms from all over the land. Great spiritual leaders of that time visited to praise the gods and give the Crown Prince their blessings. The path from the *mandap* with sacred fire to the symbolic throne was decorated with flowers. Once the prayers and hymns were done, Ujjwal gave his offerings to the gods by the ritual fire – *ghee,* saffron, grains, coconut and water touched with many flowers. When the ritual was finished by the priest, he walked on the flower path to sit on the throne. Milk and turmeric water were poured on him, and then water from Neri was poured to clean him off. Finally, the king and a priest placed the crown on his head, concluding the ceremony.

*

Sun was setting in the west, not a sign of the end of the day, but rather, welcoming a new era from the next day. The guests were either resting, cheering in the capital or had headed for home already. The sacred fire from the ritual had burned for long hours, even during that hour of dusk, it was still giving faint light. Ujjwal came to sit by the *mandap* where the sacred fire was dying slowly. His father joined him, he looked up and requested, 'Father, I can see that I have a long path to walk in this journey, one that will dwarf the quest for the flower. I am certain that with my brothers and other wise men of the court by my side, I will manage to hold a just… and *kind* rule.'

He paused for a moment, as if thinking back at some memories, then said, 'But still, in the moments where my soul wavers, I will need someone to hold me together, someone who truly understands me to be by my side. Someone to become my strength in my moments of weakness. I have a request, that someone be of my choice and not someone chosen by star charts or rituals to feed a political narrative. Someone not chosen from her birth circumstances or profession… not bound by duty, but someone who loves me.' His eyes darted to the fire as he muttered under his breath, 'And Brother Chandreya already gave his blessings anyway.'

Dharmendra looked at the sky and the stars, one of them was his wife and two were his children. He said in a reassuring voice, 'My son, I didn't bother following the customs and traditions to choose my heir, what makes you think I will say no to this. You don't need to request my boy; it is your right as a free man. Agreeing to such a heavy life decision is the least I can do after ignoring you for so long as my son. I have no doubt that your choice will be as great as you yourself.'

Ujjwal grinned as he slowly stood up, 'Thank you, Father. Pardon me then, as I start my term as the Crown Prince by running off the capital for a while. I must go find this someone soon, I have given my word.'

The king smiled and nodded, 'That does not surprise me, you

starting your duty with a leave I mean. You will always remain the unpredictable son to me.' He bowed to his father and retired for the night.

A new dawn came; a new era had started for Pandhar and the entire land. As the red sky grew brighter, the Crown Prince galloped into the horizon, in the direction of sunrise, in search of his future queen. To find and bring back Katyaki.

END

Acknowledgements

I must begin by thanking my friends who have helped shape the story. Lucia Barbieri and Swagatika Sahu, thank you for your detailed comments and suggestions that helped fine tune the story and writing. I'm also deeply grateful to Ishika Bhansali for meticulously editing the final draft.

To Severina Pociunaite, Sharon White, Pronoy Das, Bhabesh Rana and Souvik Ghosh: thank you all for your help with making the initial part of the story more engaging and accessible for general readers across different culture.

I owe a heartfelt thanks to my colleagues for being such lovely people that I could spend time working on this story without being overwhelmed by workload. Many others have helped me in various ways to bring this story to life.

I must thank Prashant Gupta for helping me with the printing and distribution of this book as a final product. Also, I am thankful to Kubra Pandit for designing the book cover.

This acknowledgement is incomplete without expressing my gratitude to my family and relatives, whose presence and influence have helped shape who I am. And finally, thank you, dear reader, for taking the time to read this far.